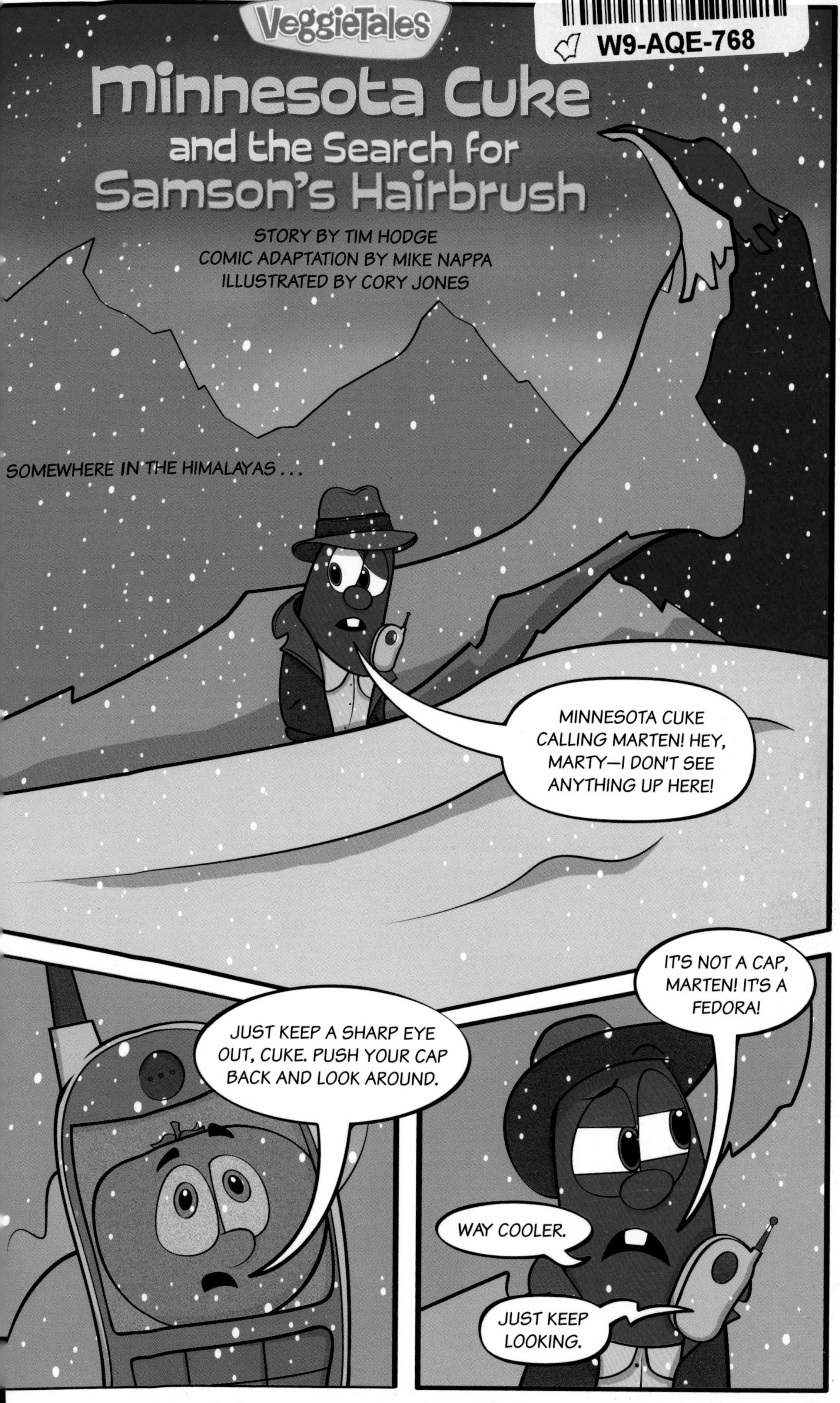
VeggieTales
Minnesota Cuke and the Search for Samson's Hairbrush
STORY BY TIM HODGE
COMIC ADAPTATION BY MIKE NAPPA
ILLUSTRATED BY CORY JONES
SOMEWHERE IN THE HIMALAYAS . . .
MINNESOTA CUKE CALLING MARTEN! HEY, MARTY—I DON'T SEE ANYTHING UP HERE!
JUST KEEP A SHARP EYE OUT, CUKE. PUSH YOUR CAP BACK AND LOOK AROUND.
IT'S NOT A CAP, MARTEN! IT'S A FEDORA!
WAY COOLER.
JUST KEEP LOOKING.

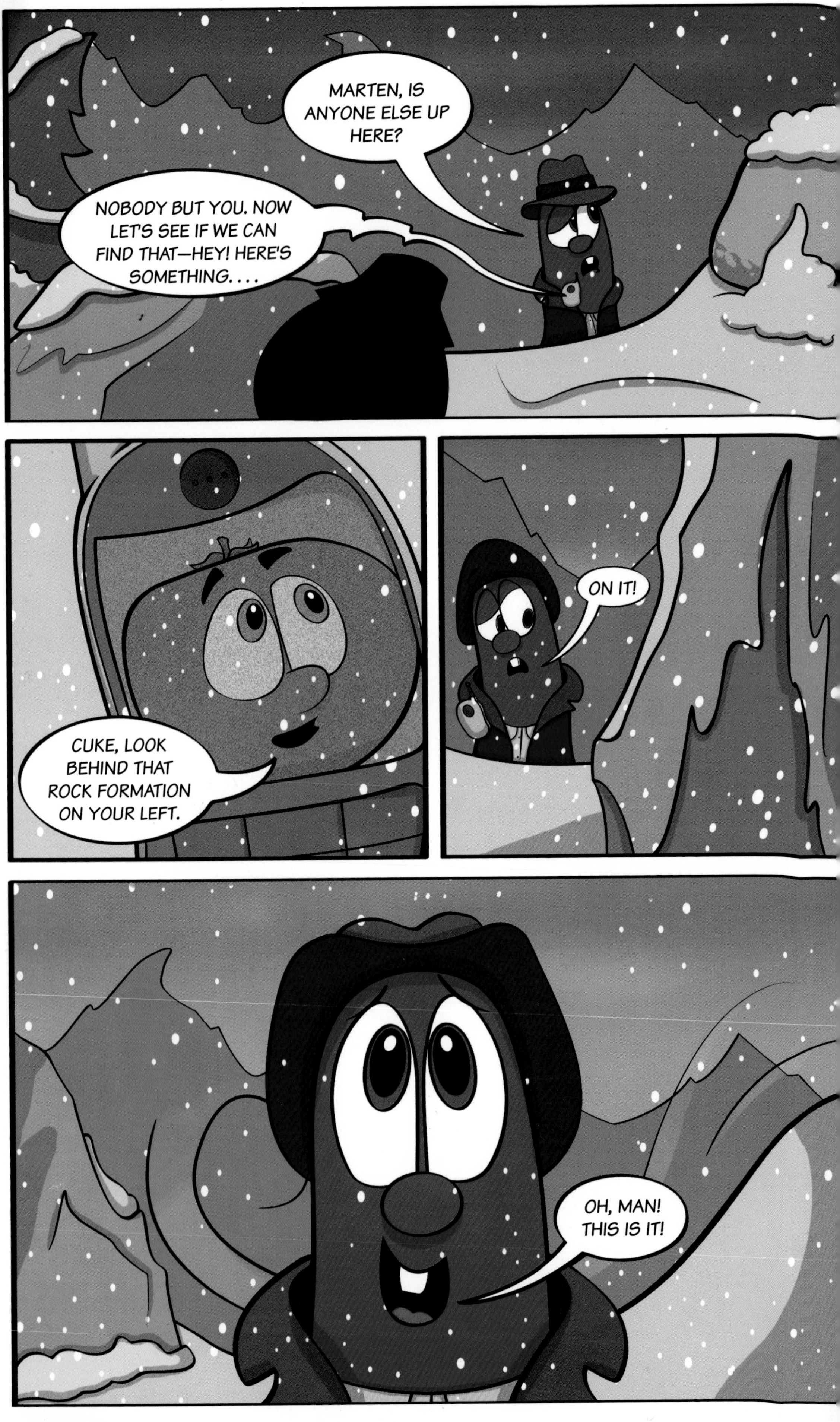
MARTEN, IS ANYONE ELSE UP HERE?
NOBODY BUT YOU. NOW LET'S SEE IF WE CAN FIND THAT—HEY! HERE'S SOMETHING. . . .
CUKE, LOOK BEHIND THAT ROCK FORMATION ON YOUR LEFT.
ON IT!
OH, MAN! THIS IS IT!

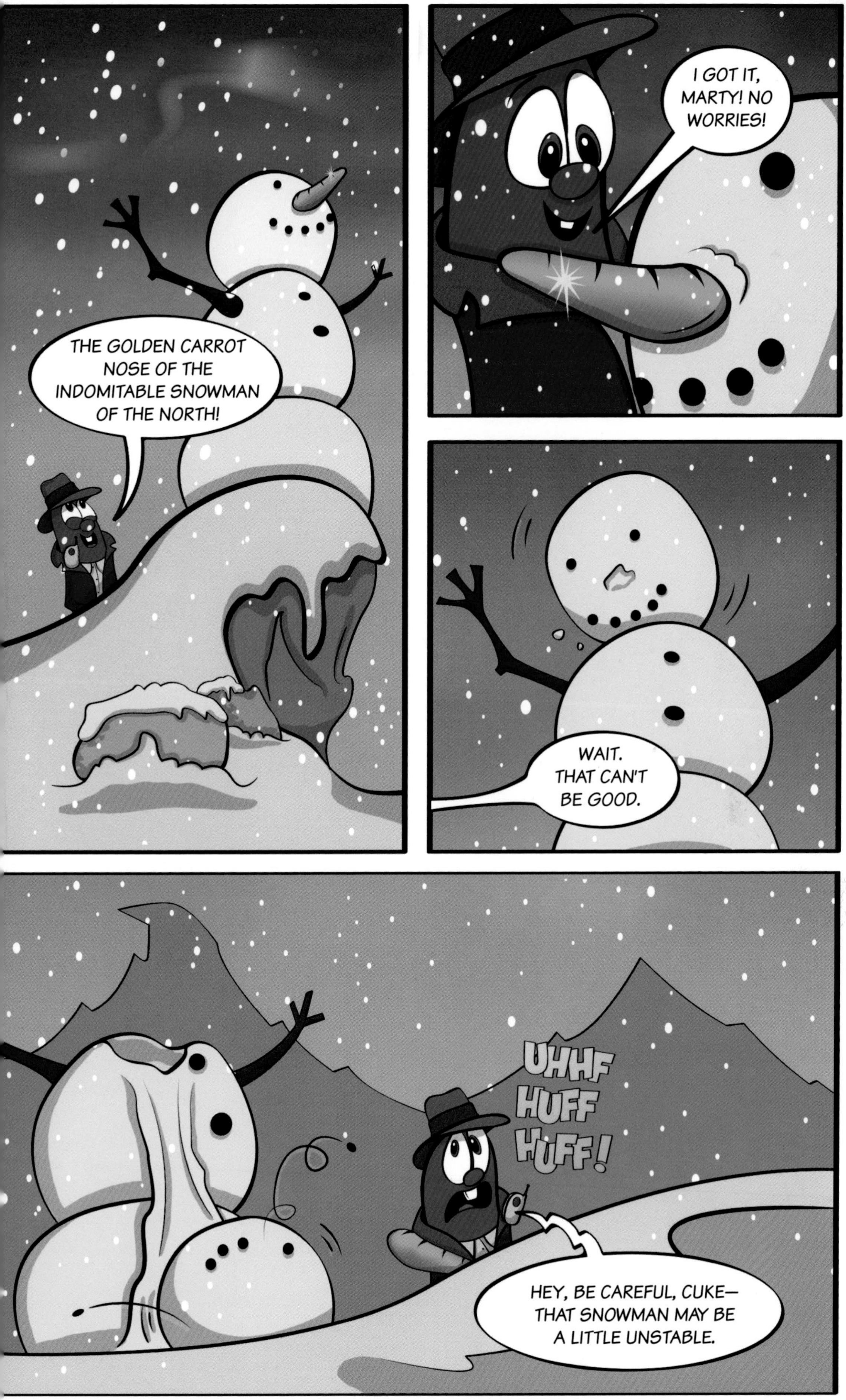
THE GOLDEN CARROT NOSE OF THE INDOMITABLE SNOWMAN OF THE NORTH!
I GOT IT, MARTY! NO WORRIES!
WAIT. THAT CAN'T BE GOOD.
UHHF HUFF HUFF!
HEY, BE CAREFUL, CUKE— THAT SNOWMAN MAY BE A LITTLE UNSTABLE.

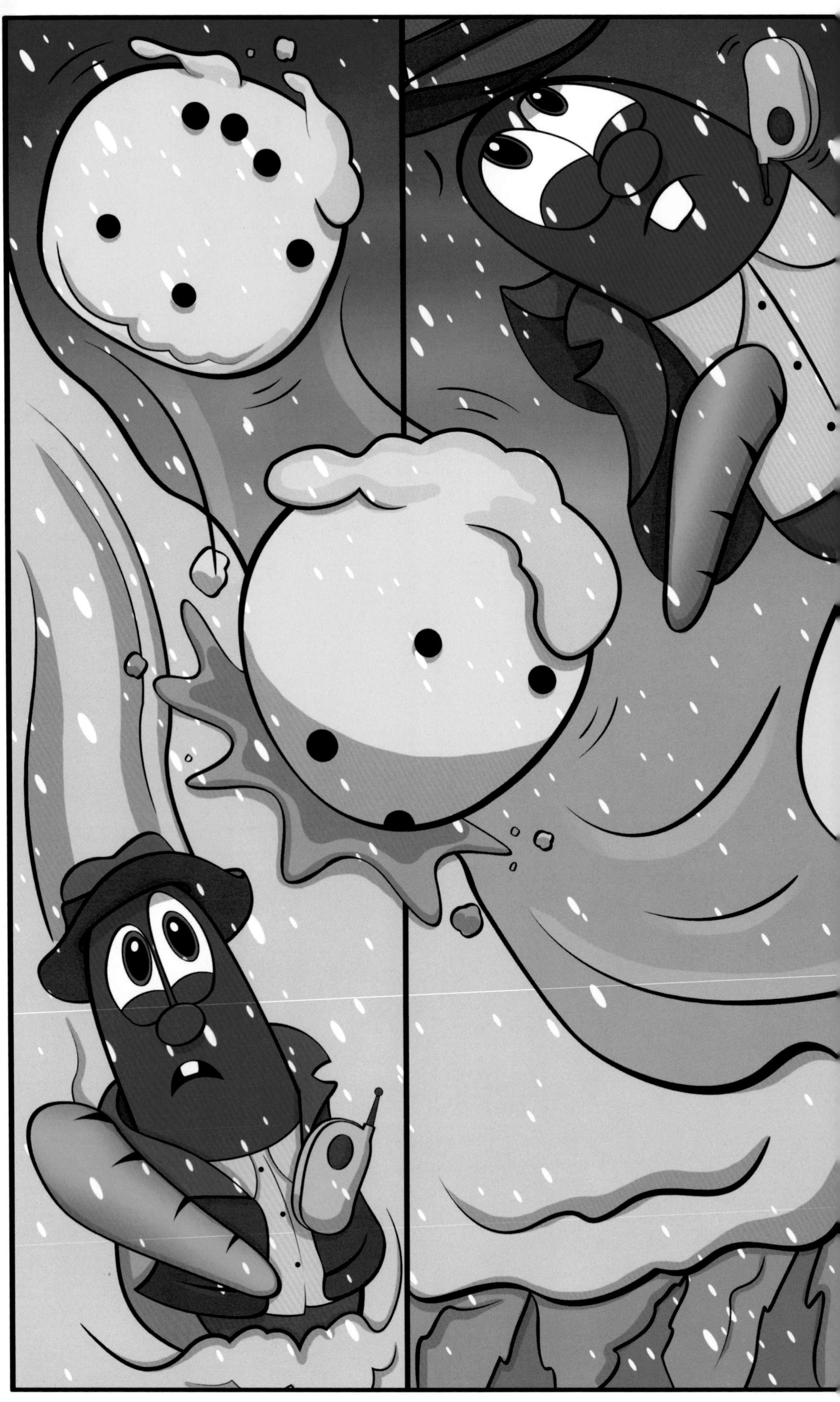

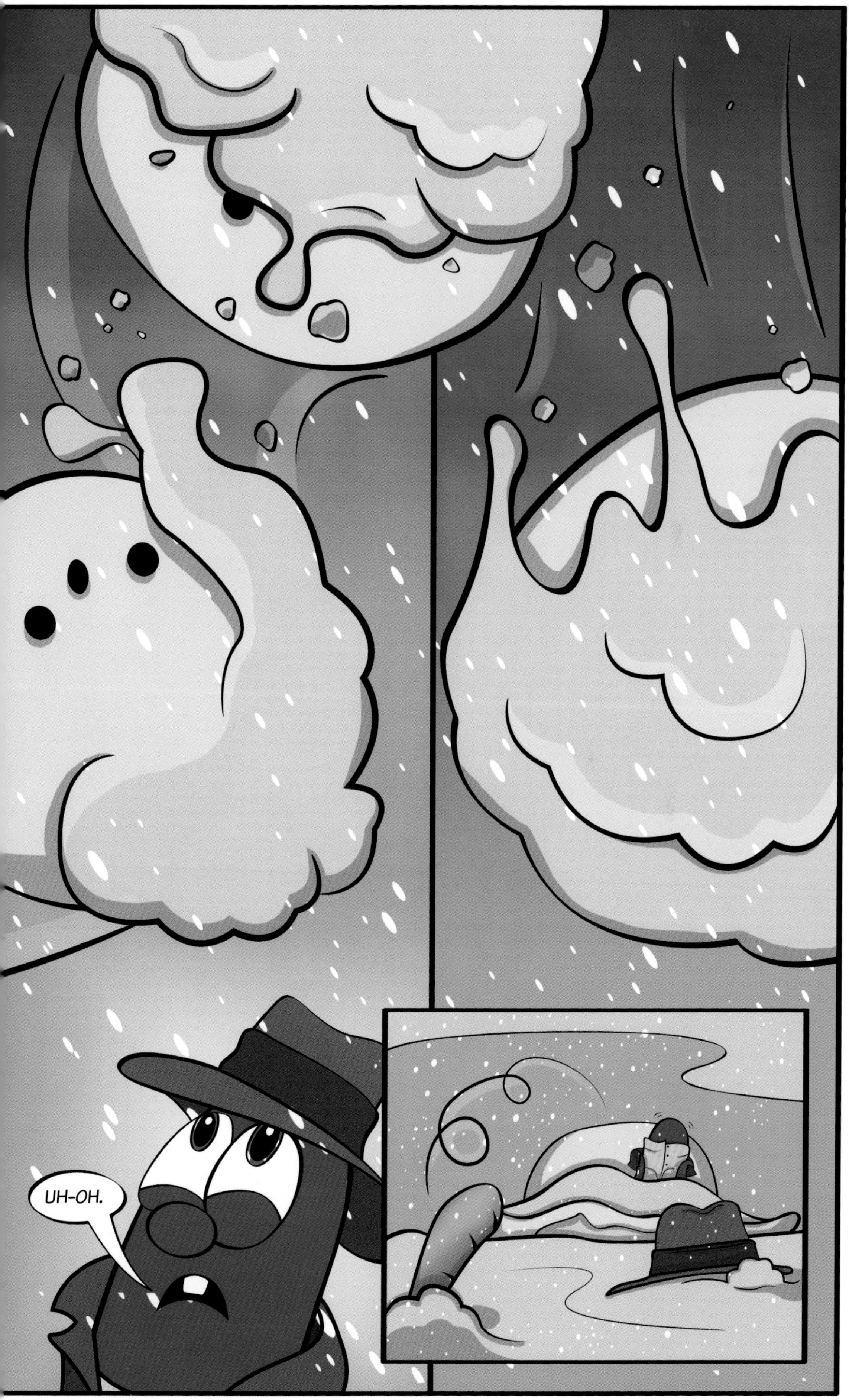
UH-OH.

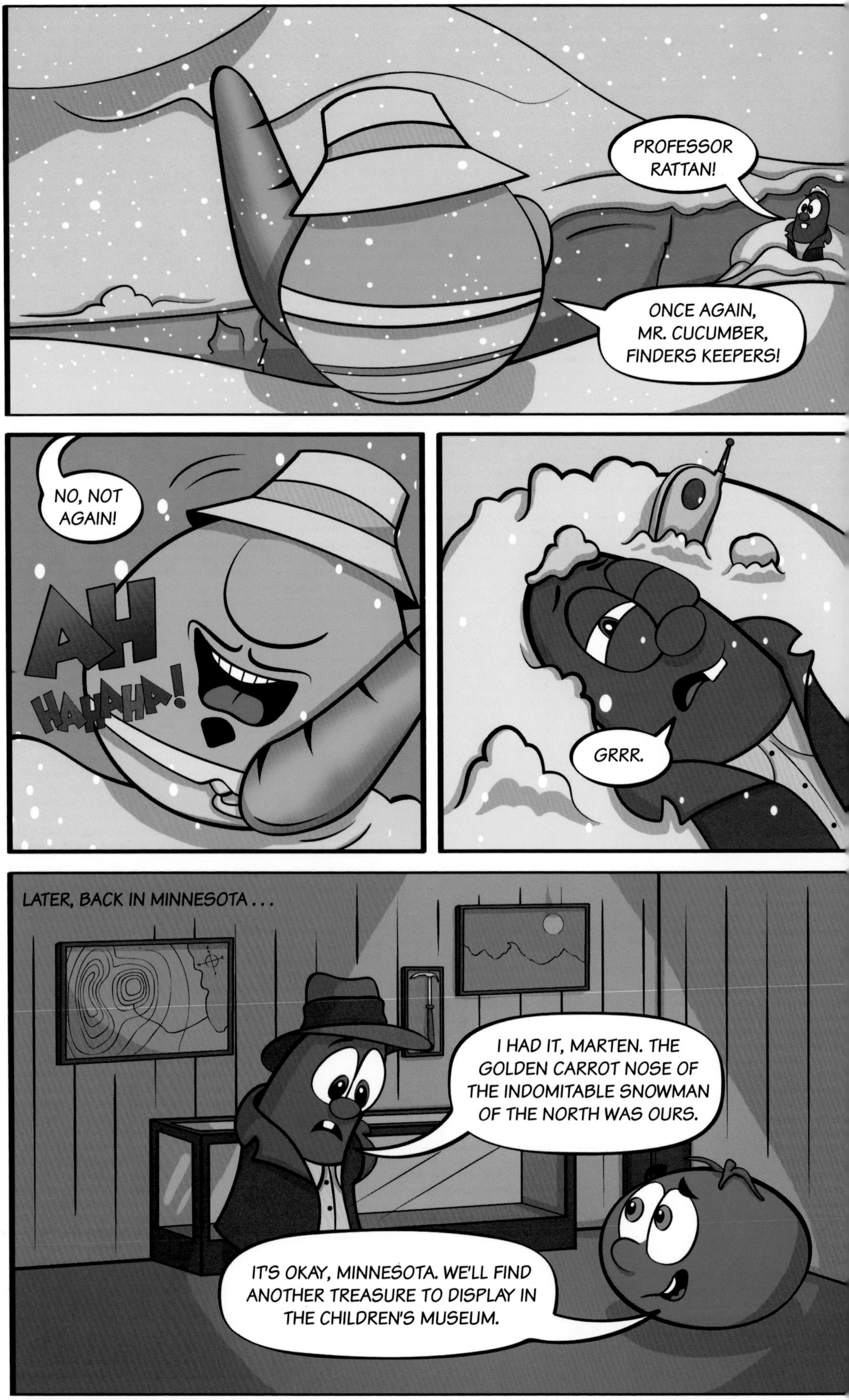
PROFESSOR RATTAN!
ONCE AGAIN, MR. CUCUMBER, FINDERS KEEPERS!
NO, NOT AGAIN!
AH HAHAHA!
GRRR.
LATER, BACK IN MINNESOTA . . .
I HAD IT, MARTEN. THE GOLDEN CARROT NOSE OF THE INDOMITABLE SNOWMAN OF THE NORTH WAS OURS.
IT'S OKAY, MINNESOTA. WE'LL FIND ANOTHER TREASURE TO DISPLAY IN THE CHILDREN'S MUSEUM.

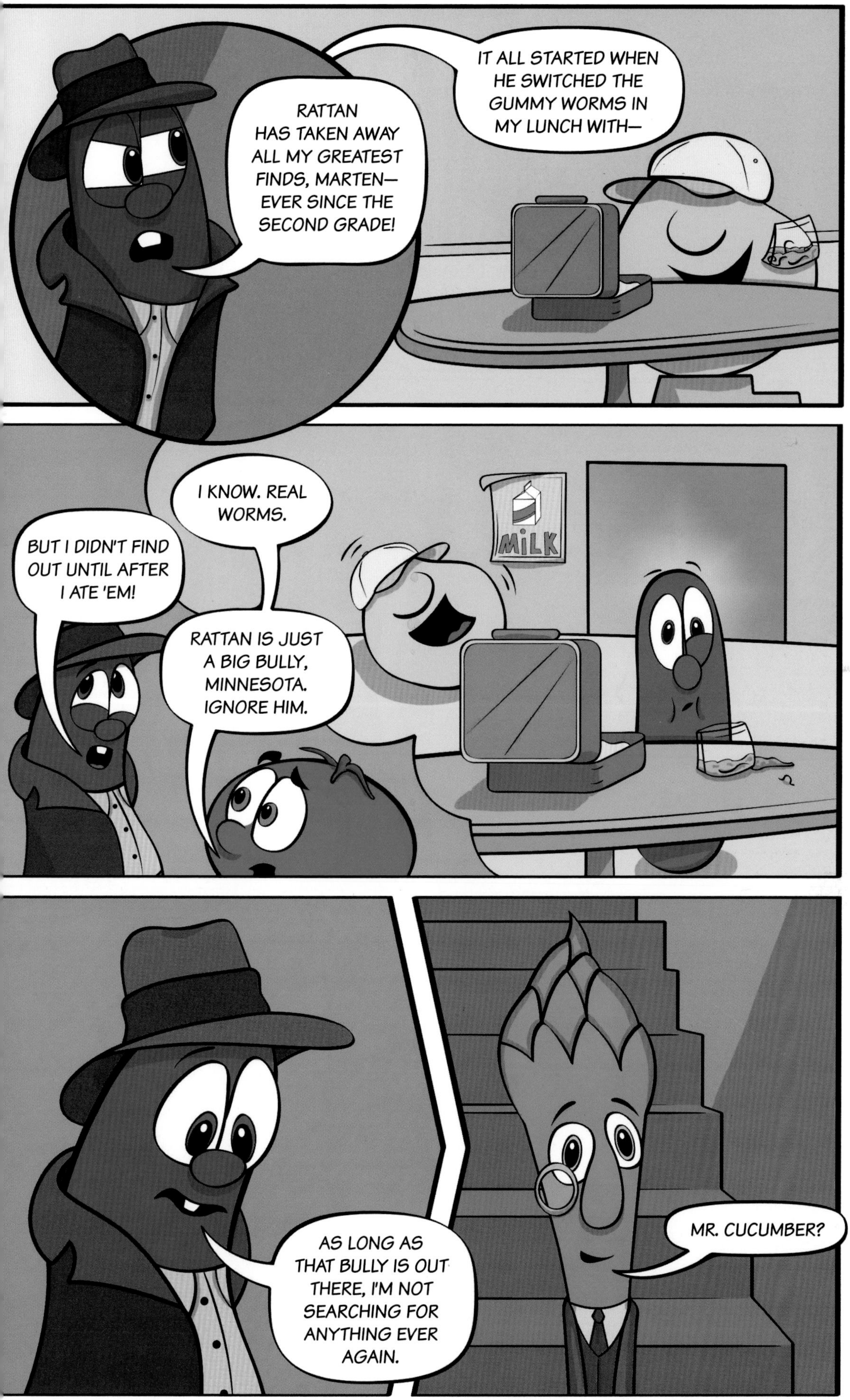
RATTAN HAS TAKEN AWAY ALL MY GREATEST FINDS, MARTEN— EVER SINCE THE SECOND GRADE!
IT ALL STARTED WHEN HE SWITCHED THE GUMMY WORMS IN MY LUNCH WITH—
I KNOW. REAL WORMS.
BUT I DIDN'T FIND OUT UNTIL AFTER I ATE 'EM!
RATTAN IS JUST A BIG BULLY, MINNESOTA. IGNORE HIM.
MILK
AS LONG AS THAT BULLY IS OUT THERE, I'M NOT SEARCHING FOR ANYTHING EVER AGAIN.
MR. CUCUMBER?

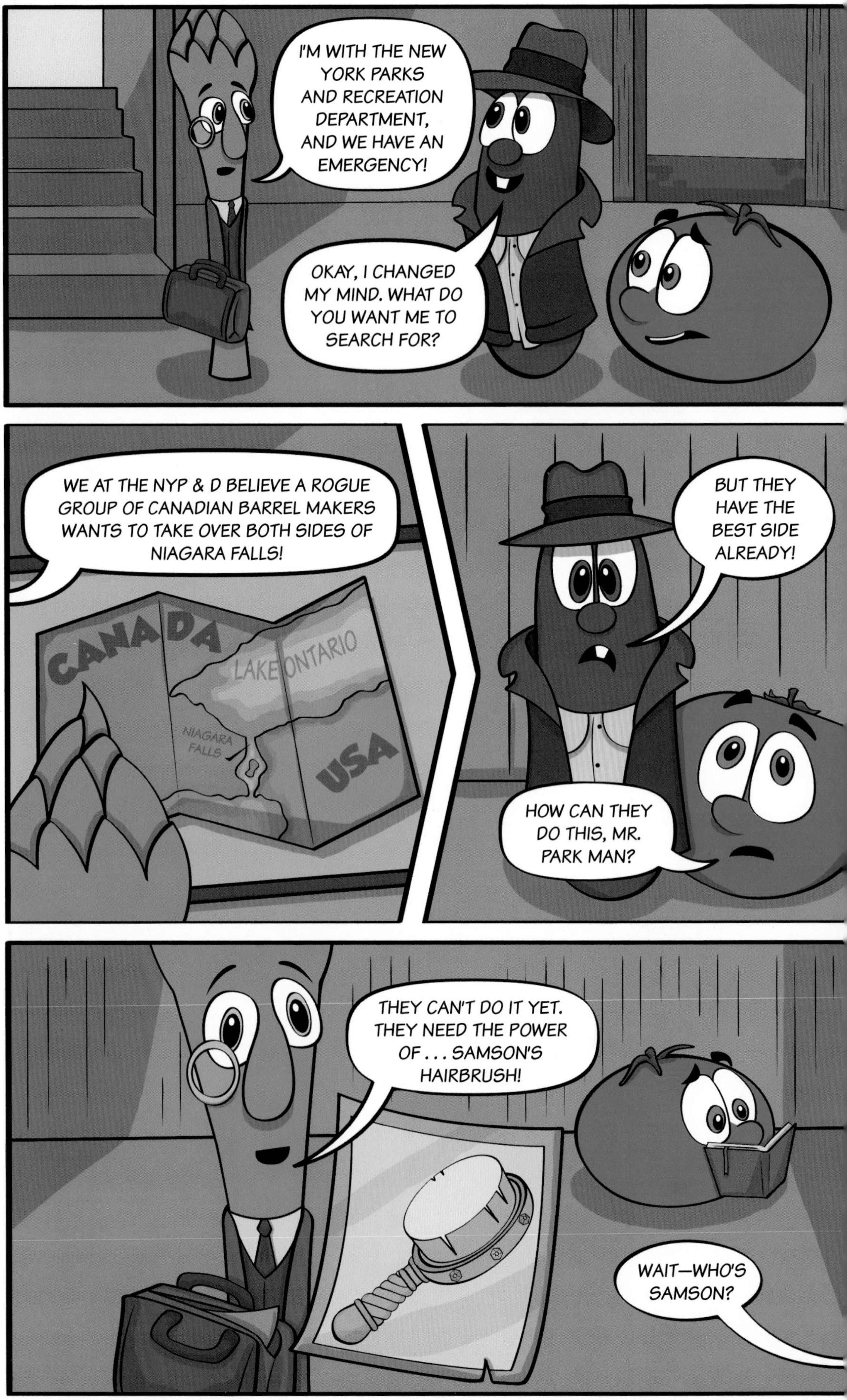
I'M WITH THE NEW YORK PARKS AND RECREATION DEPARTMENT, AND WE HAVE AN EMERGENCY!
OKAY, I CHANGED MY MIND. WHAT DO YOU WANT ME TO SEARCH FOR?
WE AT THE NYP & D BELIEVE A ROGUE GROUP OF CANADIAN BARREL MAKERS WANTS TO TAKE OVER BOTH SIDES OF NIAGARA FALLS!
CANADA
LAKE ONTARIO
NIAGARA FALLS
USA
BUT THEY HAVE THE BEST SIDE ALREADY!
HOW CAN THEY DO THIS, MR. PARK MAN?
THEY CAN'T DO IT YET. THEY NEED THE POWER OF . . . SAMSON'S HAIRBRUSH!
WAIT—WHO'S SAMSON?

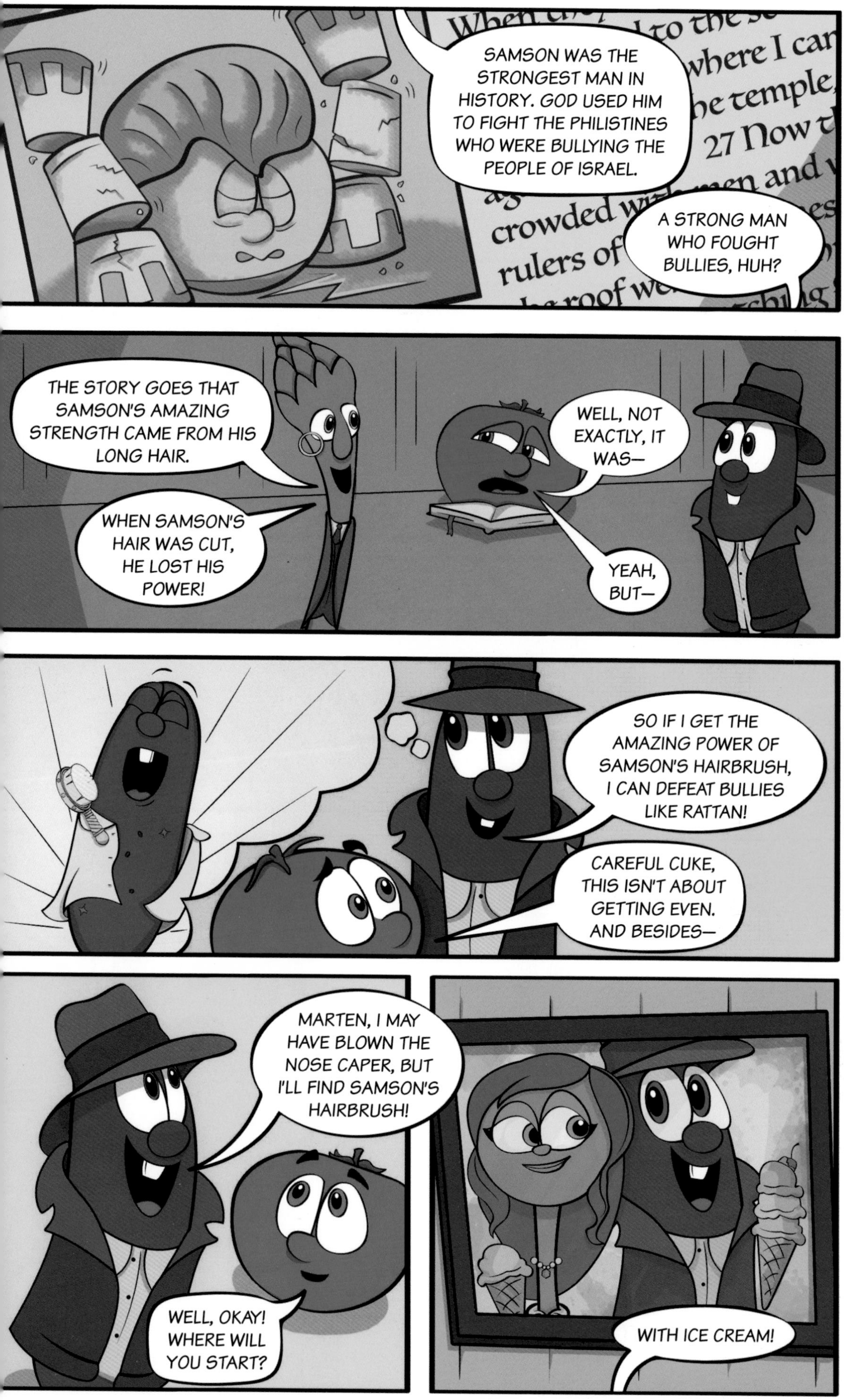
SAMSON WAS THE STRONGEST MAN IN HISTORY. GOD USED HIM TO FIGHT THE PHILISTINES WHO WERE BULLYING THE PEOPLE OF ISRAEL.
A STRONG MAN WHO FOUGHT BULLIES, HUH?
THE STORY GOES THAT SAMSON'S AMAZING STRENGTH CAME FROM HIS LONG HAIR.
WHEN SAMSON'S HAIR WAS CUT, HE LOST HIS POWER!
WELL, NOT EXACTLY, IT WAS—
YEAH, BUT—
SO IF I GET THE AMAZING POWER OF SAMSON'S HAIRBRUSH, I CAN DEFEAT BULLIES LIKE RATTAN!
CAREFUL CUKE, THIS ISN'T ABOUT GETTING EVEN. AND BESIDES—
MARTEN, I MAY HAVE BLOWN THE NOSE CAPER, BUT I'LL FIND SAMSON'S HAIRBRUSH!
WELL, OKAY! WHERE WILL YOU START?
WITH ICE CREAM!

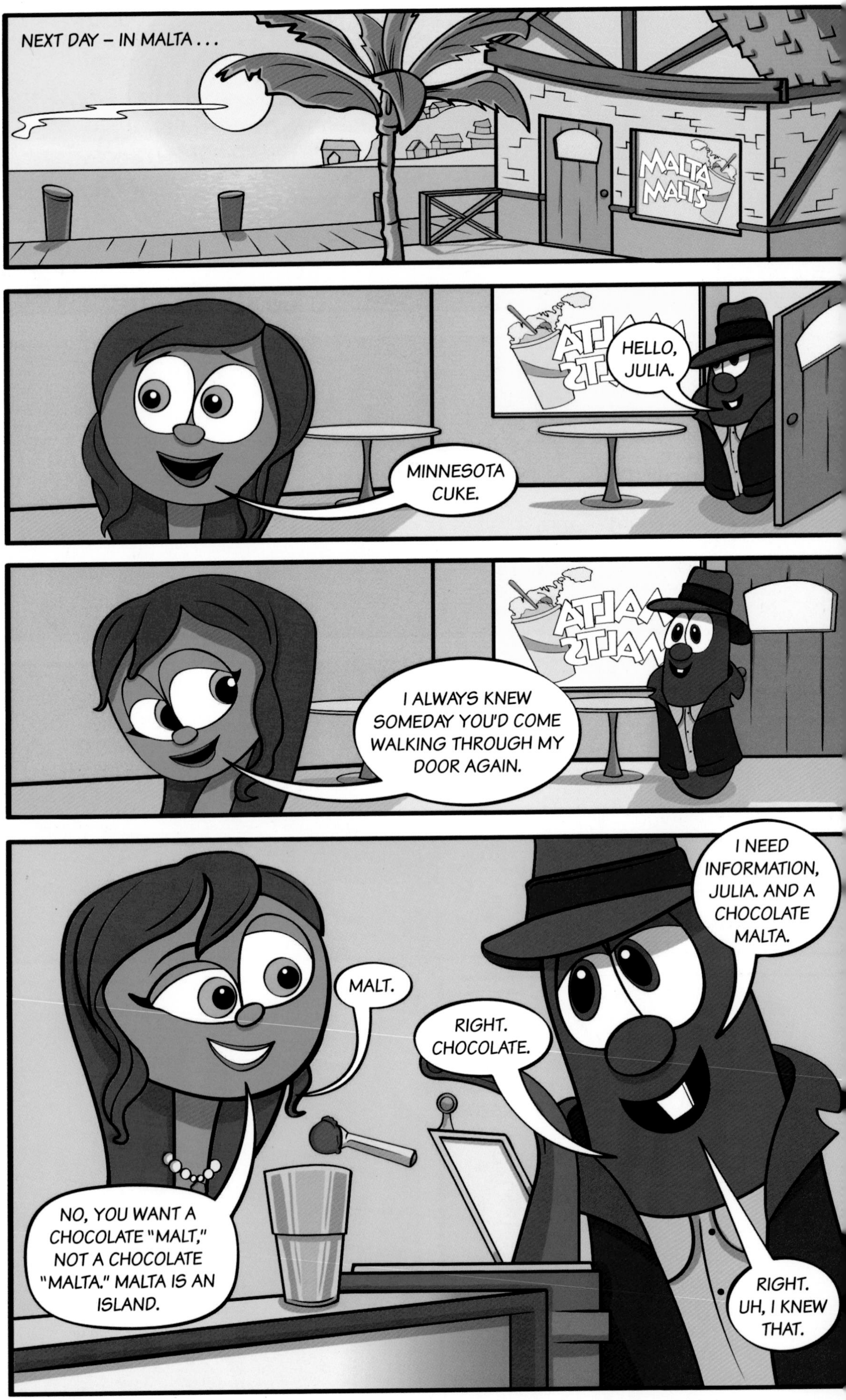
NEXT DAY – IN MALTA . . .
MALTA MALTS
HELLO, JULIA.
MINNESOTA CUKE.
I ALWAYS KNEW SOMEDAY YOU'D COME WALKING THROUGH MY DOOR AGAIN.
I NEED INFORMATION, JULIA. AND A CHOCOLATE MALTA.
MALT.
RIGHT. CHOCOLATE.
NO, YOU WANT A CHOCOLATE "MALT," NOT A CHOCOLATE "MALTA." MALTA IS AN ISLAND.
RIGHT. UH, I KNEW THAT.

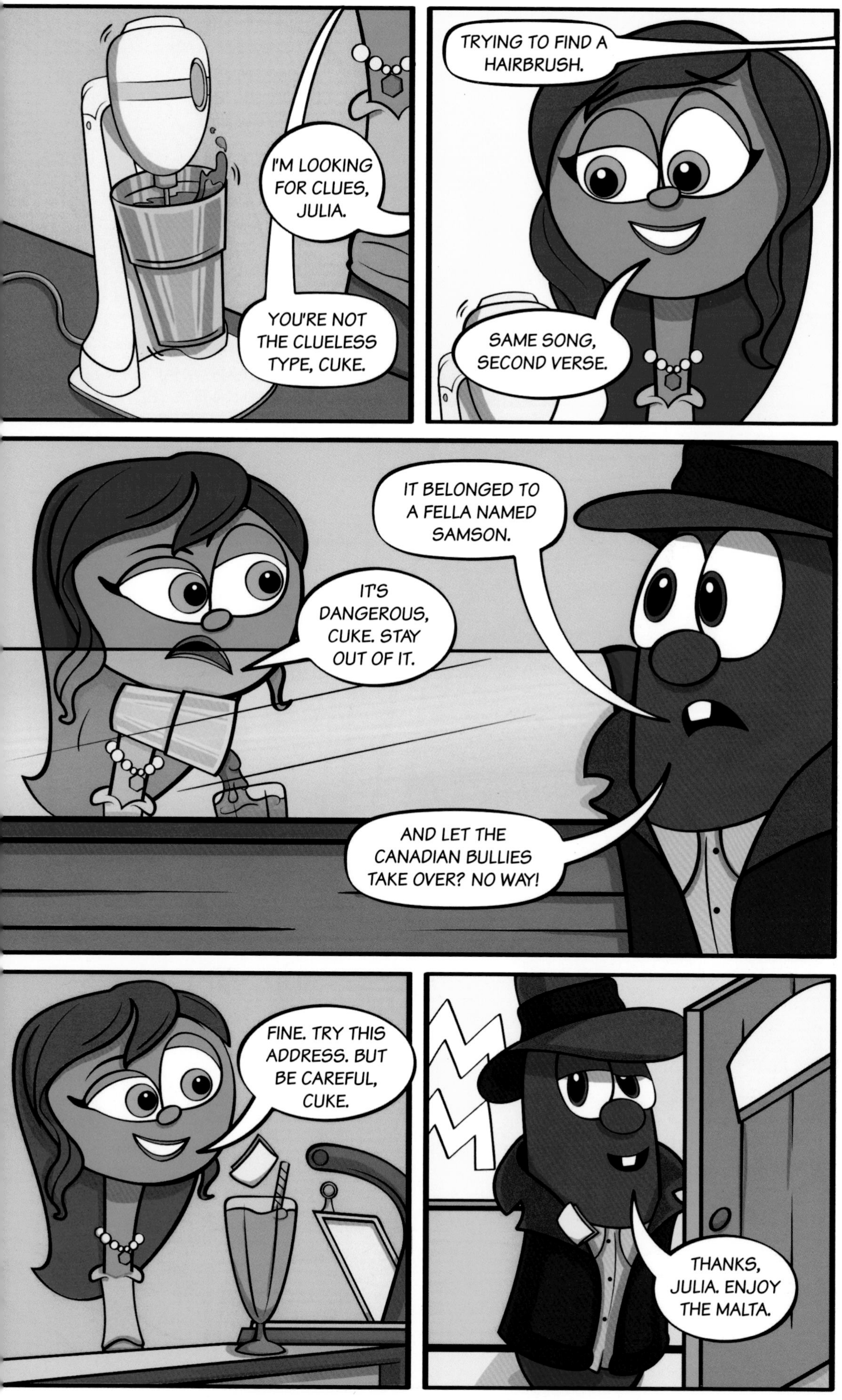
I'M LOOKING FOR CLUES, JULIA.
YOU'RE NOT THE CLUELESS TYPE, CUKE.
TRYING TO FIND A HAIRBRUSH.
SAME SONG, SECOND VERSE.
IT BELONGED TO A FELLA NAMED SAMSON.
IT'S DANGEROUS, CUKE. STAY OUT OF IT.
AND LET THE CANADIAN BULLIES TAKE OVER? NO WAY!
FINE. TRY THIS ADDRESS. BUT BE CAREFUL, CUKE.
THANKS, JULIA. ENJOY THE MALTA.

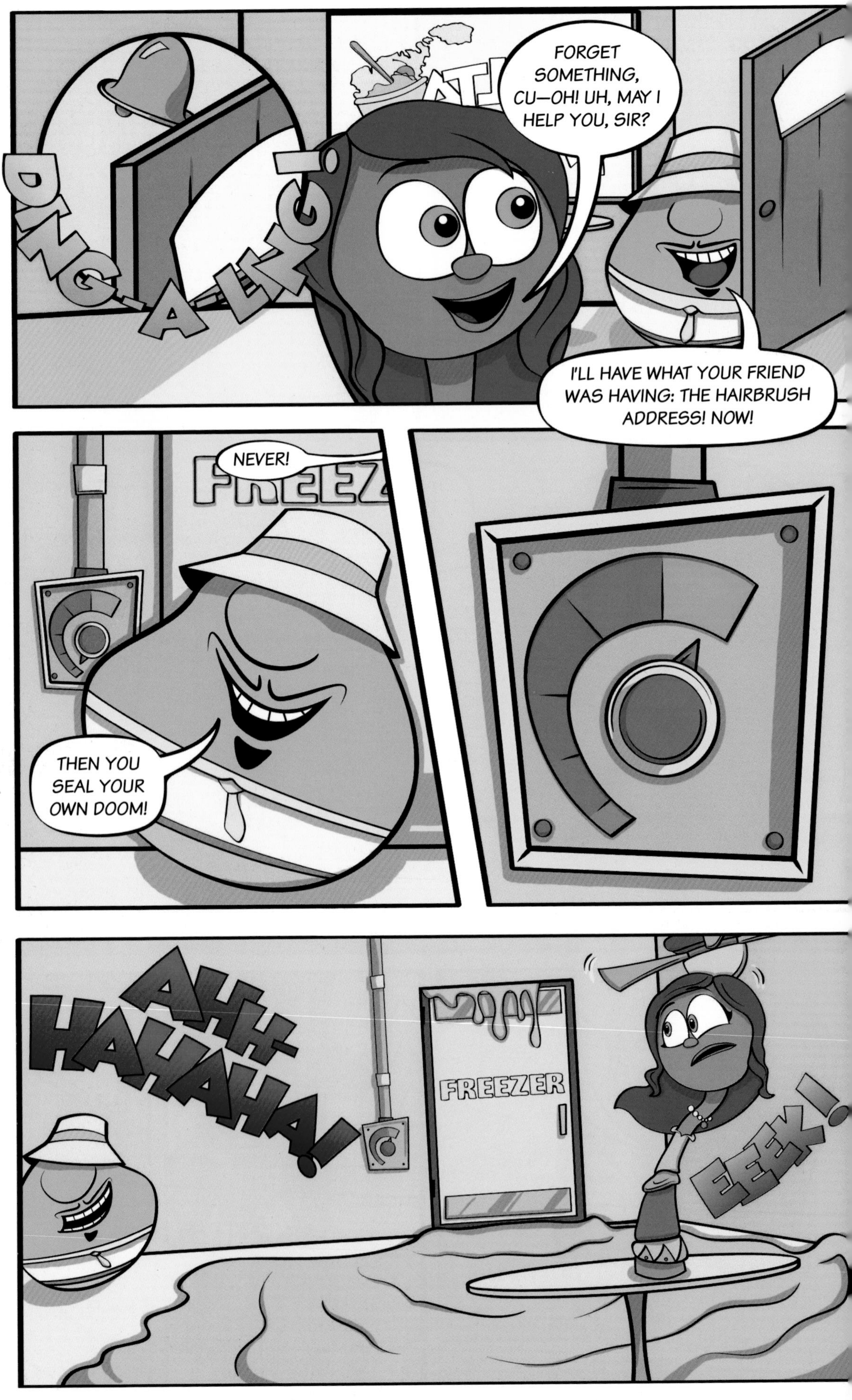
DING-A-LING
FORGET SOMETHING, CU—OH! UH, MAY I HELP YOU, SIR?
I'LL HAVE WHAT YOUR FRIEND WAS HAVING: THE HAIRBRUSH ADDRESS! NOW!
NEVER!
FREEZ
THEN YOU SEAL YOUR OWN DOOM!
AHH-HAHAHAHA!
FREEZER
EEEK!

OUTSIDE...

OKAY, MARTEN, THAT'S THE ADDRESS.

CHECKING IT NOW. AND I HAVE MORE INFO ON SAMSON!

GOD WANTED SAMSON TO BE EXTRA-SPECIAL, SO SAMSON HAD TO MAKE CERTAIN PROMISES TO GOD.

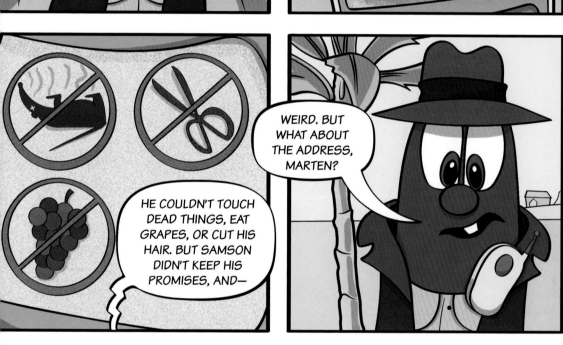

HE COULDN'T TOUCH DEAD THINGS, EAT GRAPES, OR CUT HIS HAIR. BUT SAMSON DIDN'T KEEP HIS PROMISES, AND—

WEIRD. BUT WHAT ABOUT THE ADDRESS, MARTEN?

HMM. THAT ADDRESS ISN'T IN MALTA.

RATS! I'LL CHECK WITH JULIA AGAIN.

INSIDE...

GREAT. FIRST ALL THE ICE CREAM MELTS INTO A FLOOD. THEN THE FAN TURNS INTO A CHOPPY-CRUSHY THING. WHAT'S NEXT?

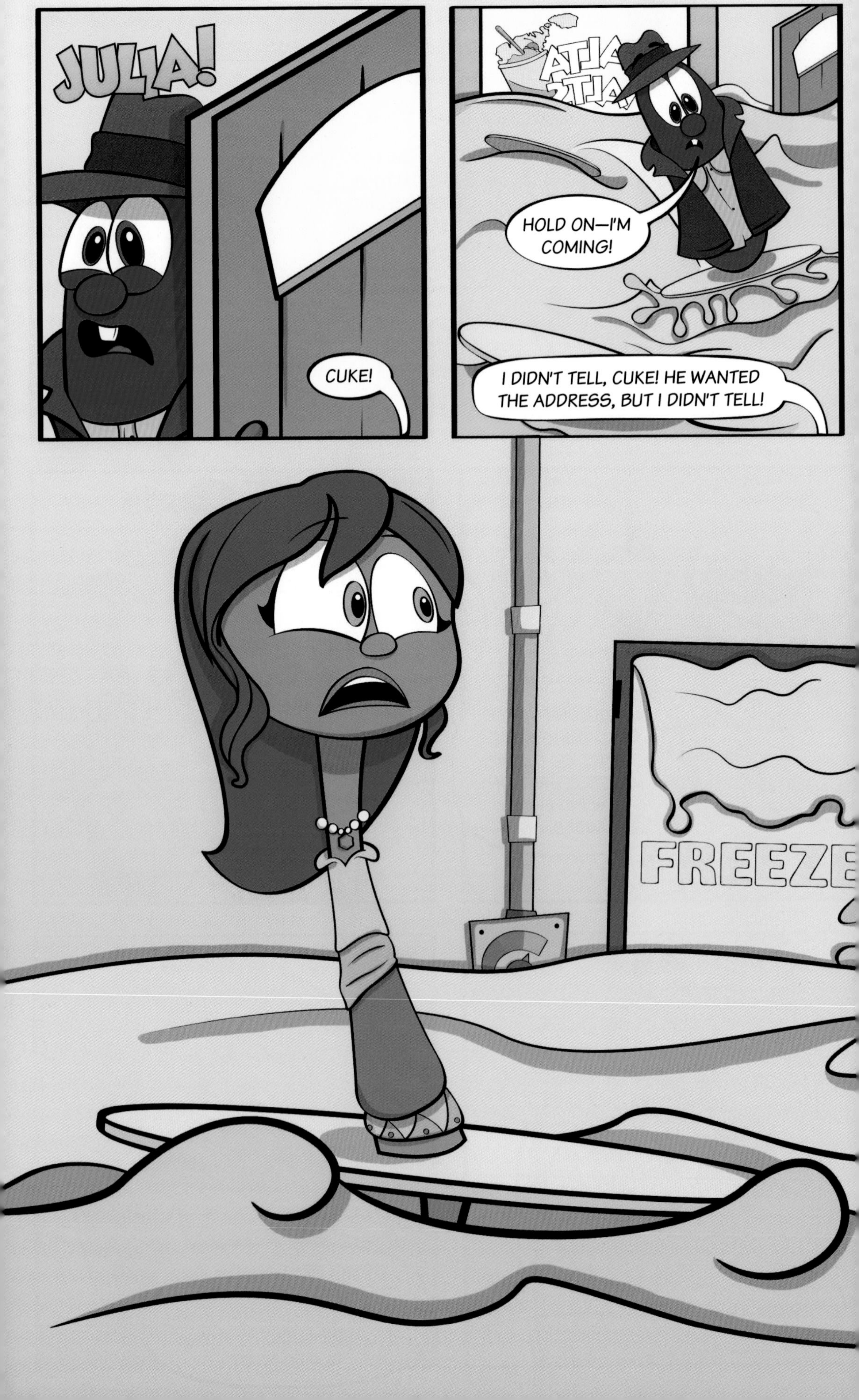
JULIA!
CUKE!
HOLD ON—I'M COMING!
I DIDN'T TELL, CUKE! HE WANTED THE ADDRESS, BUT I DIDN'T TELL!
FREEZE

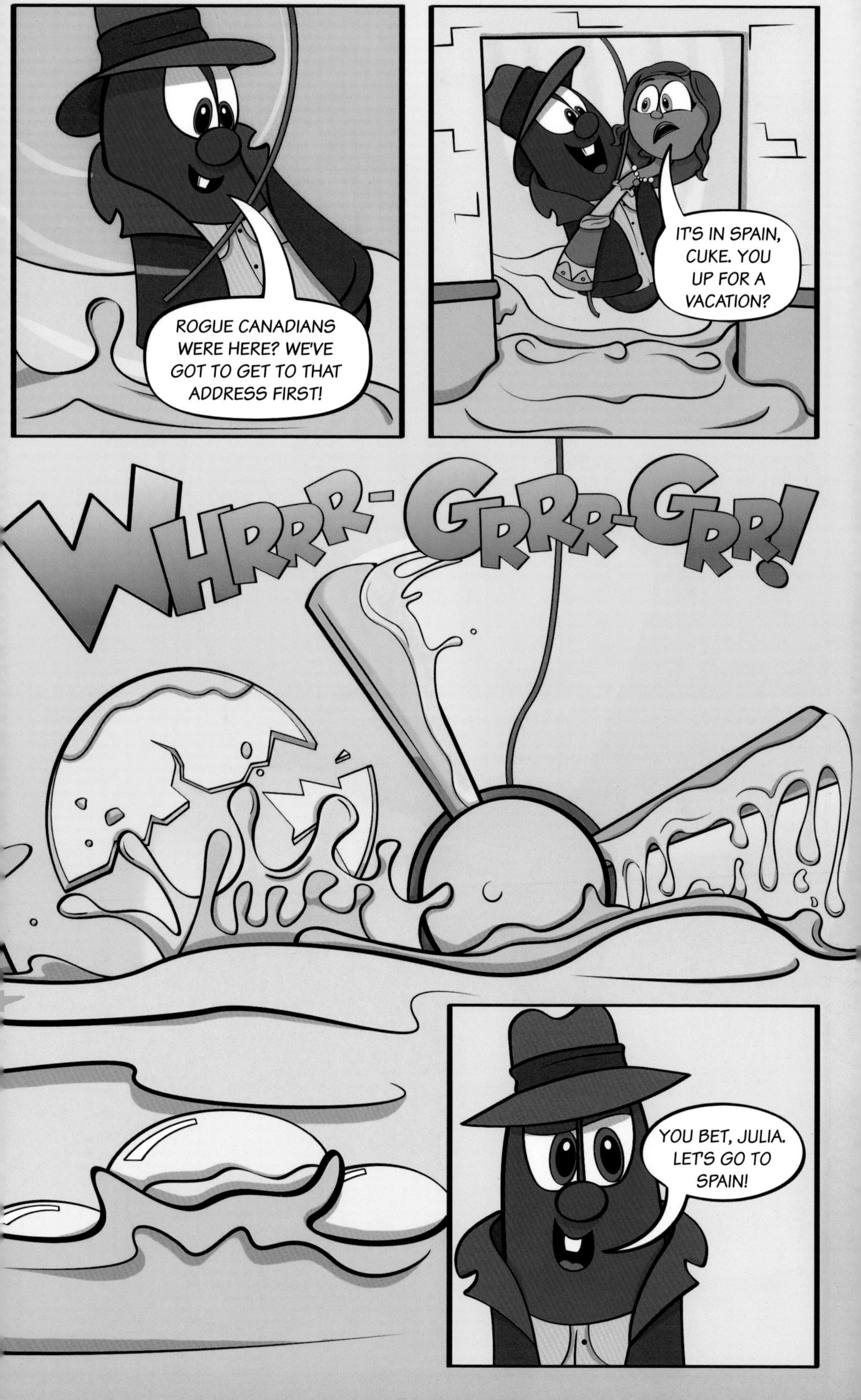
ROGUE CANADIANS WERE HERE? WE'VE GOT TO GET TO THAT ADDRESS FIRST!
IT'S IN SPAIN, CUKE. YOU UP FOR A VACATION?
WHRRR-GRRR-GRR!
YOU BET, JULIA. LET'S GO TO SPAIN!

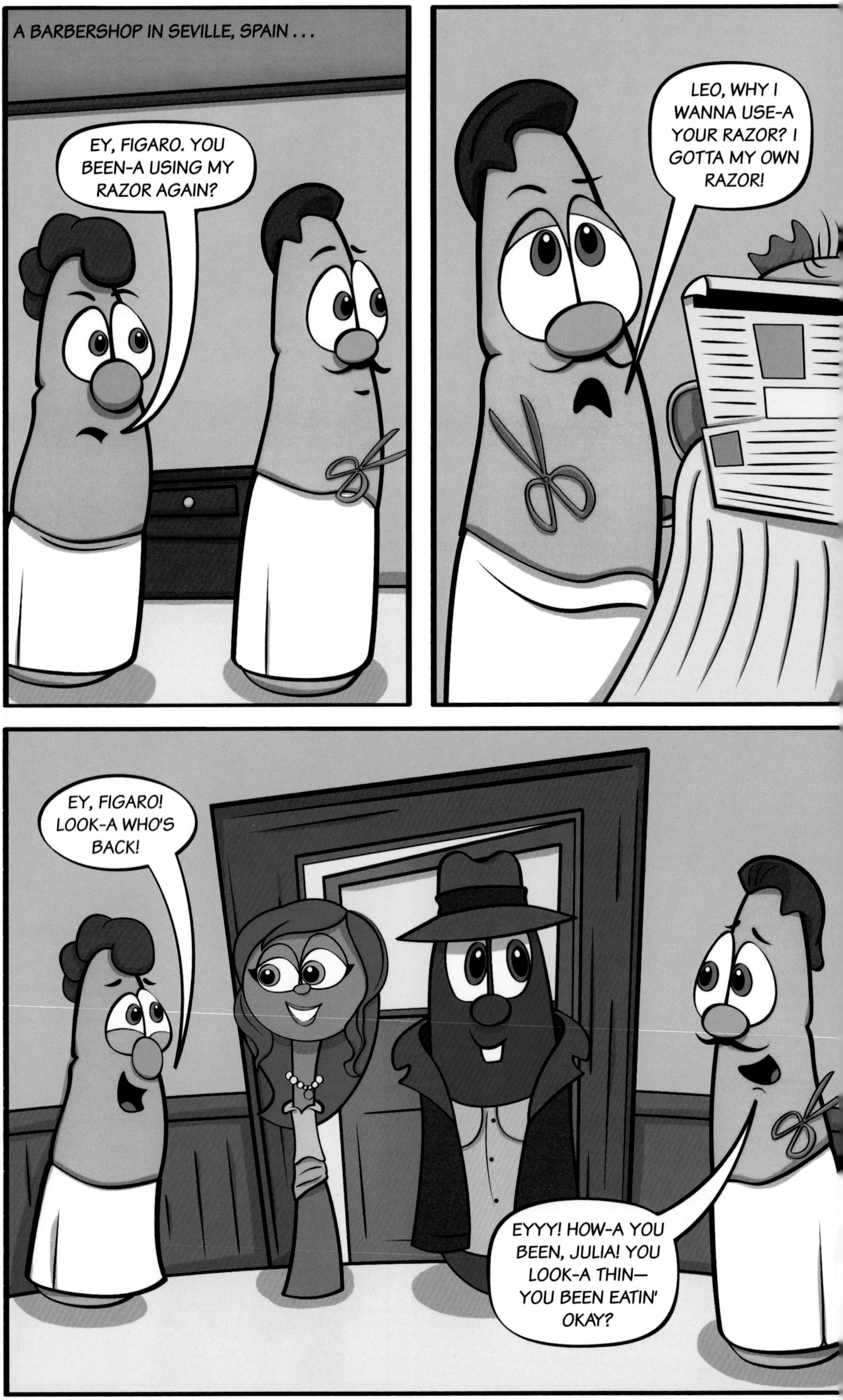
A BARBERSHOP IN SEVILLE, SPAIN . . .
EY, FIGARO. YOU BEEN-A USING MY RAZOR AGAIN?
LEO, WHY I WANNA USE-A YOUR RAZOR? I GOTTA MY OWN RAZOR!
EY, FIGARO! LOOK-A WHO'S BACK!
EYYY! HOW-A YOU BEEN, JULIA! YOU LOOK-A THIN— YOU BEEN EATIN' OKAY?

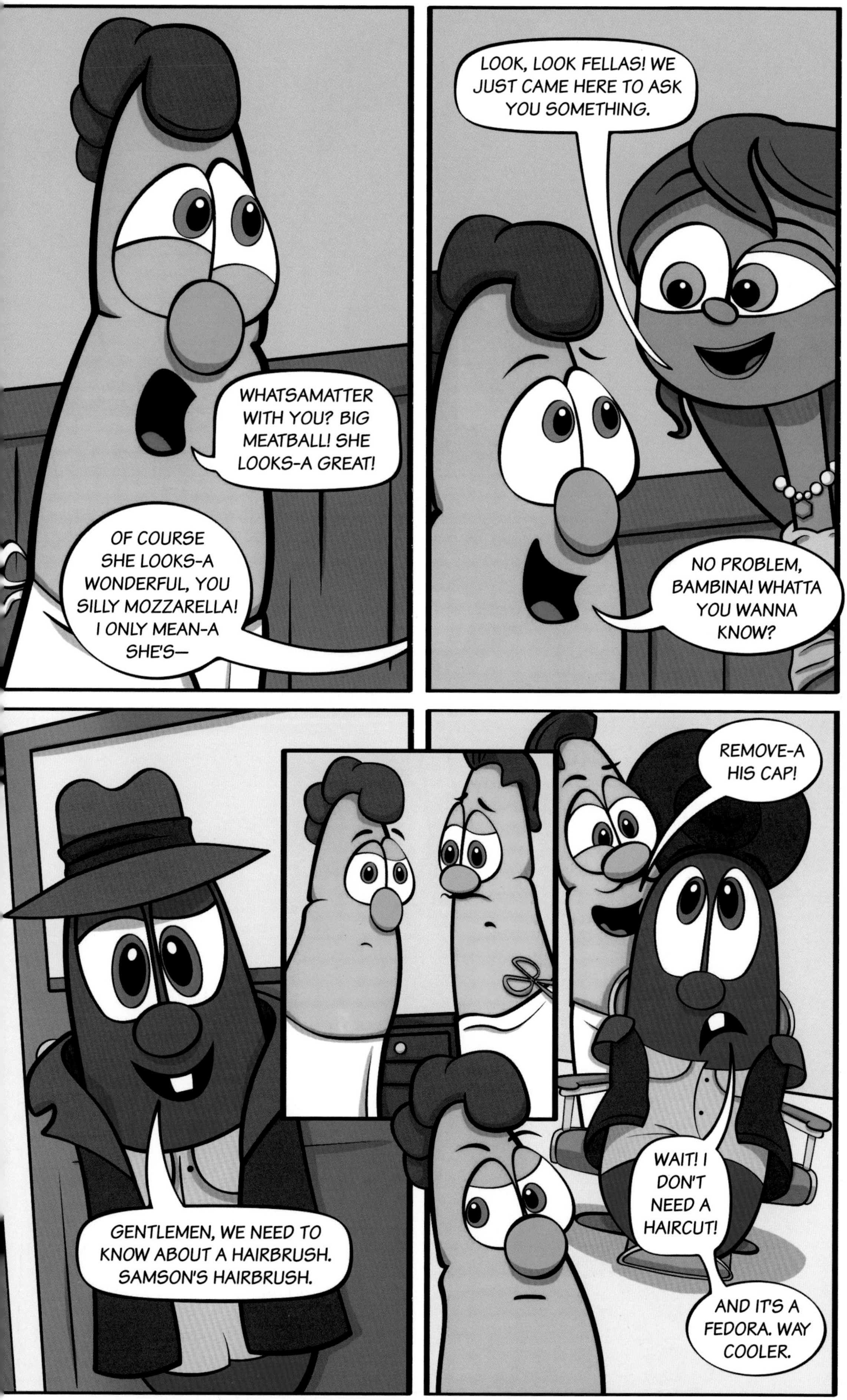
WHATSAMATTER WITH YOU? BIG MEATBALL! SHE LOOKS-A GREAT!
OF COURSE SHE LOOKS-A WONDERFUL, YOU SILLY MOZZARELLA! I ONLY MEAN-A SHE'S—
LOOK, LOOK FELLAS! WE JUST CAME HERE TO ASK YOU SOMETHING.
NO PROBLEM, BAMBINA! WHATTA YOU WANNA KNOW?
GENTLEMEN, WE NEED TO KNOW ABOUT A HAIRBRUSH. SAMSON'S HAIRBRUSH.
REMOVE-A HIS CAP!
WAIT! I DON'T NEED A HAIRCUT!
AND IT'S A FEDORA. WAY COOLER.

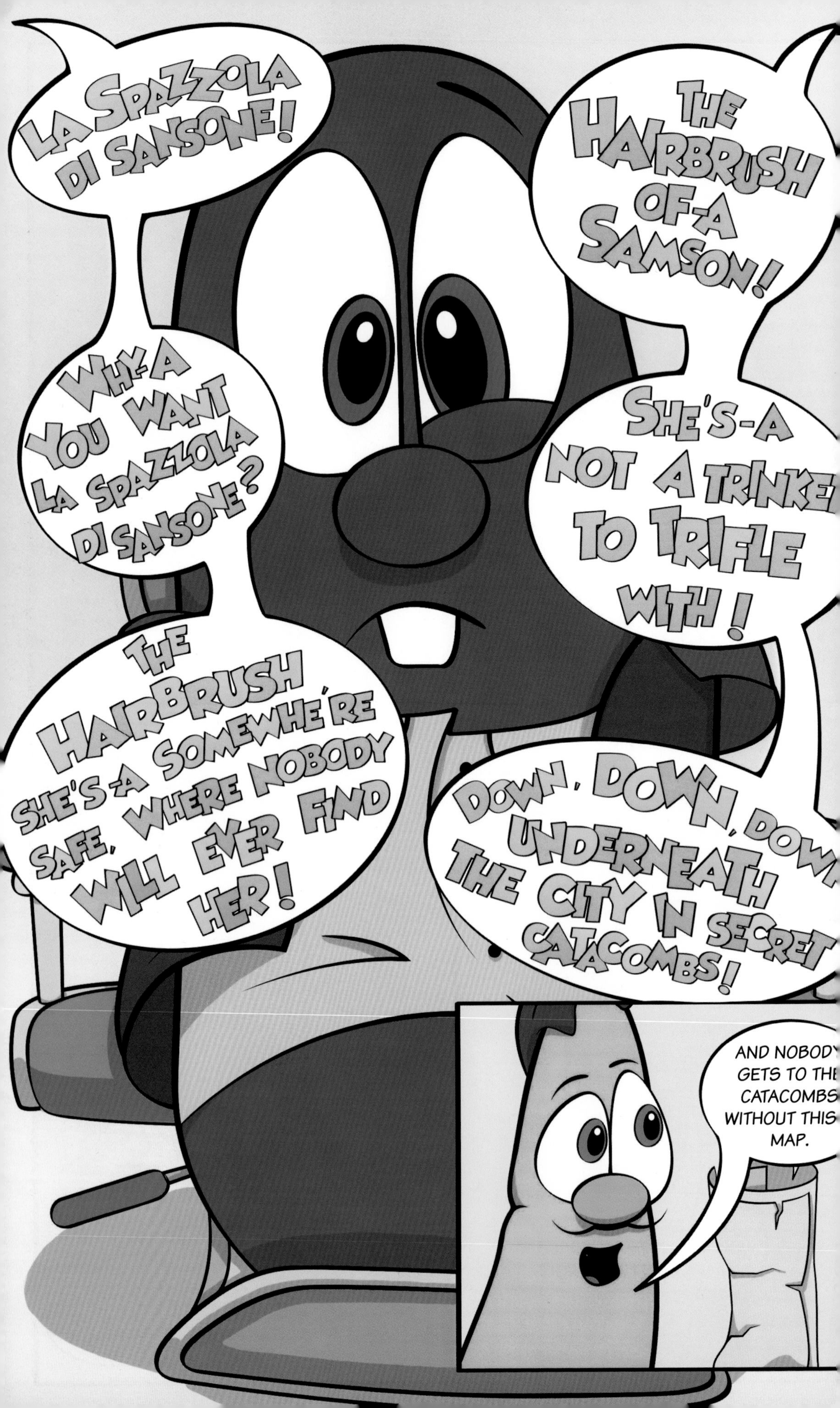
LA SPAZZOLA DI SANSONE!
THE HAIRBRUSH OF-A SAMSON!
WHY-A YOU WANT LA SPAZZOLA DI SANSONE?
SHE'S-A NOT A TRINKET TO TRIFLE WITH!
THE HAIRBRUSH SHE'S-A SOMEWHE'RE SAFE, WHERE NOBODY WILL EVER FIND HER!
DOWN, DOWN, DOWN UNDERNEATH THE CITY IN SECRET CATACOMBS!
AND NOBODY GETS TO THE CATACOMBS WITHOUT THIS MAP.

WAIT A MINUTE, FELLAS. I DON'T WANT A CAT COMB. . . .

ONCE AGAIN YOU LOSE, MINNESOTA FLUKE!

MAMA MIA!

LEMME OUTTA THIS CHAIR! FIGARO! FIGARO! FI-GA-RO! HE'S GETTING AWAY!

AGGH!

OKAY, THAT WAS EMBARRASSING.

YAH. GOOD THING THERE'S ANOTHER WAY TO THE CATACOMBS.

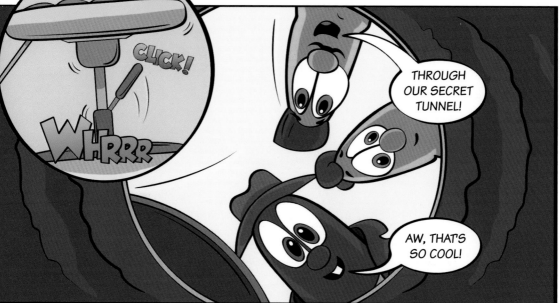

CLICK!

WHRRR

THROUGH OUR SECRET TUNNEL!

AW, THAT'S SO COOL!

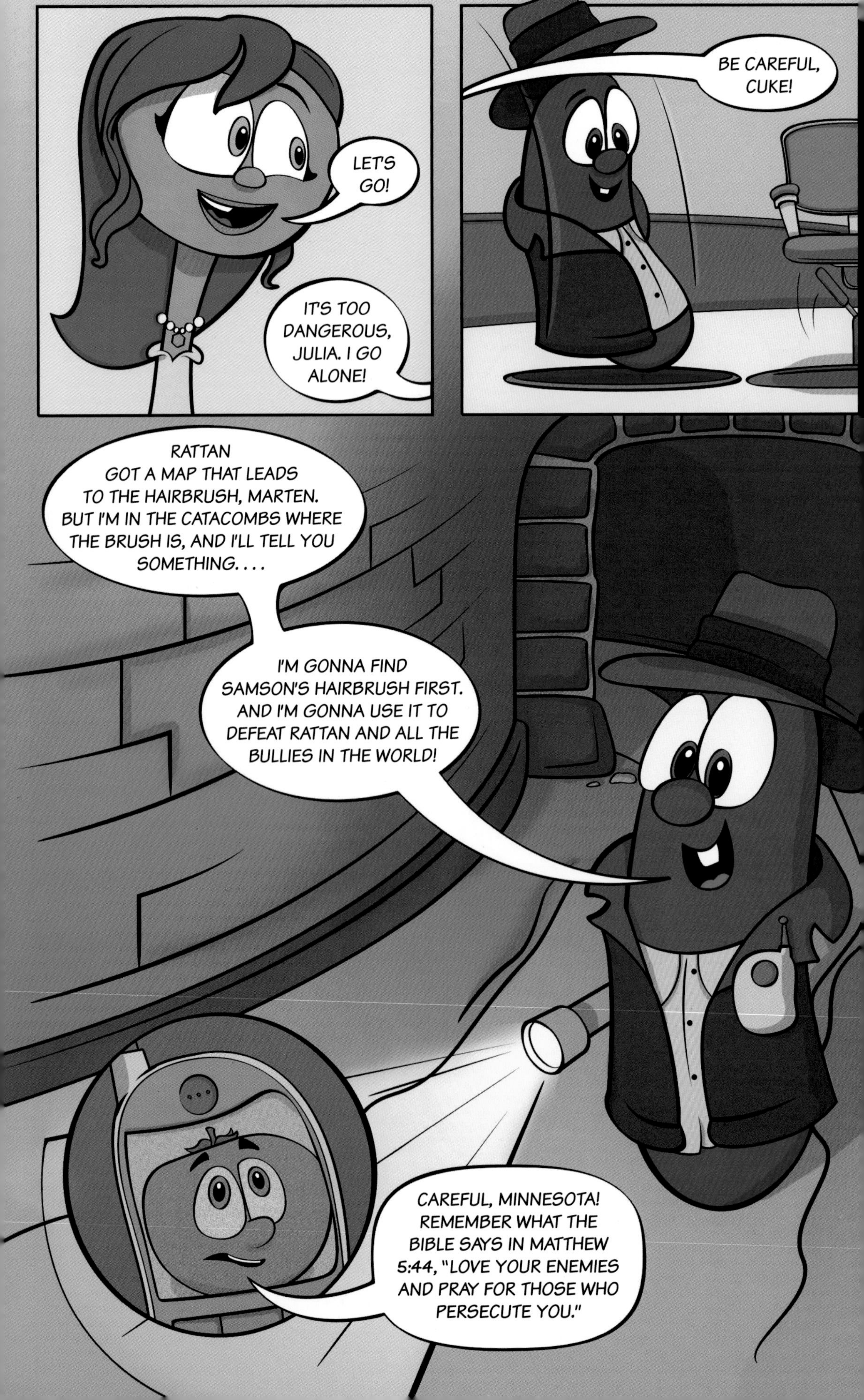
LET'S GO!
IT'S TOO DANGEROUS, JULIA. I GO ALONE!
BE CAREFUL, CUKE!
RATTAN GOT A MAP THAT LEADS TO THE HAIRBRUSH, MARTEN. BUT I'M IN THE CATACOMBS WHERE THE BRUSH IS, AND I'LL TELL YOU SOMETHING. . . .
I'M GONNA FIND SAMSON'S HAIRBRUSH FIRST. AND I'M GONNA USE IT TO DEFEAT RATTAN AND ALL THE BULLIES IN THE WORLD!
CAREFUL, MINNESOTA! REMEMBER WHAT THE BIBLE SAYS IN MATTHEW 5:44, "LOVE YOUR ENEMIES AND PRAY FOR THOSE WHO PERSECUTE YOU."

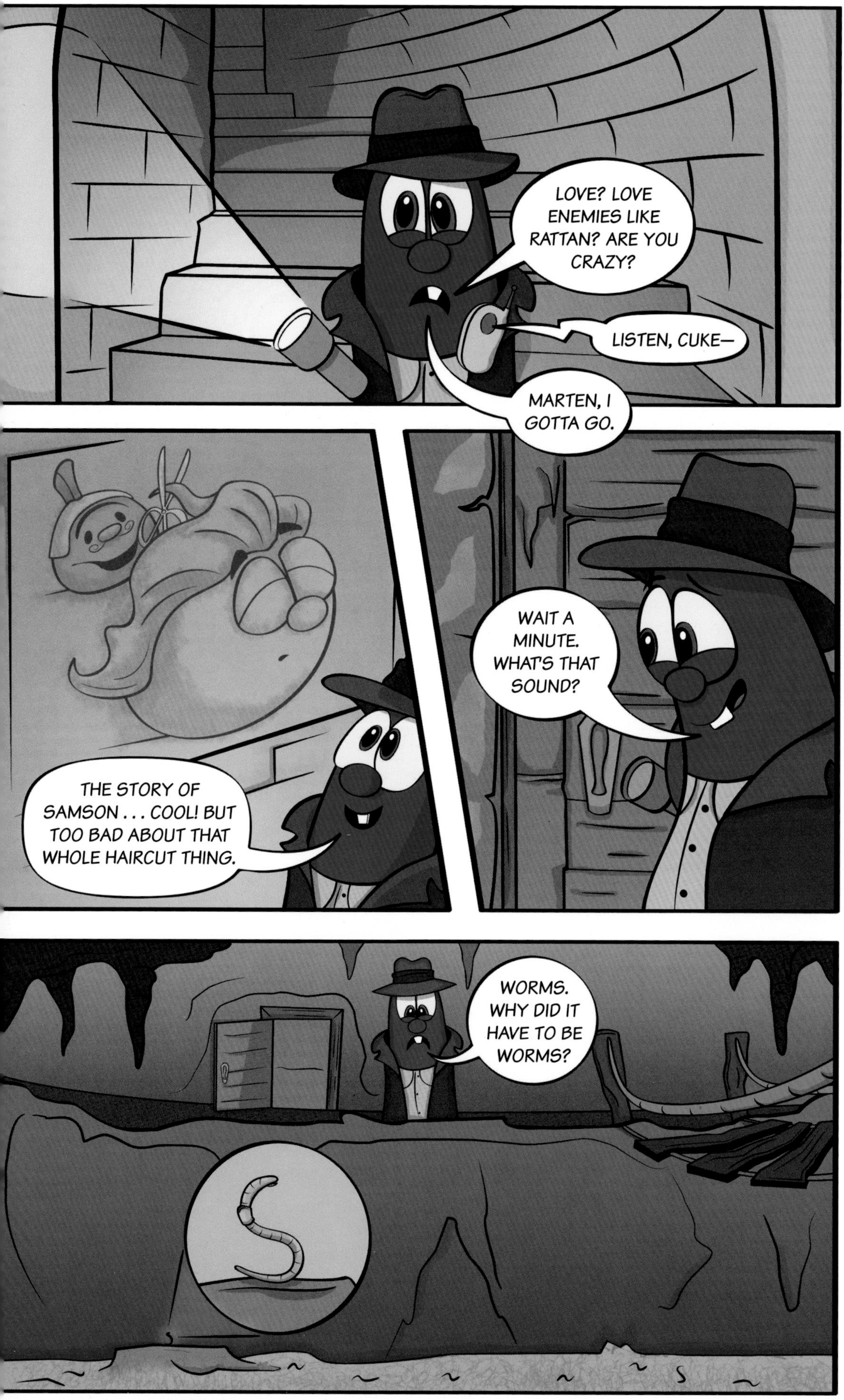
LOVE? LOVE ENEMIES LIKE RATTAN? ARE YOU CRAZY?
LISTEN, CUKE—
MARTEN, I GOTTA GO.
THE STORY OF SAMSON . . . COOL! BUT TOO BAD ABOUT THAT WHOLE HAIRCUT THING.
WAIT A MINUTE. WHAT'S THAT SOUND?
WORMS. WHY DID IT HAVE TO BE WORMS?

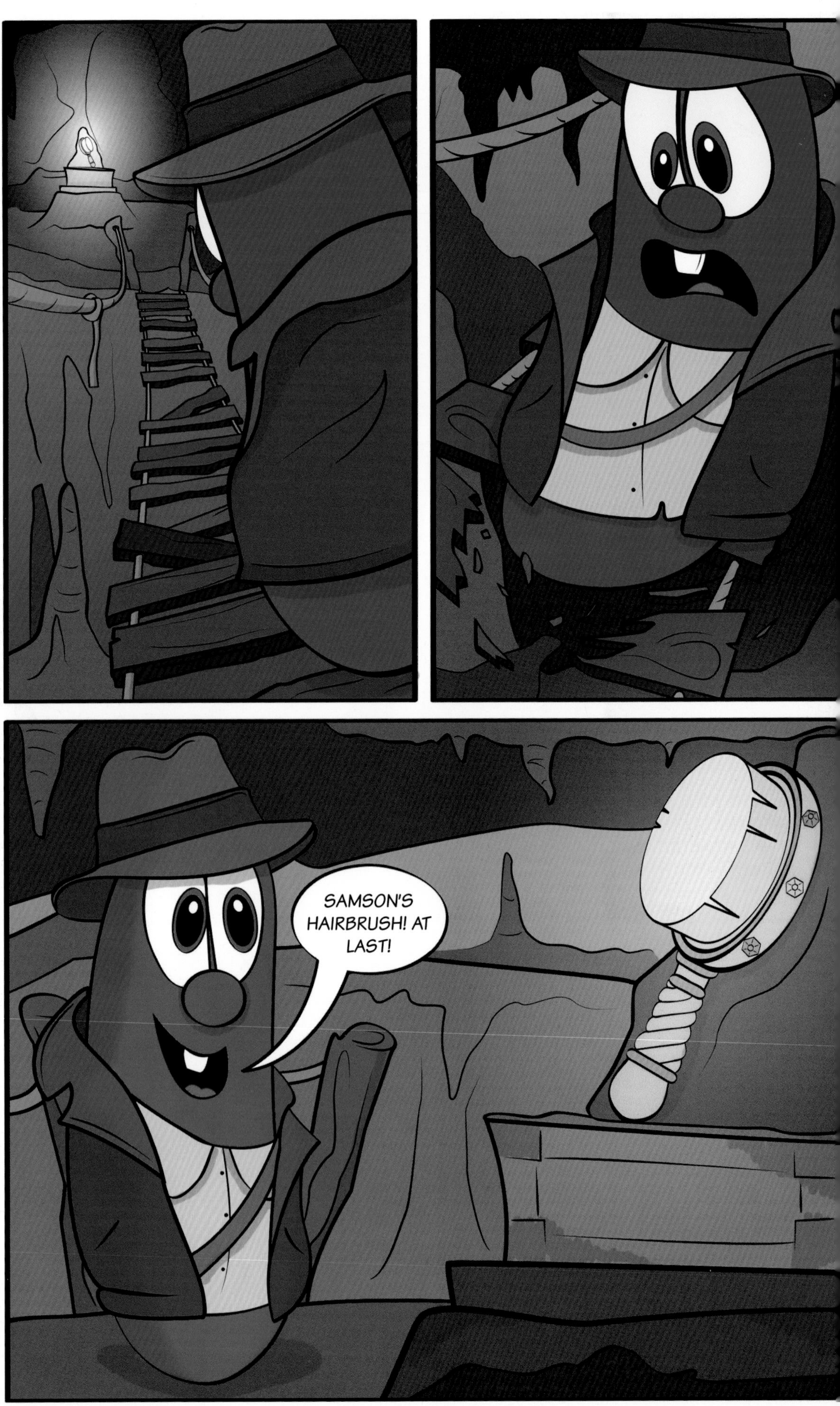
SAMSON'S HAIRBRUSH! AT LAST!

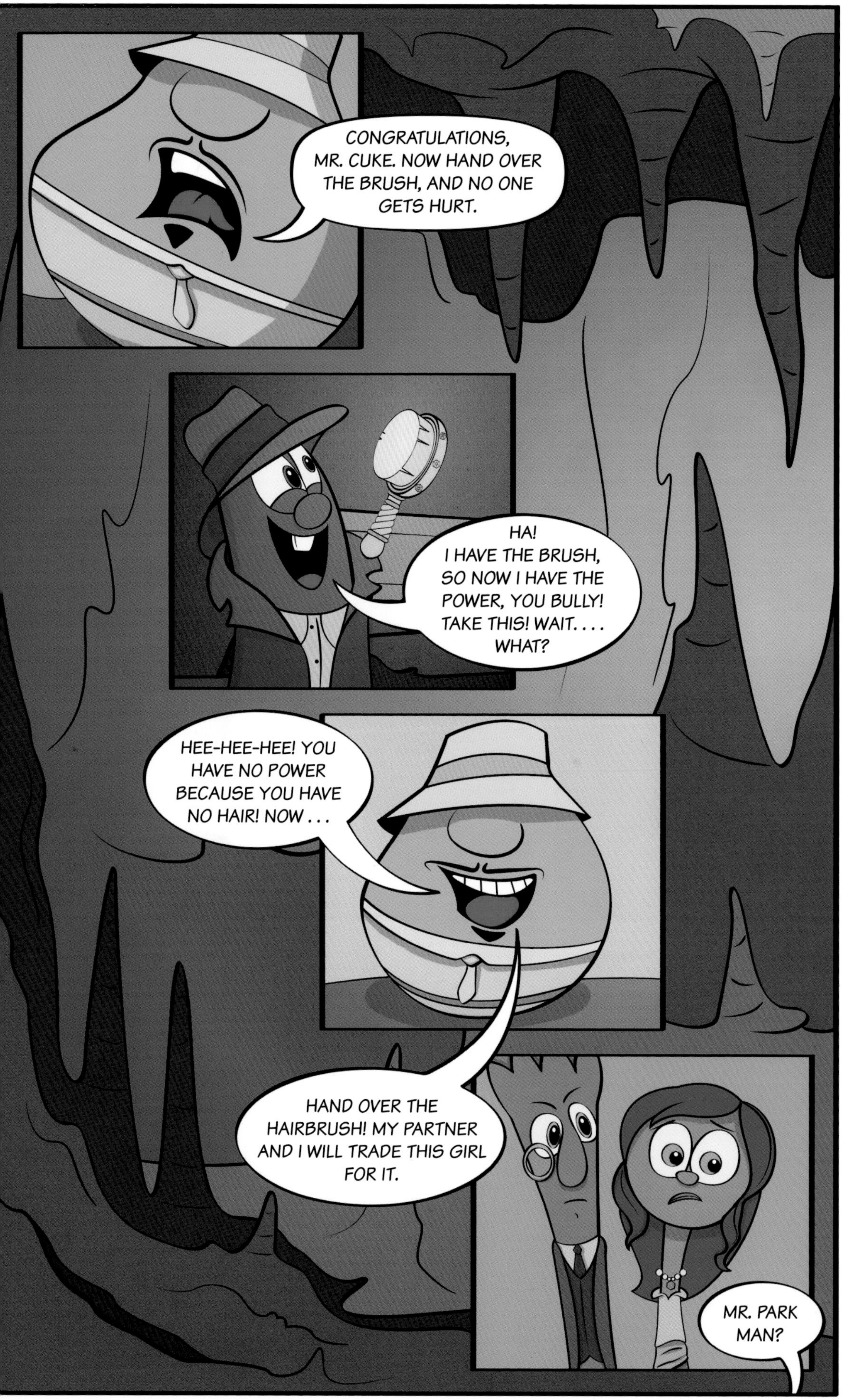

CONGRATULATIONS, MR. CUKE. NOW HAND OVER THE BRUSH, AND NO ONE GETS HURT.
HA! I HAVE THE BRUSH, SO NOW I HAVE THE POWER, YOU BULLY! TAKE THIS! WAIT. . . . WHAT?
HEE-HEE-HEE! YOU HAVE NO POWER BECAUSE YOU HAVE NO HAIR! NOW . . .
HAND OVER THE HAIRBRUSH! MY PARTNER AND I WILL TRADE THIS GIRL FOR IT.
MR. PARK MAN?

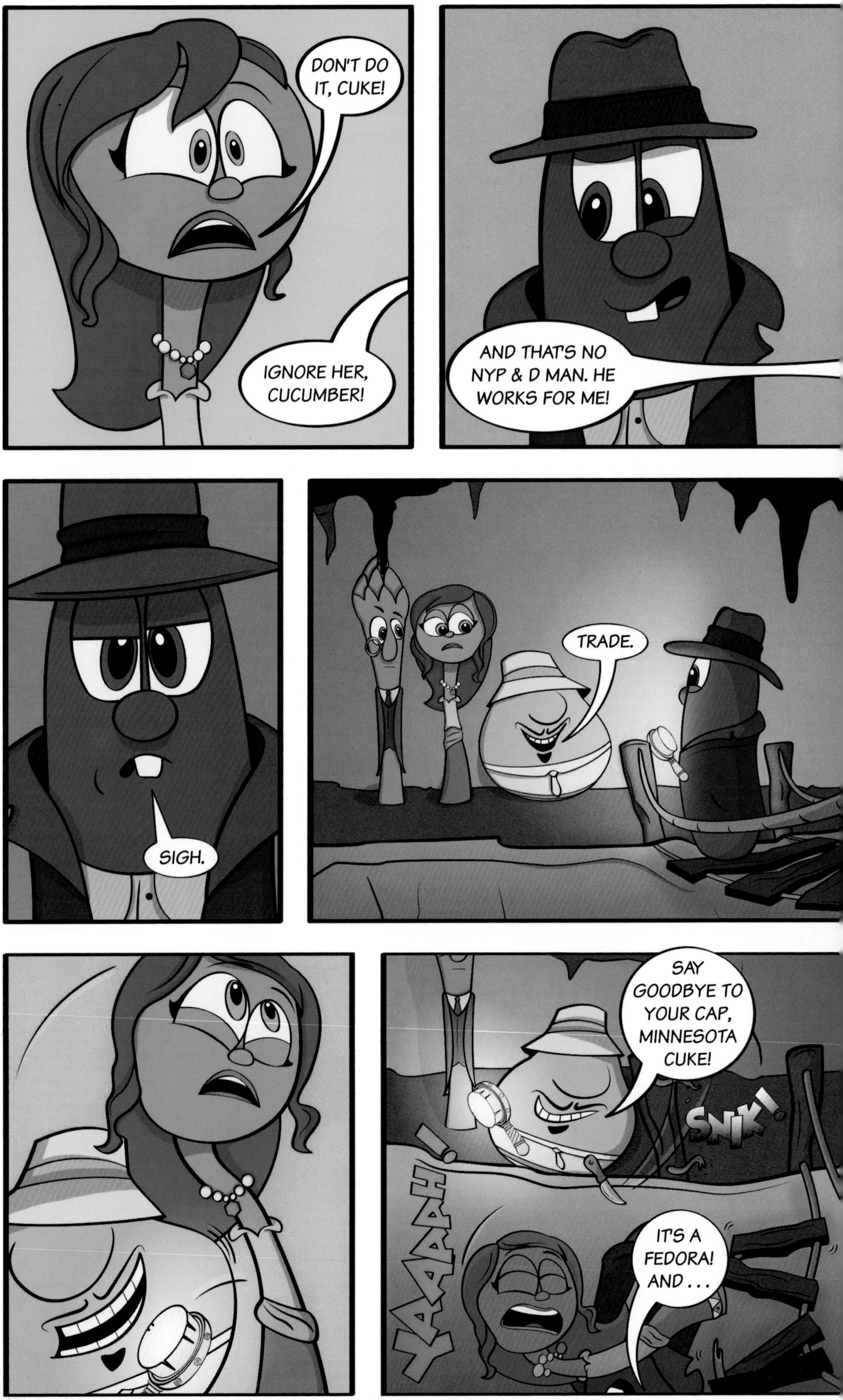
DON'T DO IT, CUKE!
IGNORE HER, CUCUMBER!
AND THAT'S NO NYP & D MAN. HE WORKS FOR ME!
SIGH.
TRADE.
SAY GOODBYE TO YOUR CAP, MINNESOTA CUKE!
SNIK!
YAAAAH!
IT'S A FEDORA! AND . . .

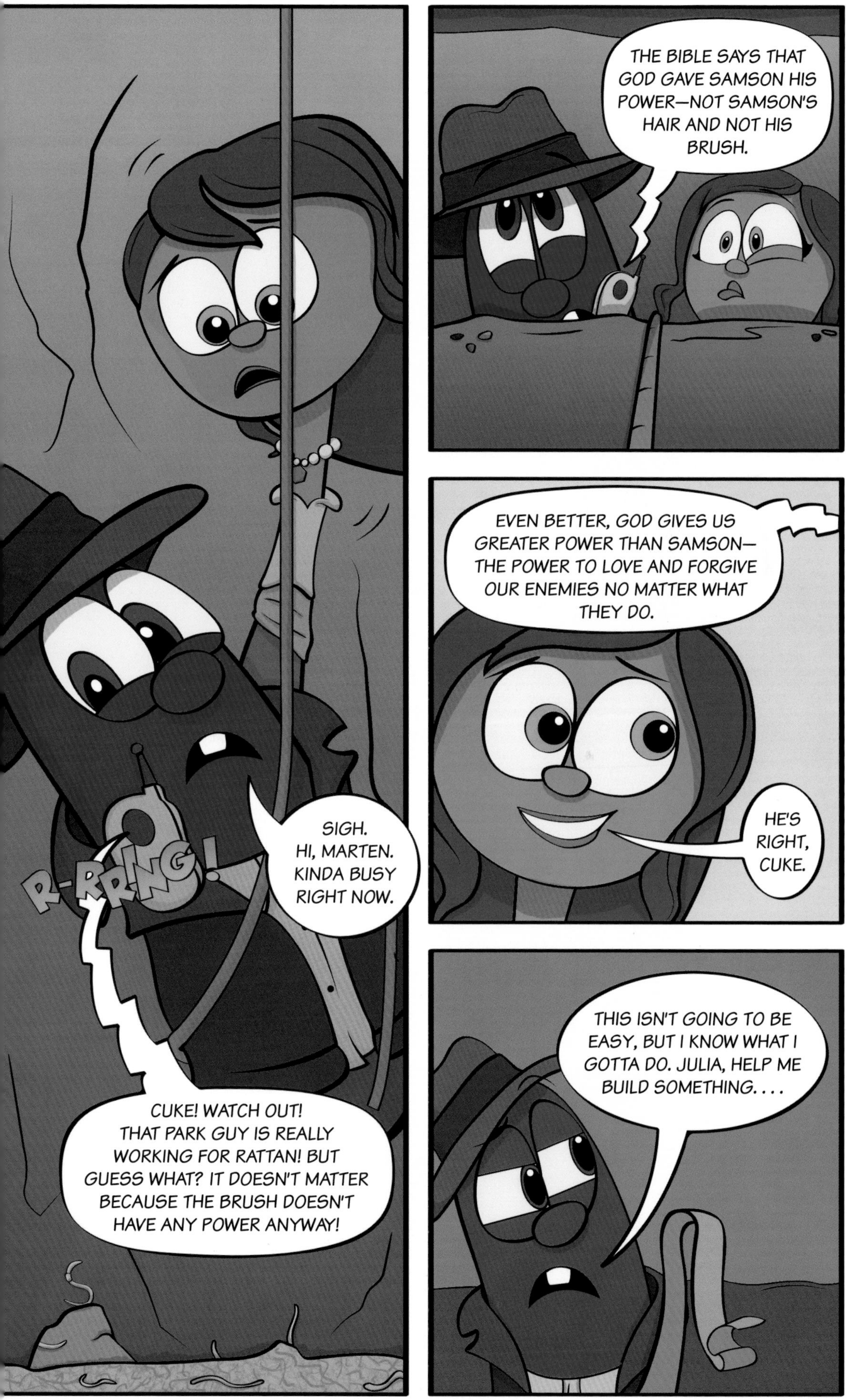
R-RRING!
SIGH. HI, MARTEN. KINDA BUSY RIGHT NOW.
CUKE! WATCH OUT! THAT PARK GUY IS REALLY WORKING FOR RATTAN! BUT GUESS WHAT? IT DOESN'T MATTER BECAUSE THE BRUSH DOESN'T HAVE ANY POWER ANYWAY!
THE BIBLE SAYS THAT GOD GAVE SAMSON HIS POWER—NOT SAMSON'S HAIR AND NOT HIS BRUSH.
EVEN BETTER, GOD GIVES US GREATER POWER THAN SAMSON—THE POWER TO LOVE AND FORGIVE OUR ENEMIES NO MATTER WHAT THEY DO.
HE'S RIGHT, CUKE.
THIS ISN'T GOING TO BE EASY, BUT I KNOW WHAT I GOTTA DO. JULIA, HELP ME BUILD SOMETHING. . . .

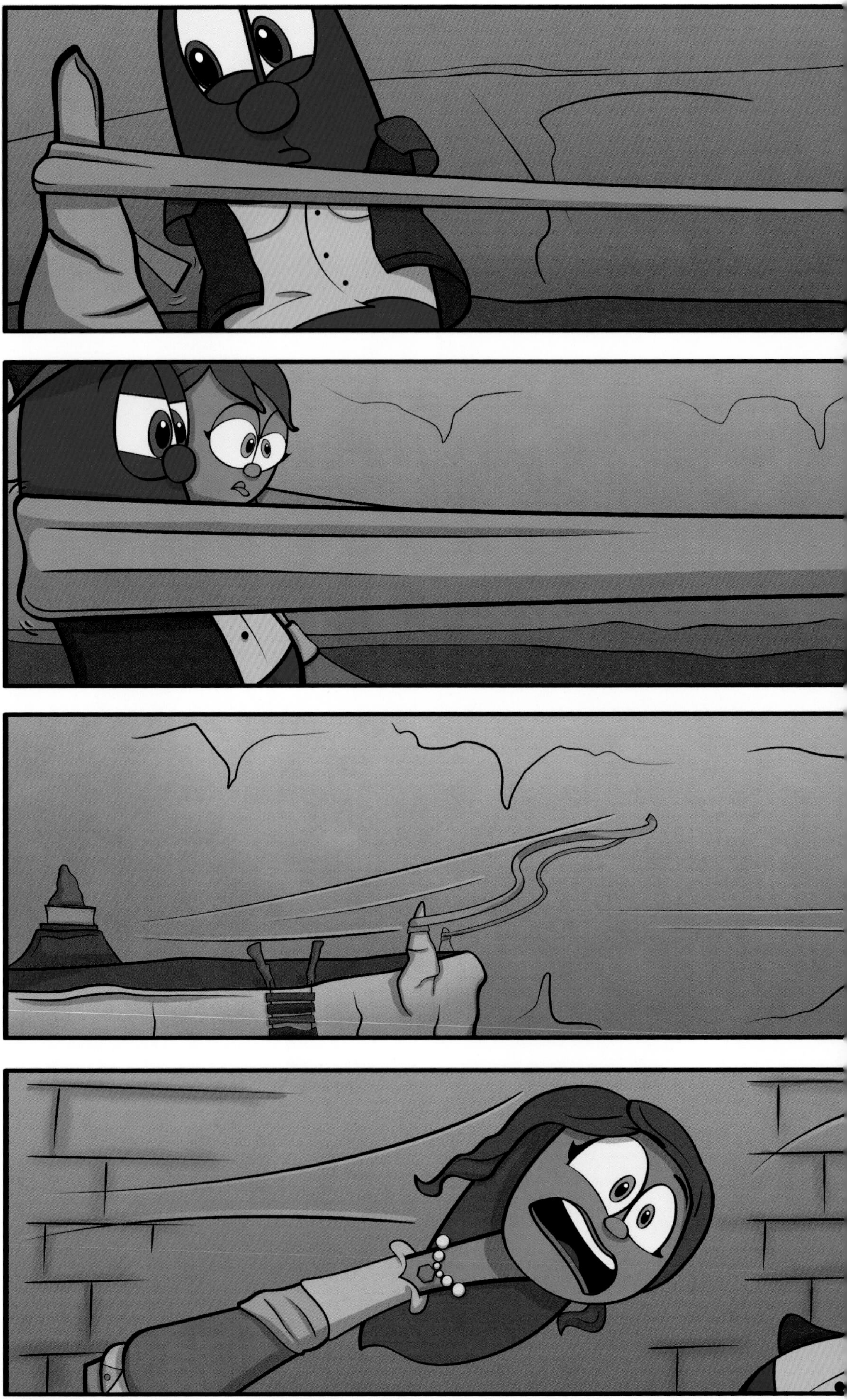

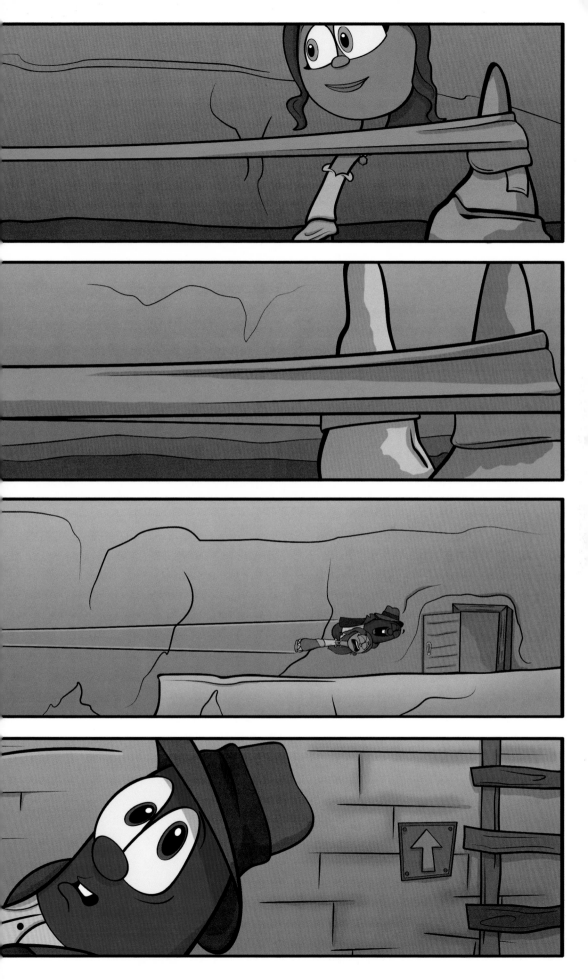

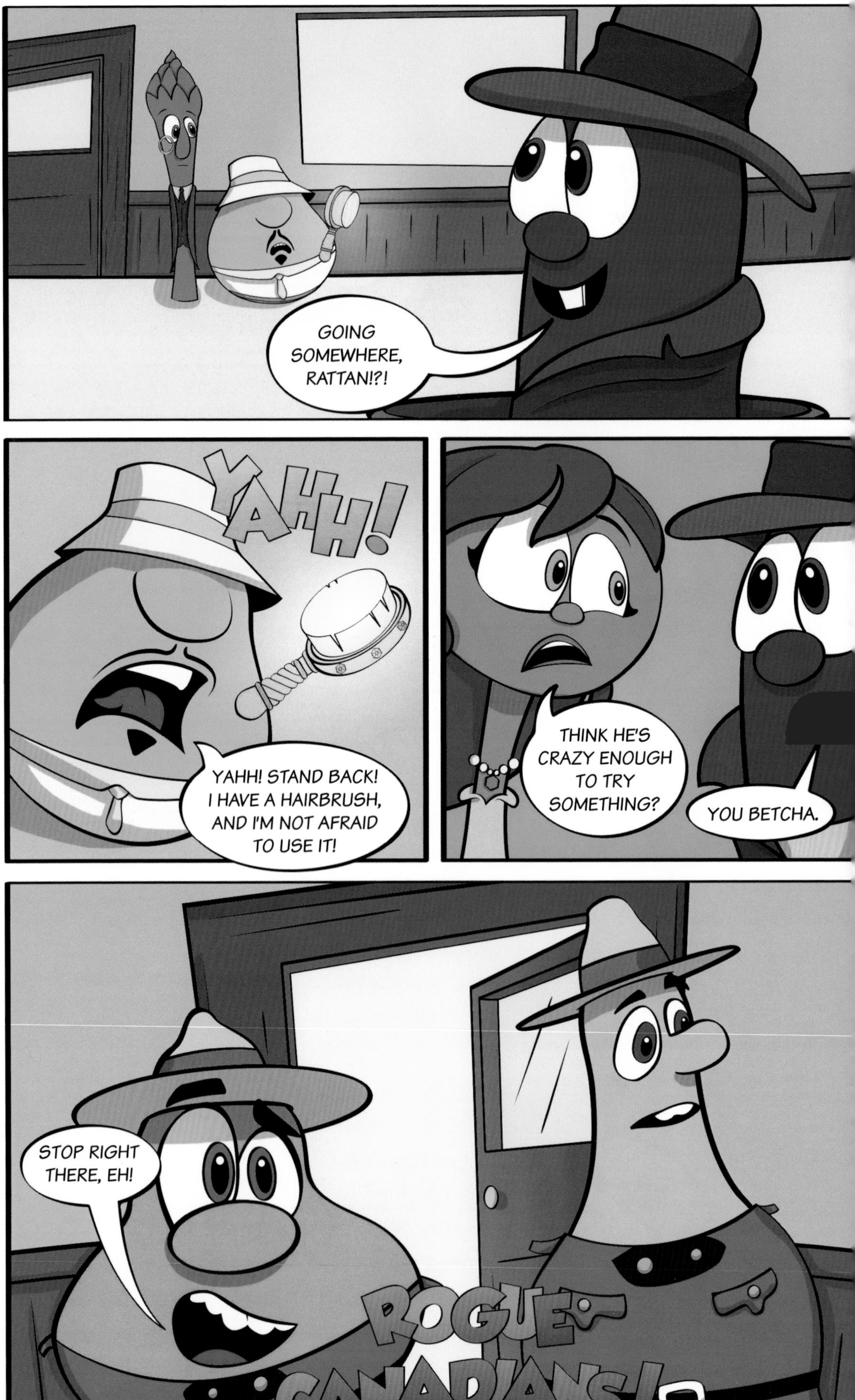
GOING SOMEWHERE, RATTAN!?!
YAHH!
YAHH! STAND BACK! I HAVE A HAIRBRUSH, AND I'M NOT AFRAID TO USE IT!
THINK HE'S CRAZY ENOUGH TO TRY SOMETHING?
YOU BETCHA.
STOP RIGHT THERE, EH!
ROGUE CANADIANS!

NO, NO, NO, MY FRIEND! THEY'RE THE GOOD GUYS.

WE CALL-A THE CALVARY!

NOBODY COMES TO THE RESCUE BETTER THAN THE ROYAL CANADIAN MOUNTIES, EH?

GET HIM!

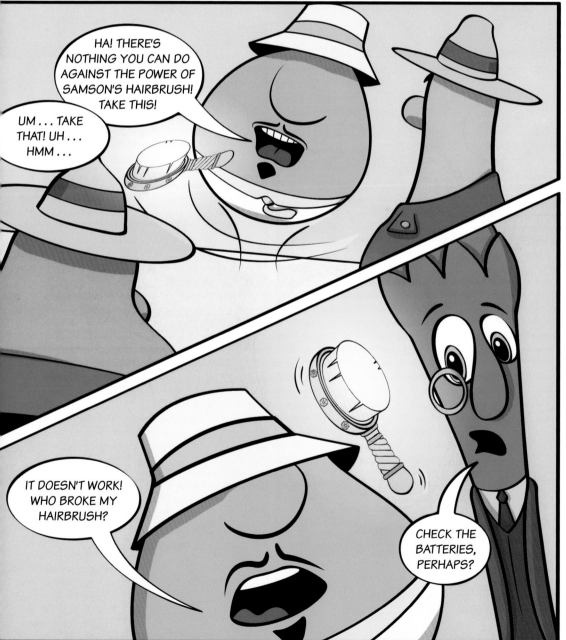

HA! THERE'S NOTHING YOU CAN DO AGAINST THE POWER OF SAMSON'S HAIRBRUSH! TAKE THIS!

UM . . . TAKE THAT! UH . . . HMM . . .

IT DOESN'T WORK! WHO BROKE MY HAIRBRUSH?

CHECK THE BATTERIES, PERHAPS?

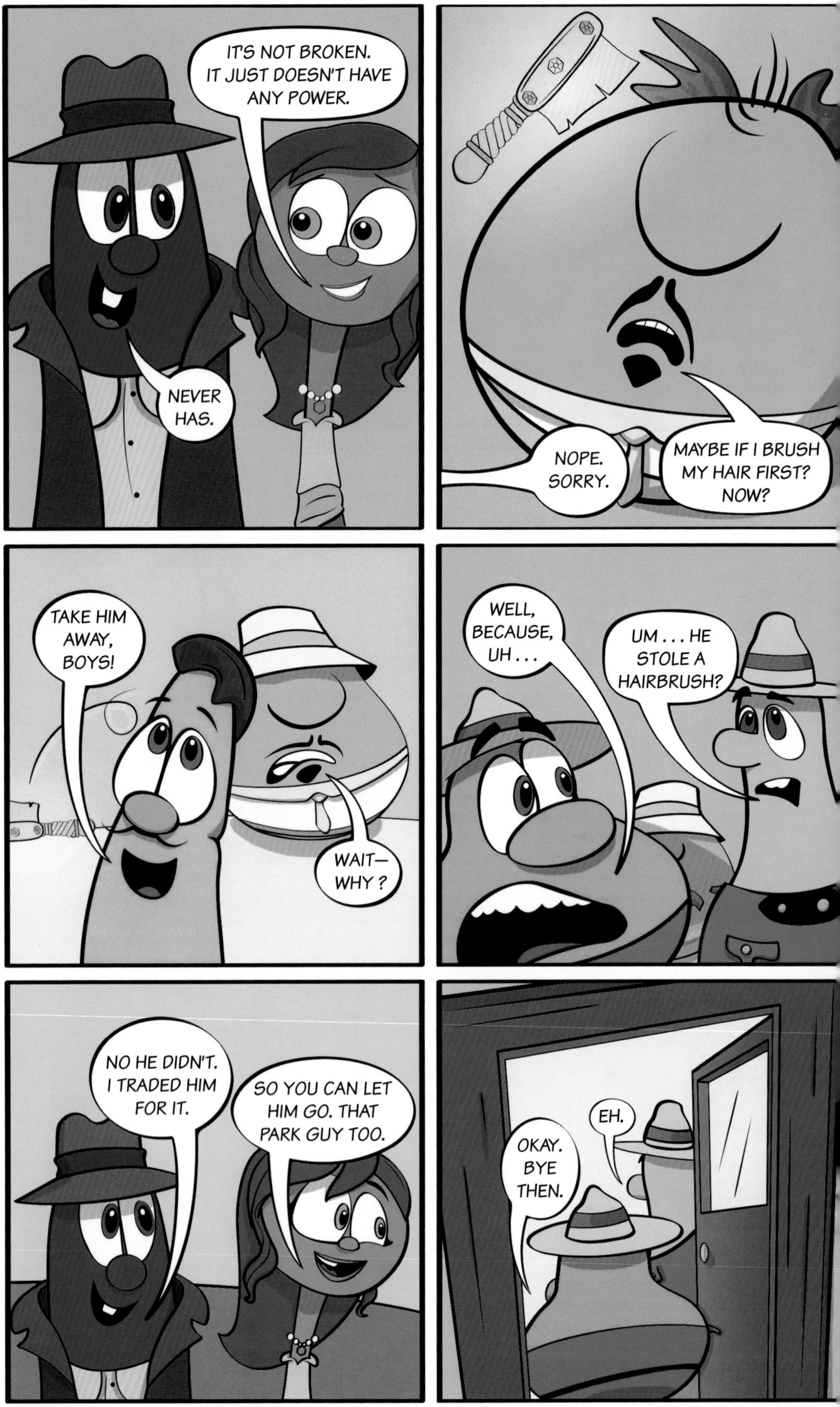
IT'S NOT BROKEN. IT JUST DOESN'T HAVE ANY POWER.
NEVER HAS.
MAYBE IF I BRUSH MY HAIR FIRST? NOW?
NOPE. SORRY.
TAKE HIM AWAY, BOYS!
WAIT— WHY ?
WELL, BECAUSE, UH . . .
UM . . . HE STOLE A HAIRBRUSH?
NO HE DIDN'T. I TRADED HIM FOR IT.
SO YOU CAN LET HIM GO. THAT PARK GUY TOO.
EH.
OKAY. BYE THEN.

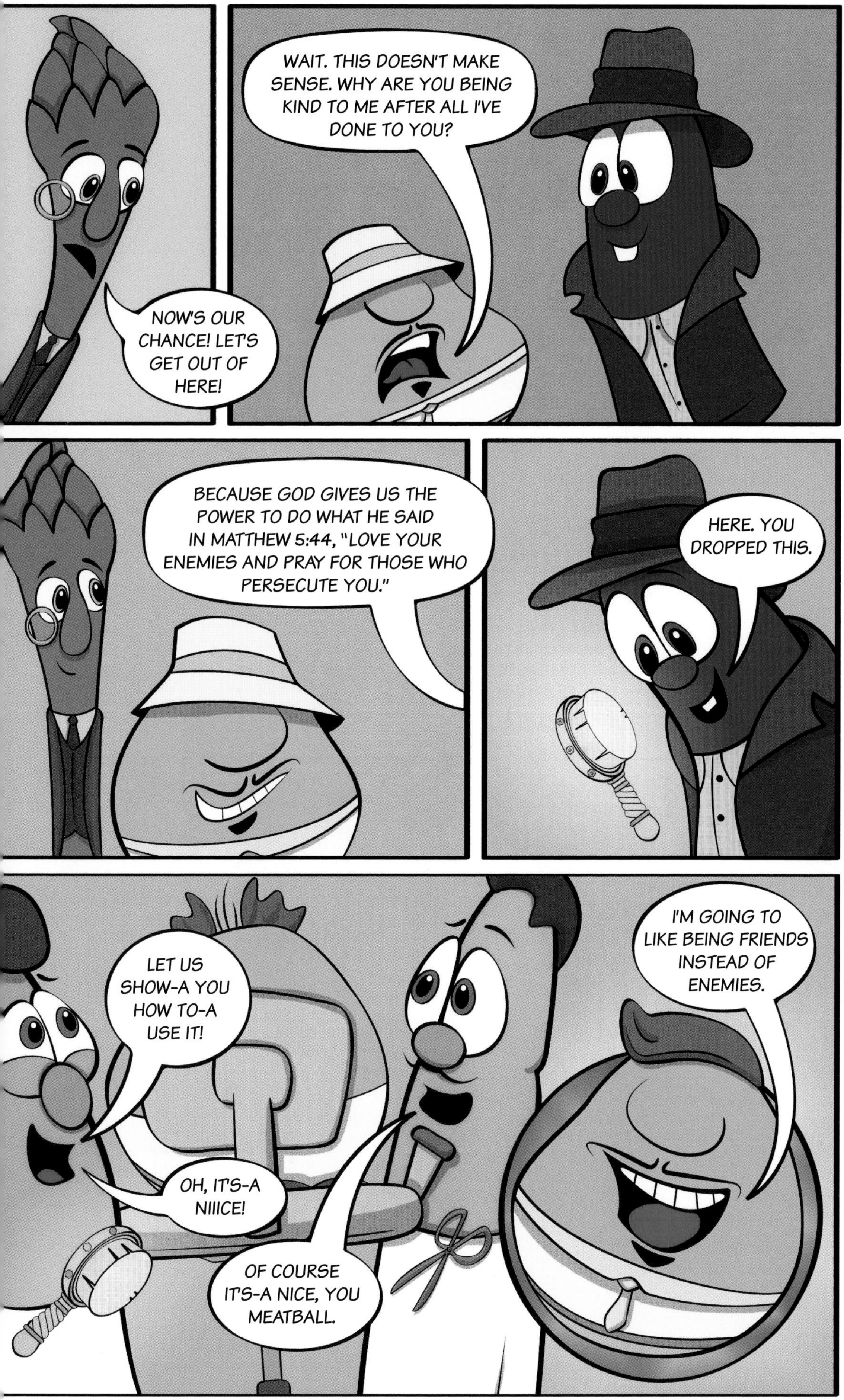
WAIT. THIS DOESN'T MAKE SENSE. WHY ARE YOU BEING KIND TO ME AFTER ALL I'VE DONE TO YOU?
NOW'S OUR CHANCE! LET'S GET OUT OF HERE!
BECAUSE GOD GIVES US THE POWER TO DO WHAT HE SAID IN MATTHEW 5:44, "LOVE YOUR ENEMIES AND PRAY FOR THOSE WHO PERSECUTE YOU."
HERE. YOU DROPPED THIS.
LET US SHOW-A YOU HOW TO-A USE IT!
OH, IT'S-A NIIICE!
OF COURSE IT'S-A NICE, YOU MEATBALL.
I'M GOING TO LIKE BEING FRIENDS INSTEAD OF ENEMIES.

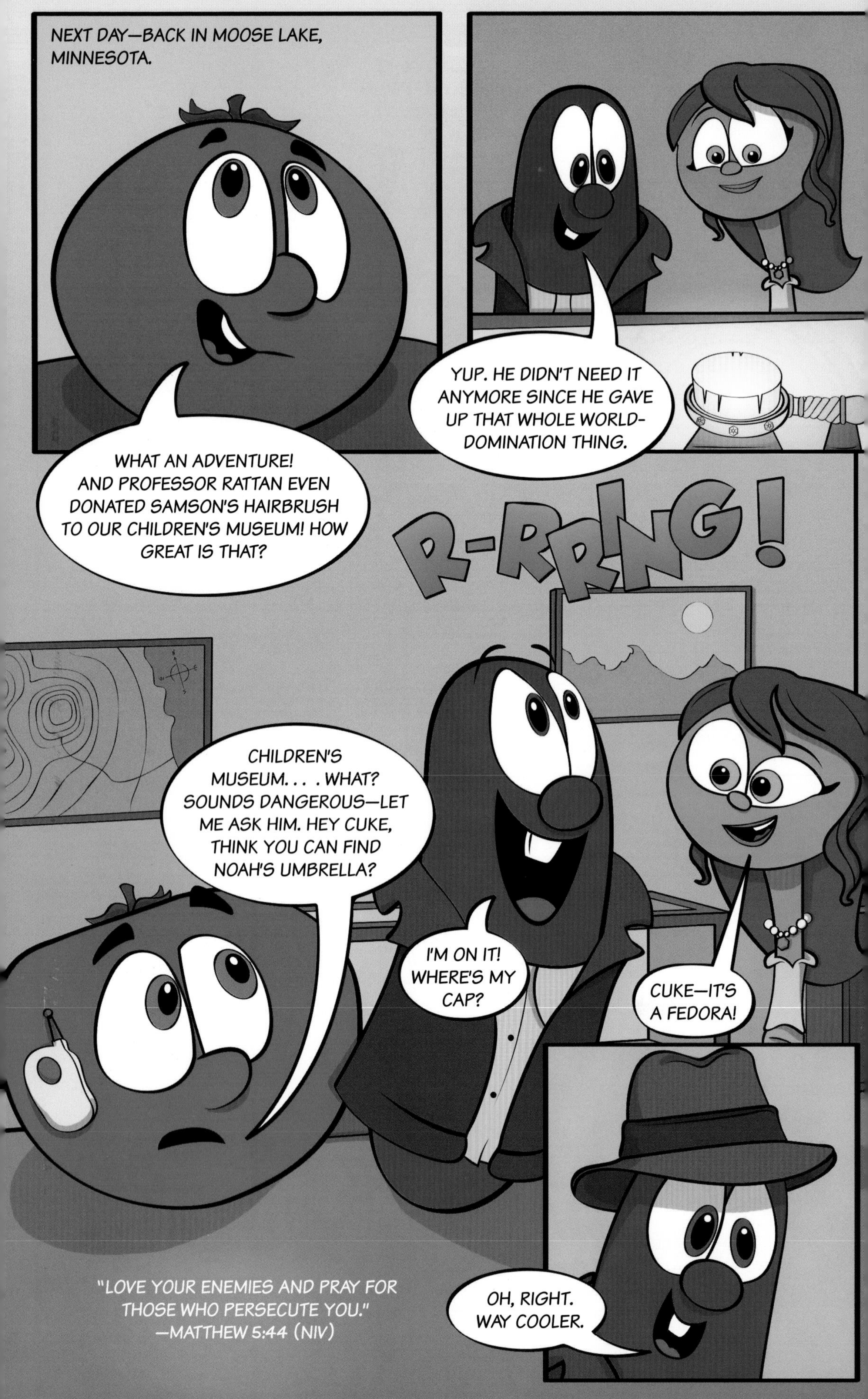

NEXT DAY—BACK IN MOOSE LAKE, MINNESOTA.
WHAT AN ADVENTURE! AND PROFESSOR RATTAN EVEN DONATED SAMSON'S HAIRBRUSH TO OUR CHILDREN'S MUSEUM! HOW GREAT IS THAT?
YUP. HE DIDN'T NEED IT ANYMORE SINCE HE GAVE UP THAT WHOLE WORLD-DOMINATION THING.
R-RRING!
CHILDREN'S MUSEUM. . . . WHAT? SOUNDS DANGEROUS—LET ME ASK HIM. HEY CUKE, THINK YOU CAN FIND NOAH'S UMBRELLA?
I'M ON IT! WHERE'S MY CAP?
CUKE—IT'S A FEDORA!
OH, RIGHT. WAY COOLER.
"LOVE YOUR ENEMIES AND PRAY FOR THOSE WHO PERSECUTE YOU." —MATTHEW 5:44 (NIV)

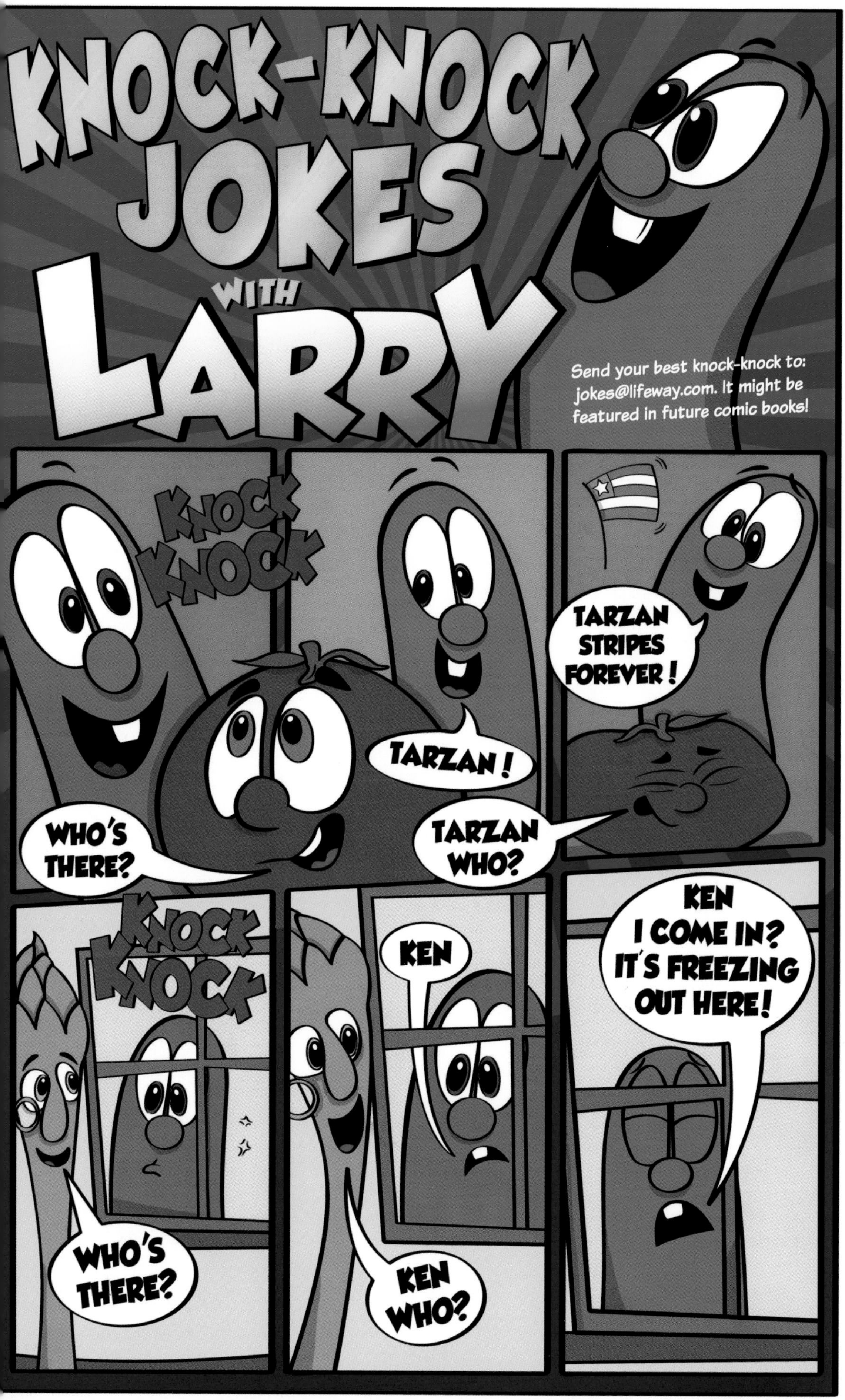
KNOCK-KNOCK JOKES WITH LARRY
Send your best knock-knock to: jokes@lifeway.com. It might be featured in future comic books!
KNOCK KNOCK
WHO'S THERE?
TARZAN!
TARZAN WHO?
TARZAN STRIPES FOREVER!
KNOCK KNOCK
WHO'S THERE?
KEN
KEN WHO?
KEN I COME IN? IT'S FREEZING OUT HERE!

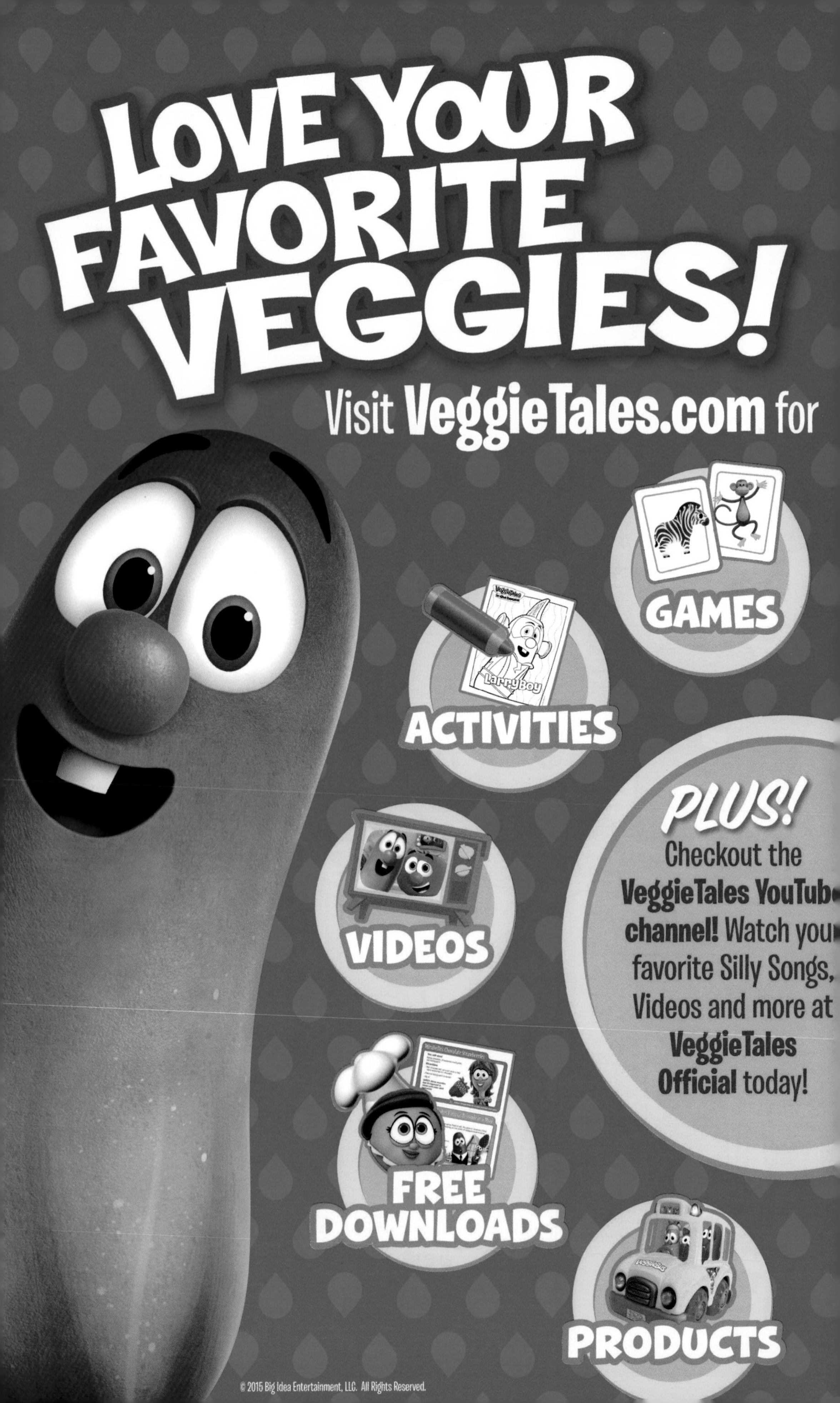
LOVE YOUR FAVORITE VEGGIES!
Visit VeggieTales.com for
GAMES
ACTIVITIES
LarryBoy
VIDEOS
FREE DOWNLOADS
PRODUCTS
PLUS!
Checkout the VeggieTales YouTube channel! Watch your favorite Silly Songs, Videos and more at VeggieTales Official today!
© 2015 Big Idea Entertainment, LLC. All Rights Reserved.

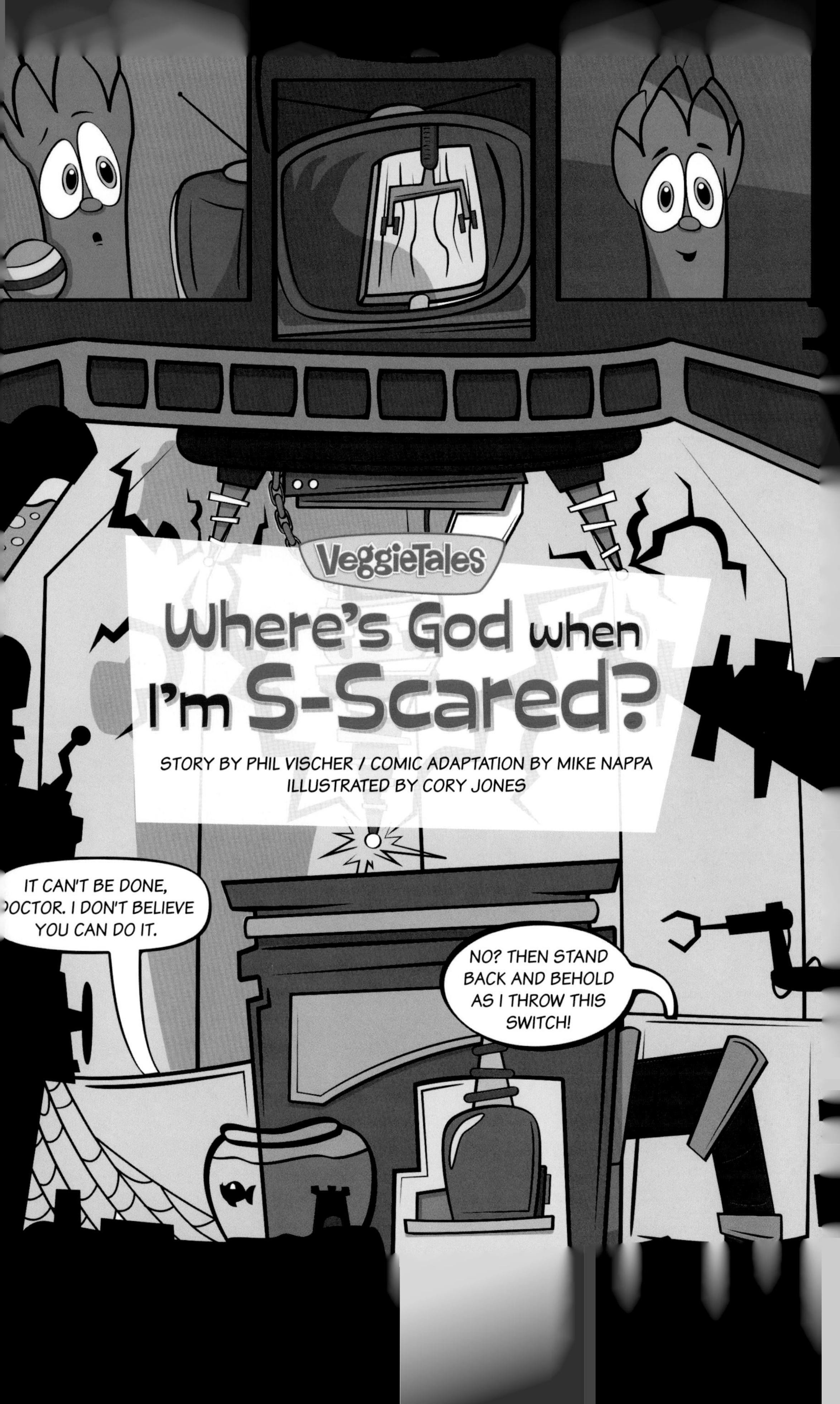
VeggieTales
Where's God when I'm S-Scared?
STORY BY PHIL VISCHER / COMIC ADAPTATION BY MIKE NAPPA
ILLUSTRATED BY CORY JONES
IT CAN'T BE DONE, DOCTOR. I DON'T BELIEVE YOU CAN DO IT.
NO? THEN STAND BACK AND BEHOLD AS I THROW THIS SWITCH!

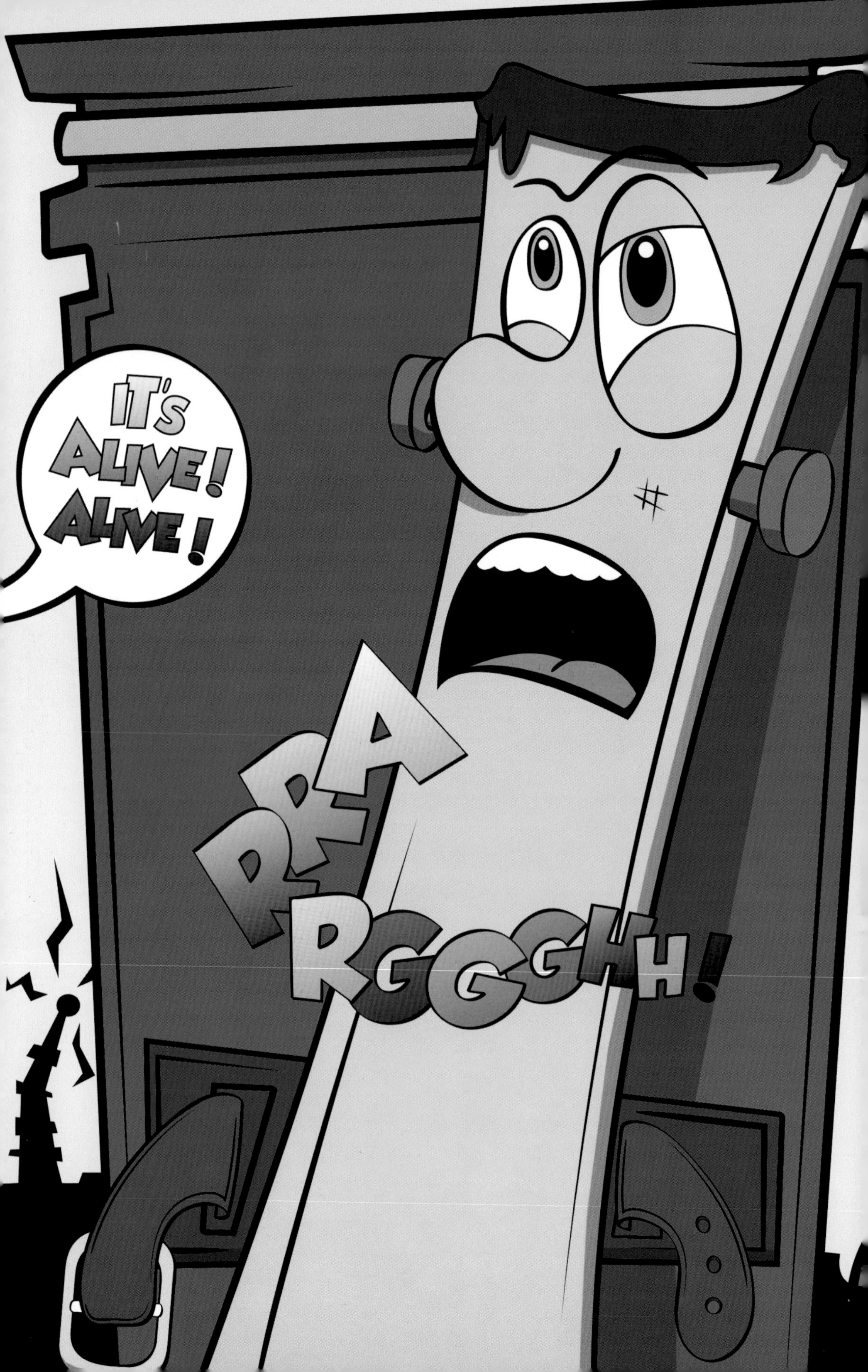
IT'S ALIVE! ALIVE!
RRARGGGHH!

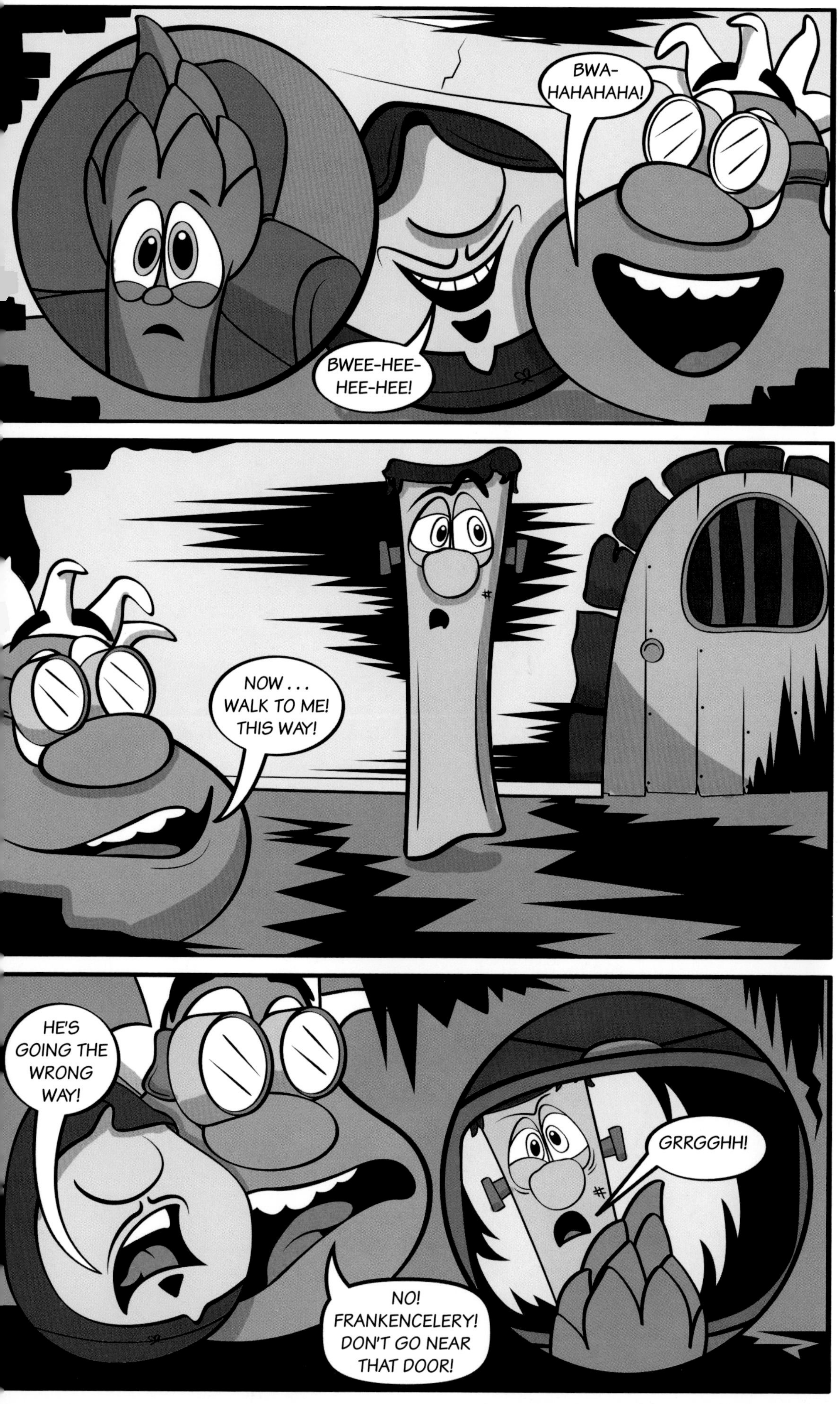
BWA-
HAHAHAHA!
BWEE-HEE-
HEE-HEE!
NOW . . .
WALK TO ME!
THIS WAY!
HE'S
GOING THE
WRONG
WAY!
GRRGGHH!
NO!
FRANKENCELERY!
DON'T GO NEAR
THAT DOOR!

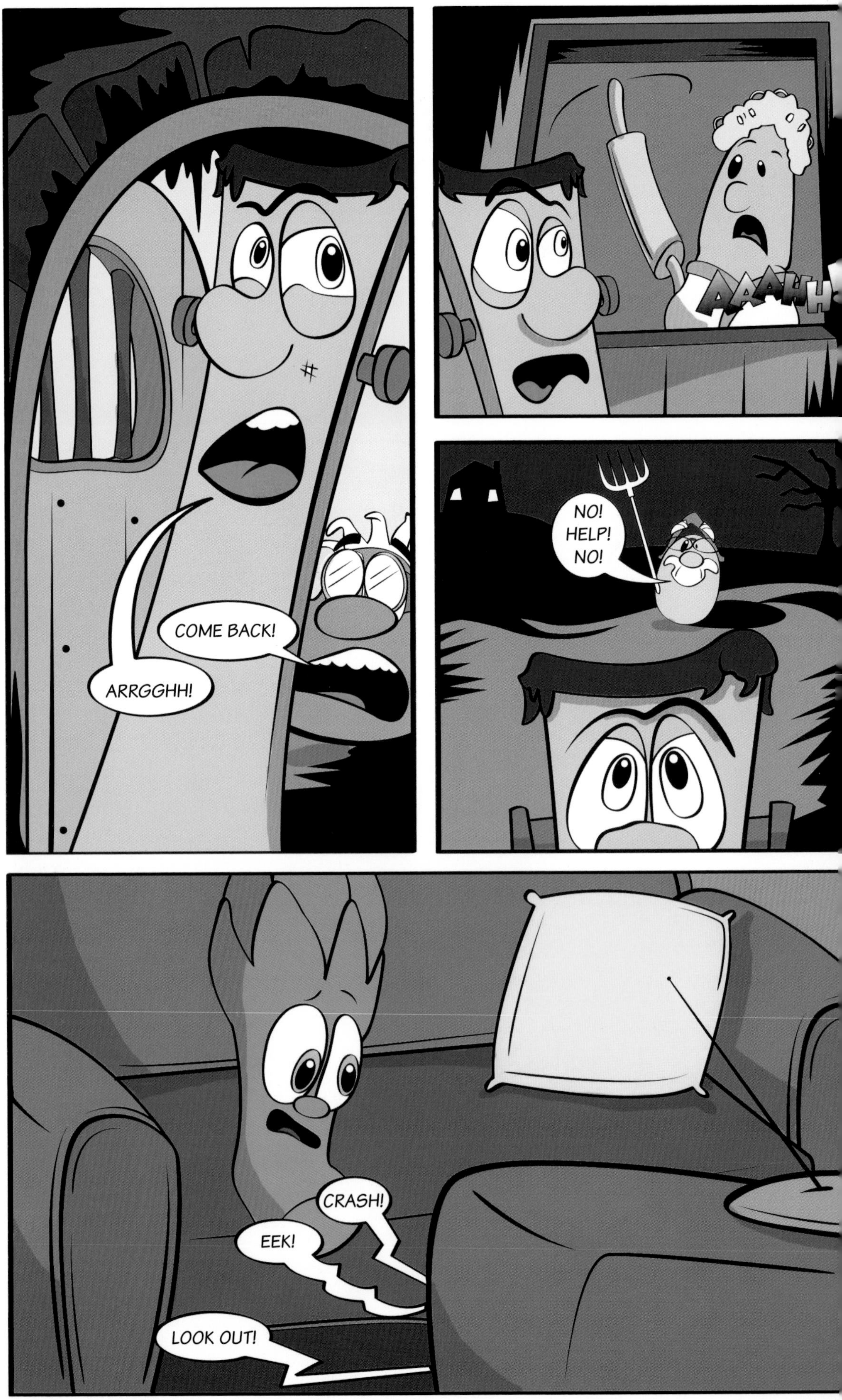
COME BACK!
ARRGGHH!
AAAHH
NO!
HELP!
NO!
CRASH!
EEK!
LOOK OUT!

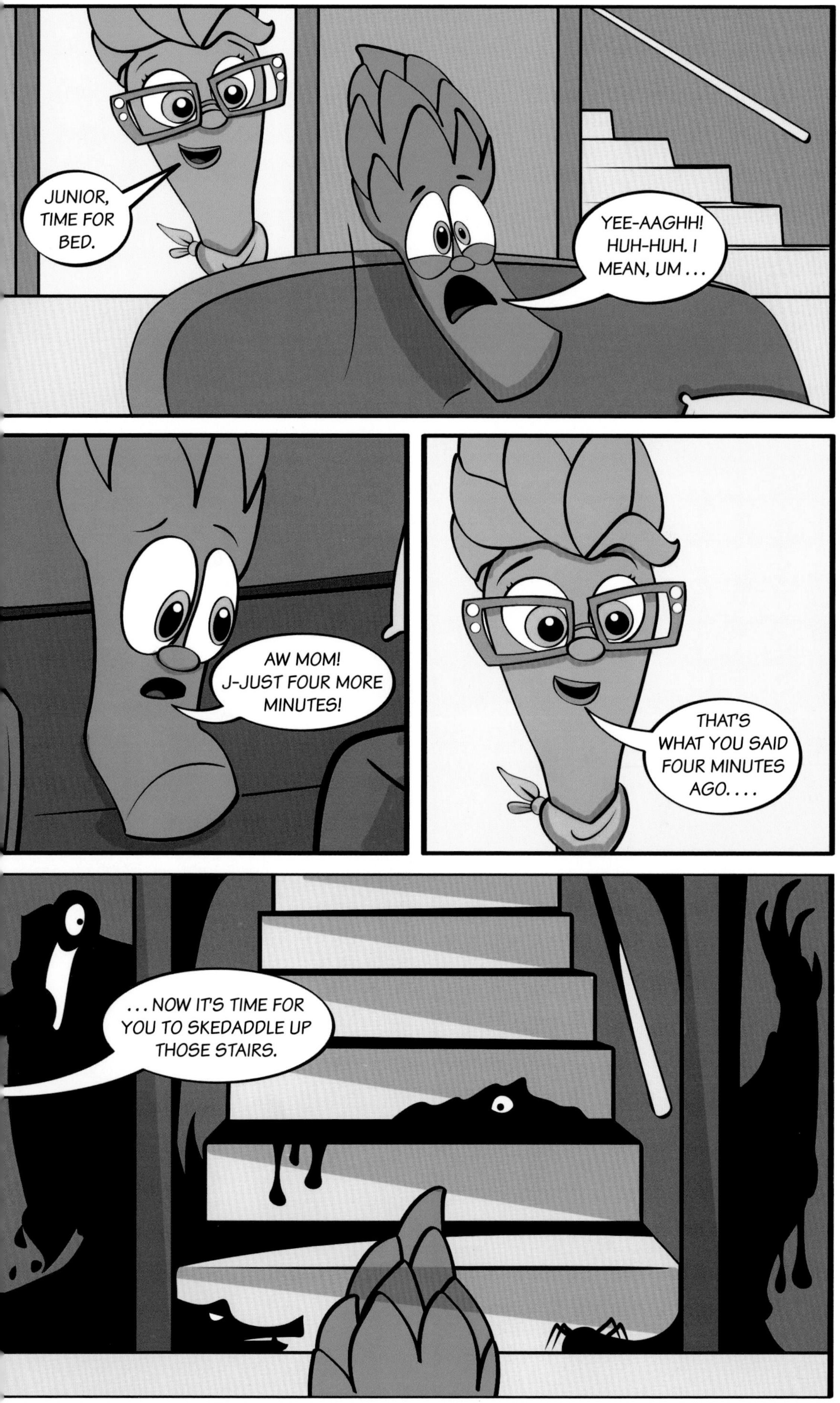
JUNIOR, TIME FOR BED.
YEE-AAGHH! HUH-HUH. I MEAN, UM . . .
AW MOM! J-JUST FOUR MORE MINUTES!
THAT'S WHAT YOU SAID FOUR MINUTES AGO. . . .
. . . NOW IT'S TIME FOR YOU TO SKEDADDLE UP THOSE STAIRS.

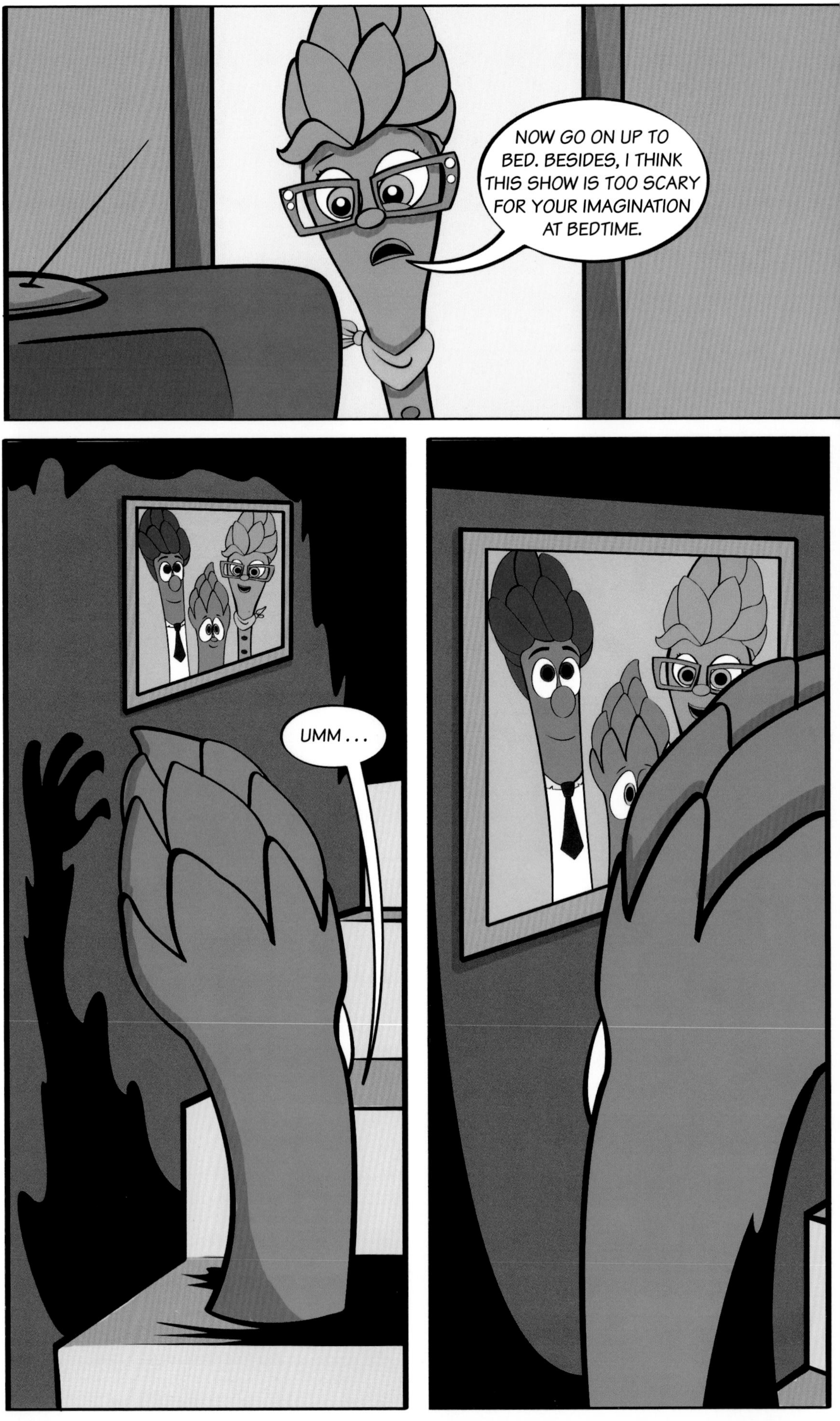
NOW GO ON UP TO BED. BESIDES, I THINK THIS SHOW IS TOO SCARY FOR YOUR IMAGINATION AT BEDTIME.
UMM . . .

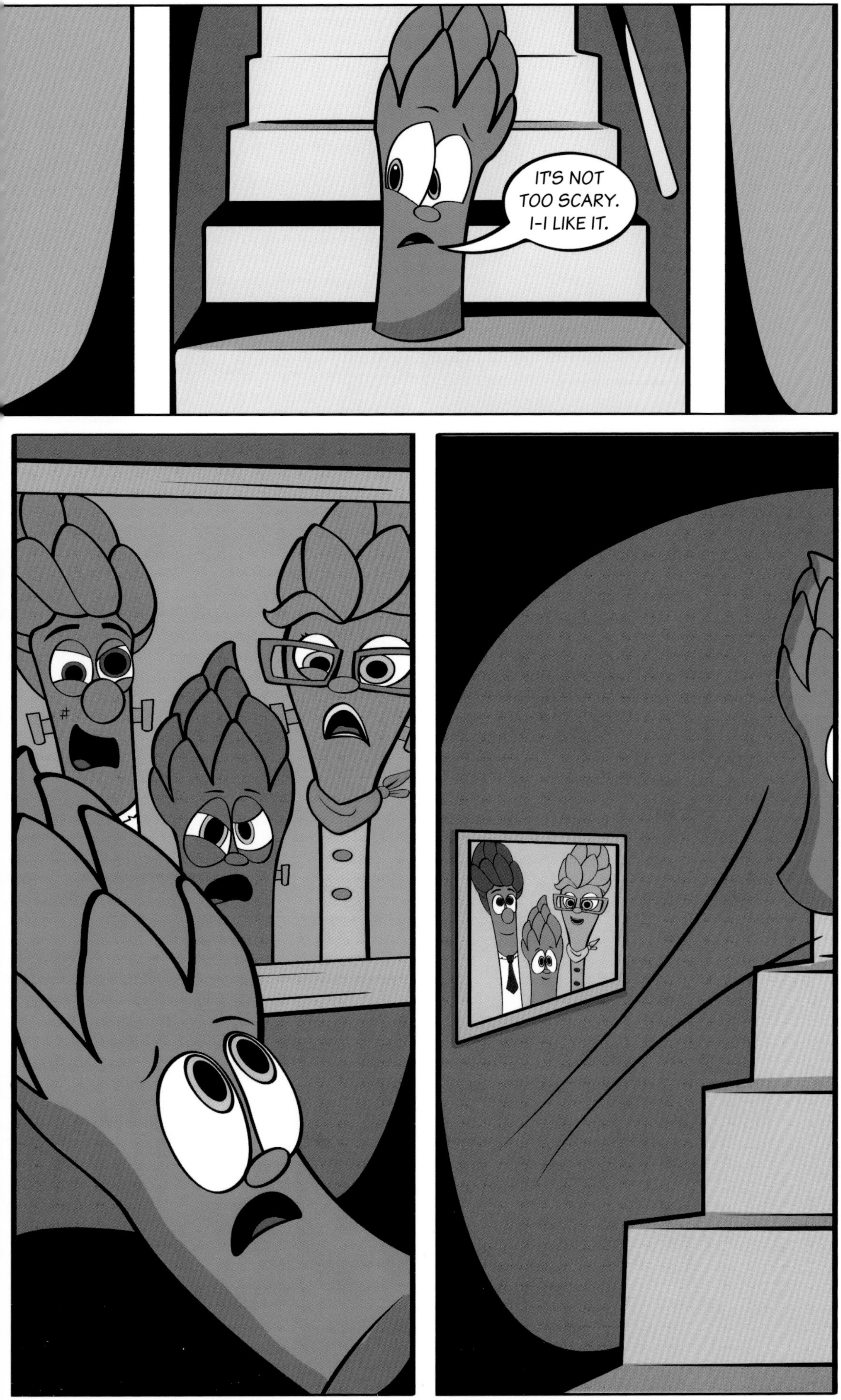
IT'S NOT TOO SCARY. I-I LIKE IT.

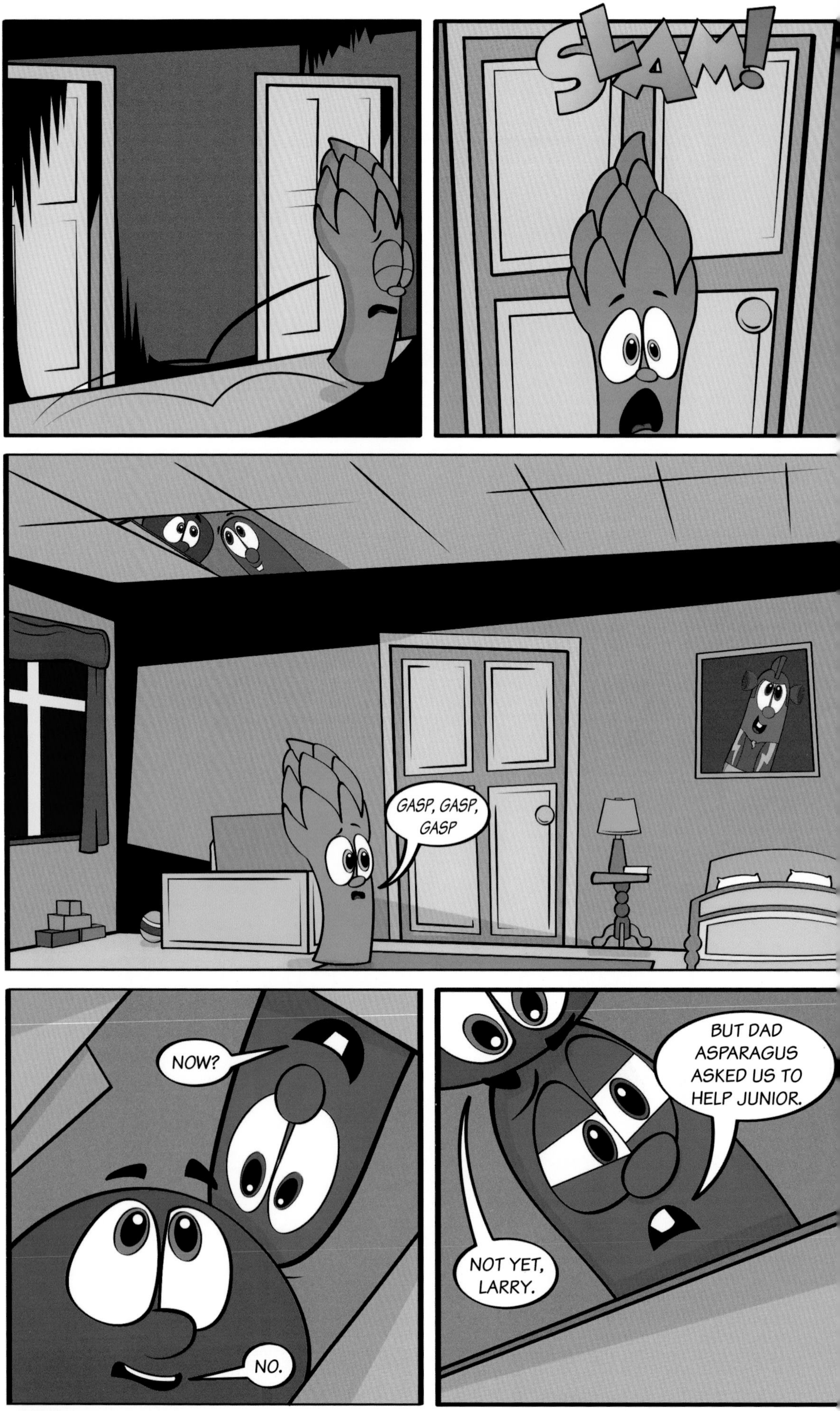
SLAM!
GASP, GASP, GASP
NOW?
NO.
BUT DAD ASPARAGUS ASKED US TO HELP JUNIOR.
NOT YET, LARRY.

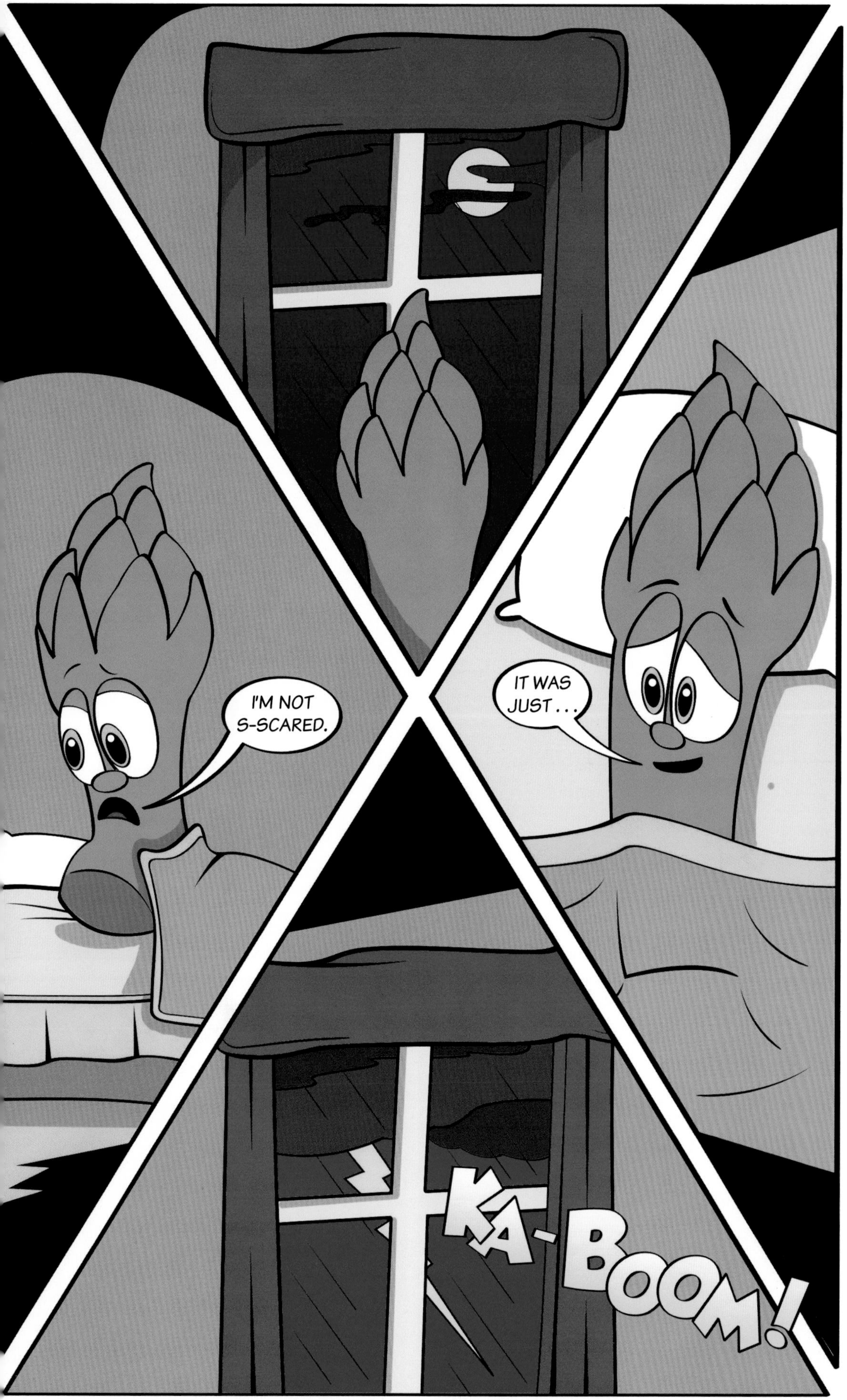
I'M NOT S-SCARED.
IT WAS JUST . . .
KA-BOOM!

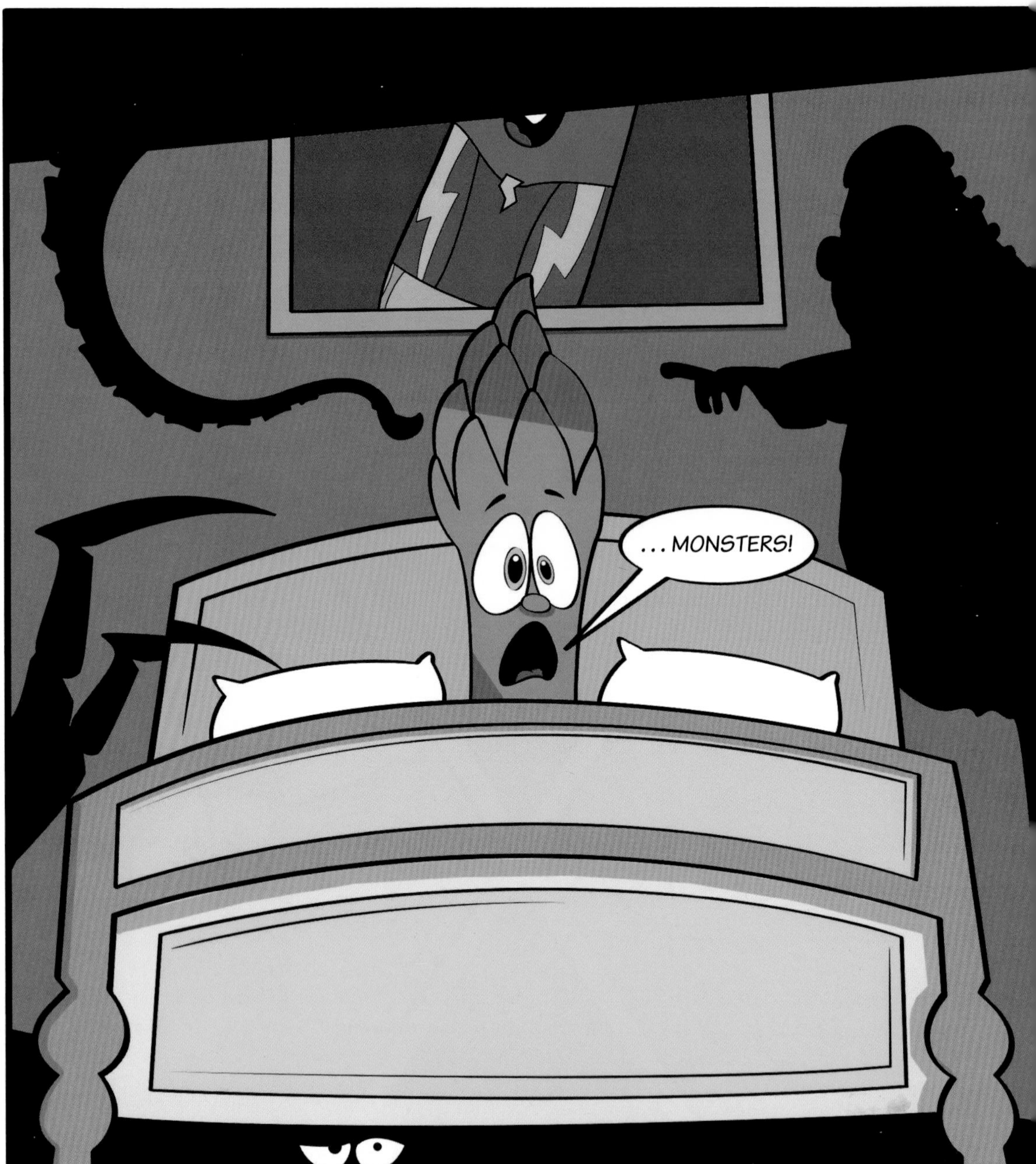
. . . MONSTERS!

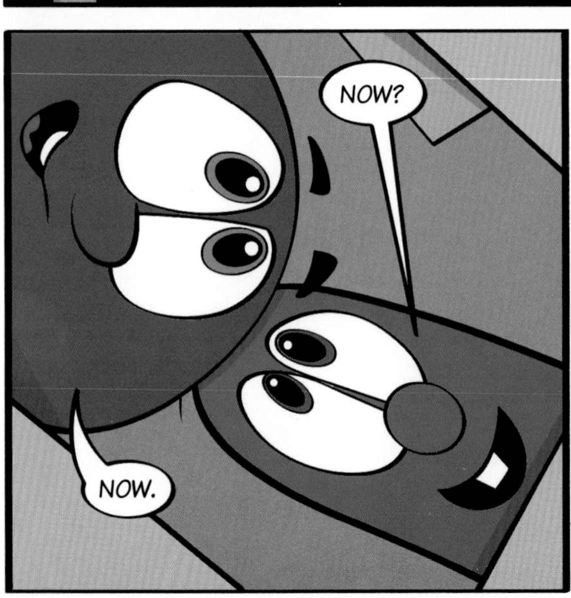
NOW?
NOW.

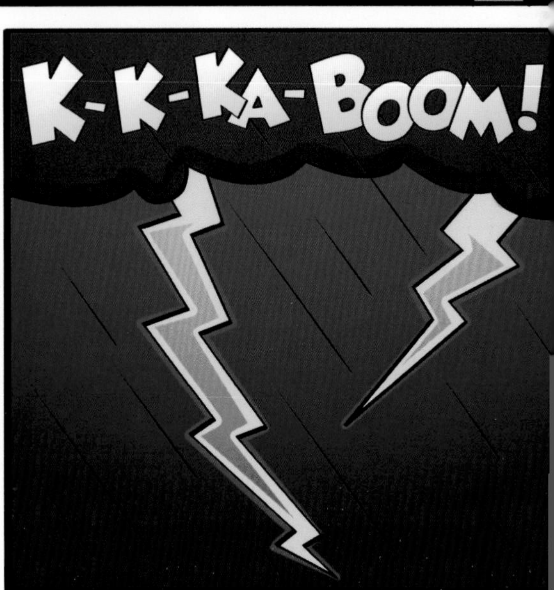
K-K-KA-BOOM!

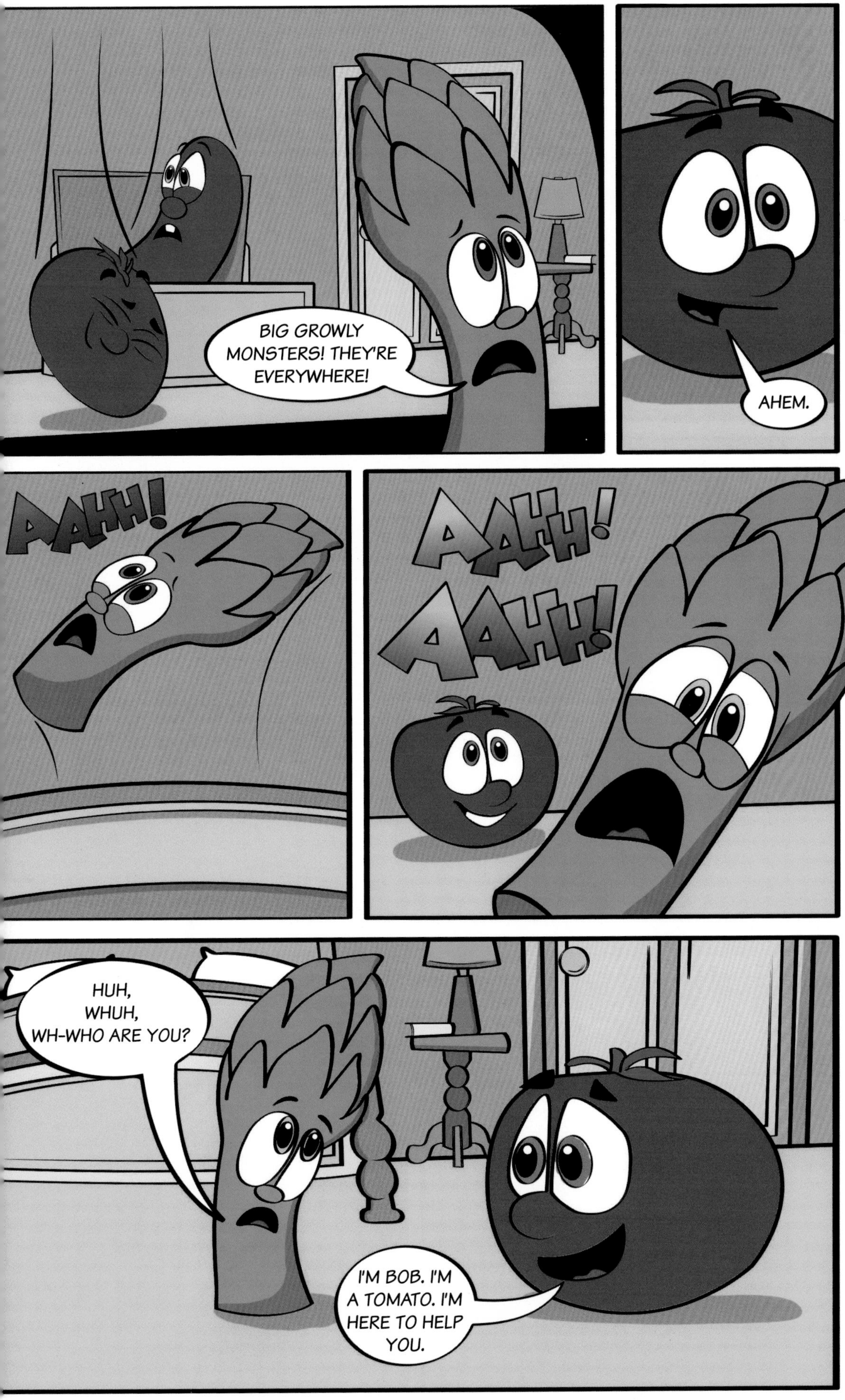

BIG GROWLY MONSTERS! THEY'RE EVERYWHERE!
AHEM.
AAHH!
AAHH!
AAHH!
HUH, WHUH, WH-WHO ARE YOU?
I'M BOB. I'M A TOMATO. I'M HERE TO HELP YOU.

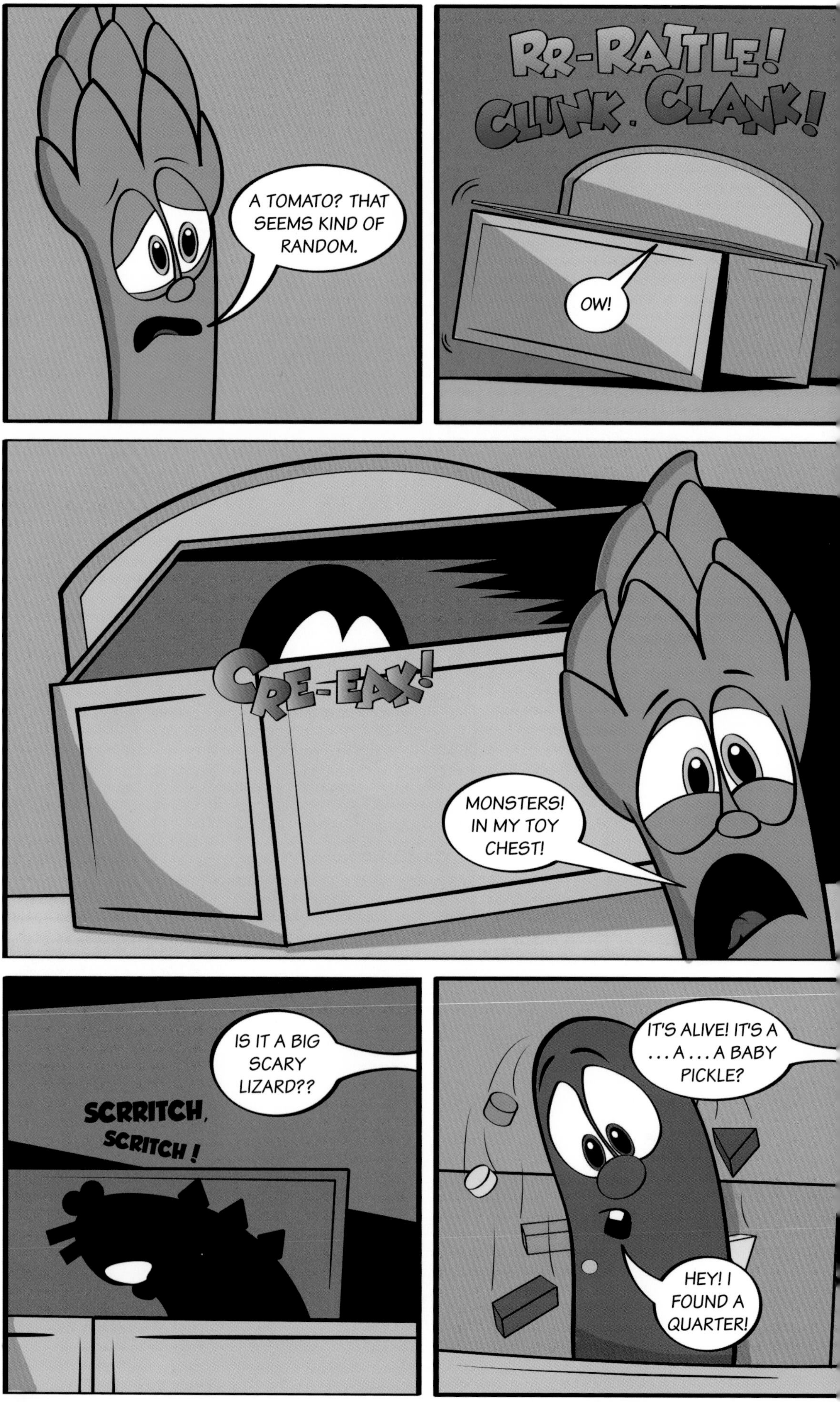
A TOMATO? THAT SEEMS KIND OF RANDOM.
RR-RATTLE! CLUNK. CLANK!
OW!
CRE-EAK!
MONSTERS! IN MY TOY CHEST!
IS IT A BIG SCARY LIZARD??
SCRRITCH, SCRITCH!
IT'S ALIVE! IT'S A . . . A . . . A BABY PICKLE?
HEY! I FOUND A QUARTER!

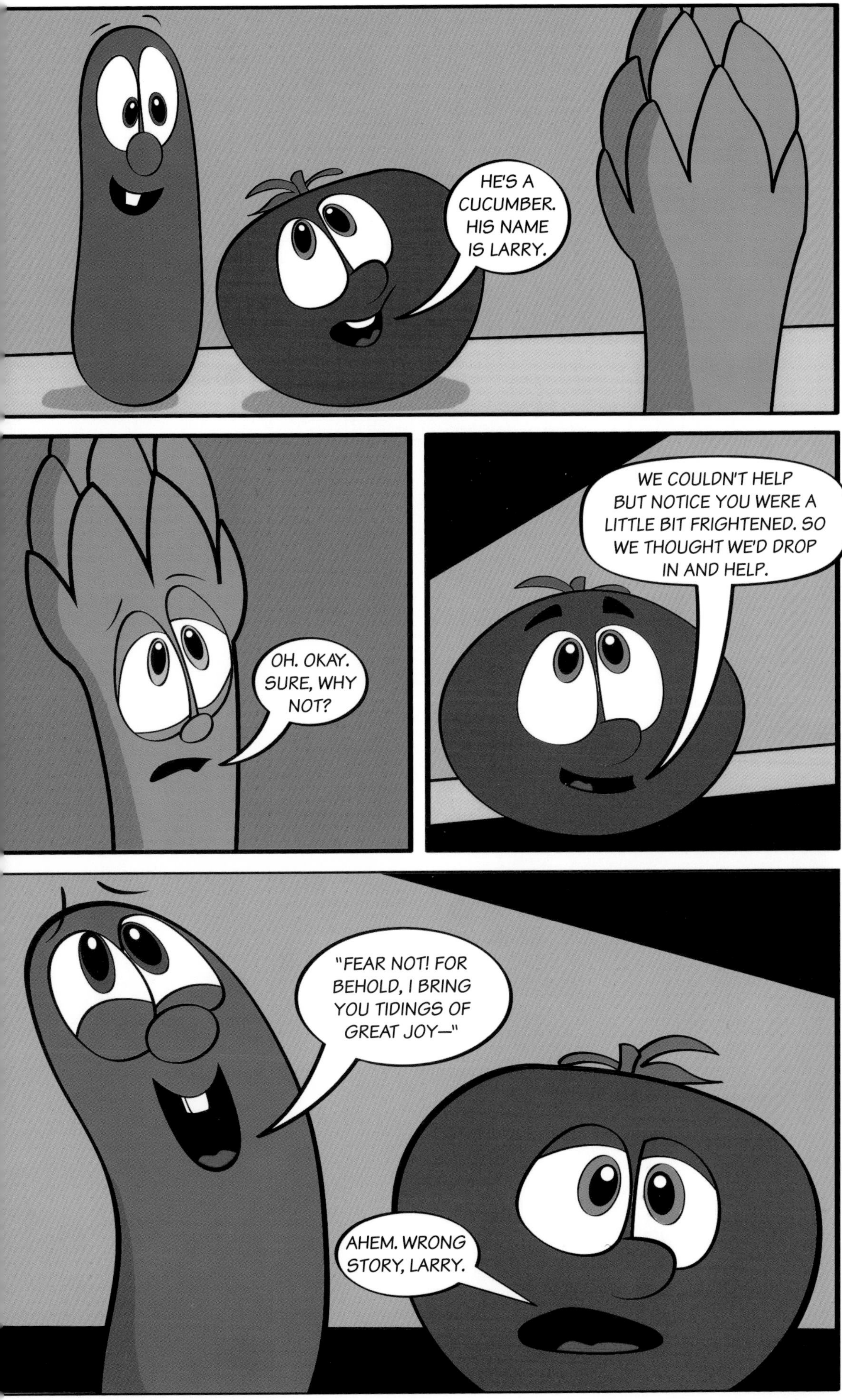
HE'S A CUCUMBER. HIS NAME IS LARRY.
OH. OKAY. SURE, WHY NOT?
WE COULDN'T HELP BUT NOTICE YOU WERE A LITTLE BIT FRIGHTENED. SO WE THOUGHT WE'D DROP IN AND HELP.
"FEAR NOT! FOR BEHOLD, I BRING YOU TIDINGS OF GREAT JOY—"
AHEM. WRONG STORY, LARRY.

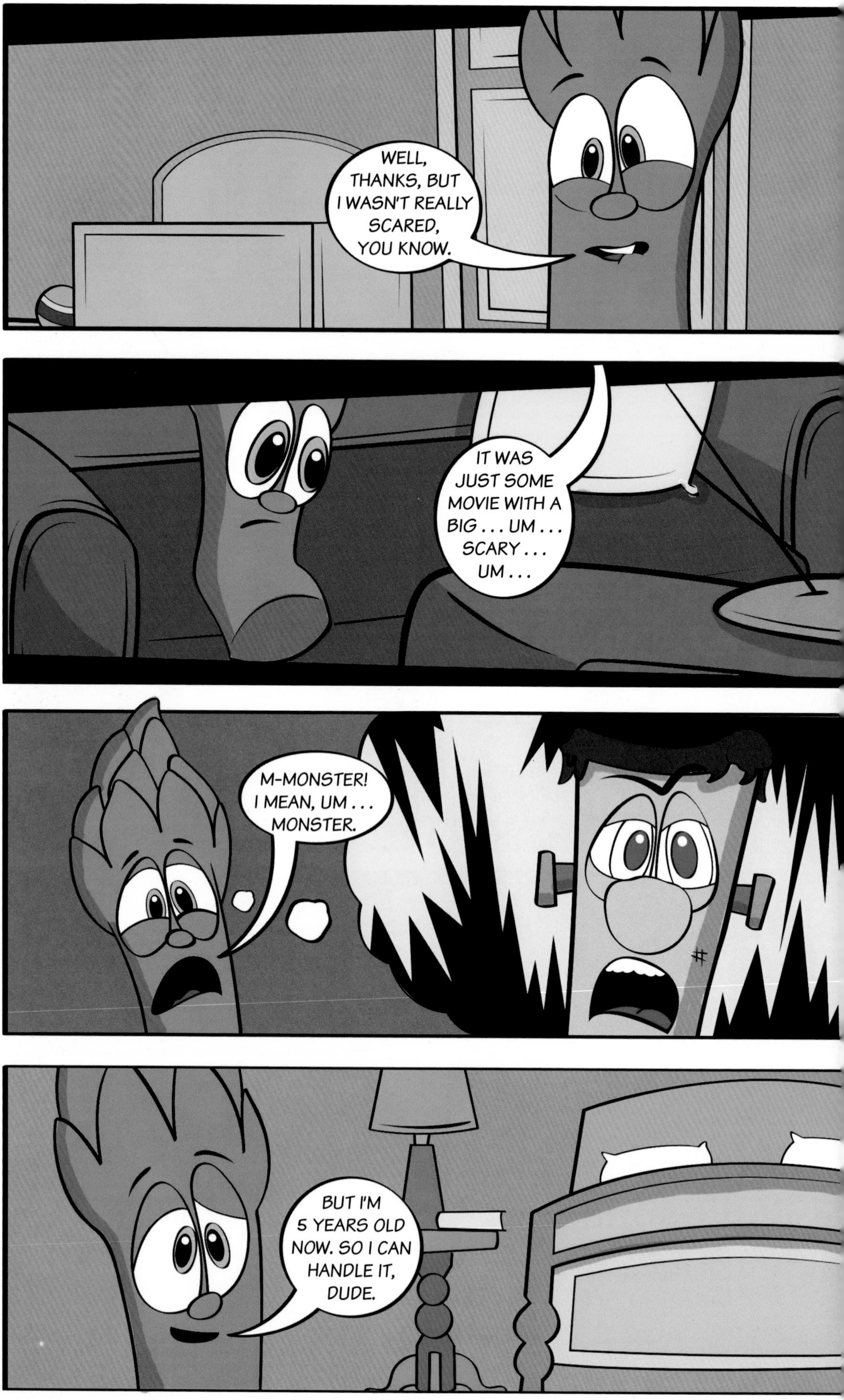
WELL, THANKS, BUT I WASN'T REALLY SCARED, YOU KNOW.
IT WAS JUST SOME MOVIE WITH A BIG . . . UM . . . SCARY . . . UM . . .
M-MONSTER! I MEAN, UM . . . MONSTER.
BUT I'M 5 YEARS OLD NOW. SO I CAN HANDLE IT, DUDE.

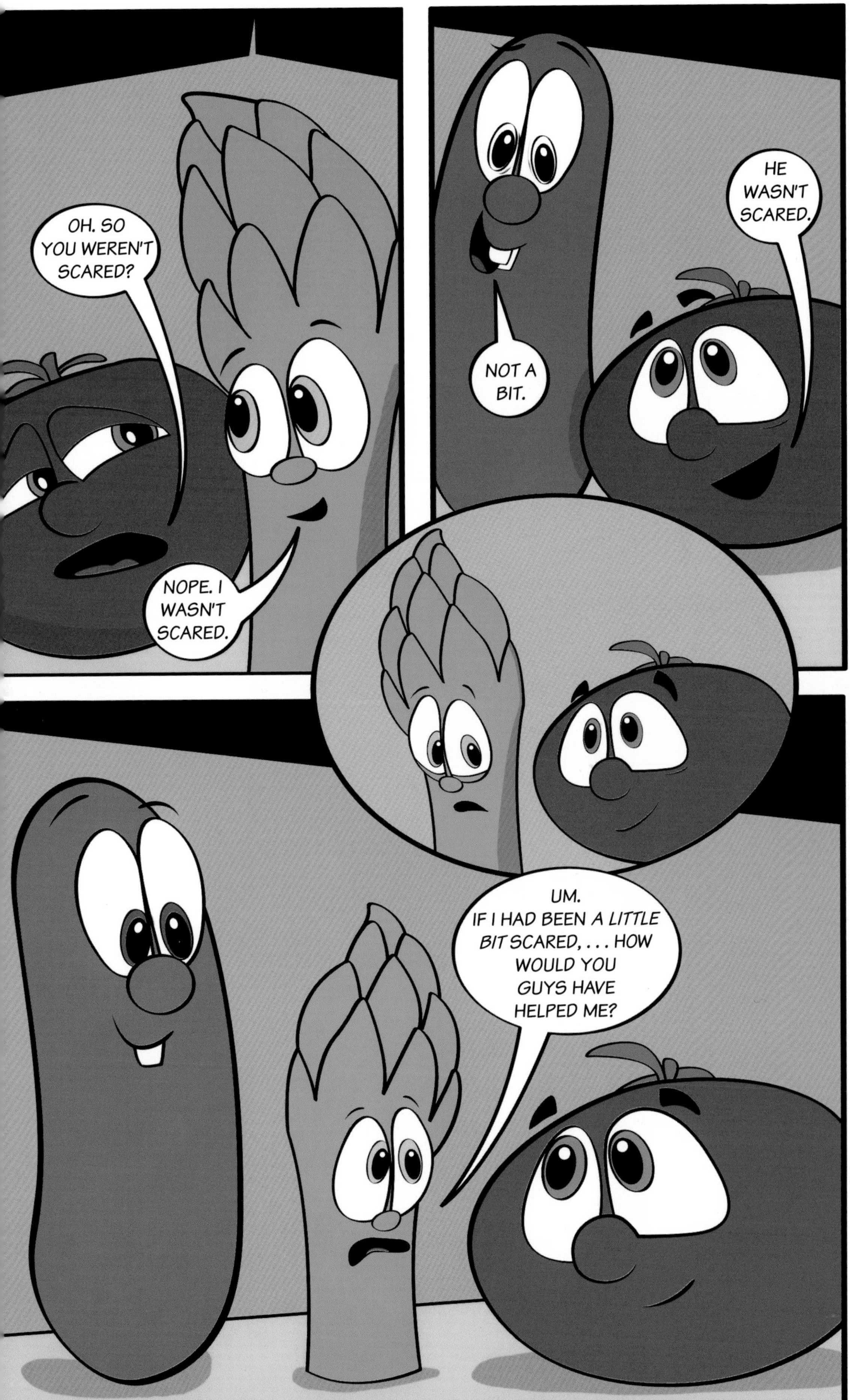
OH. SO YOU WEREN'T SCARED?
NOPE. I WASN'T SCARED.
NOT A BIT.
HE WASN'T SCARED.
UM. IF I HAD BEEN A *LITTLE BIT* SCARED, . . . HOW WOULD YOU GUYS HAVE HELPED ME?

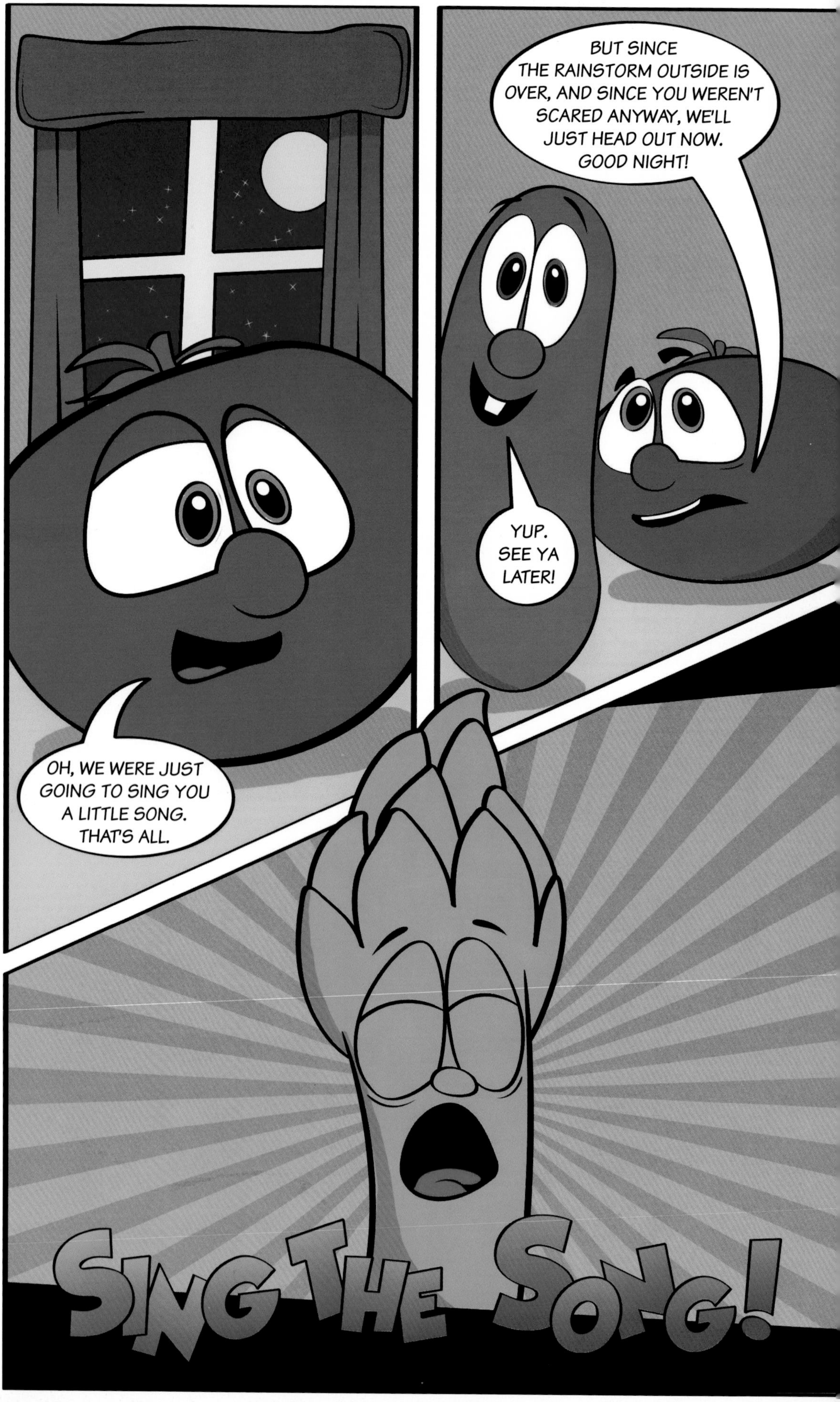
OH, WE WERE JUST GOING TO SING YOU A LITTLE SONG. THAT'S ALL.
BUT SINCE THE RAINSTORM OUTSIDE IS OVER, AND SINCE YOU WEREN'T SCARED ANYWAY, WE'LL JUST HEAD OUT NOW. GOOD NIGHT!
YUP. SEE YA LATER!
SING THE SONG!

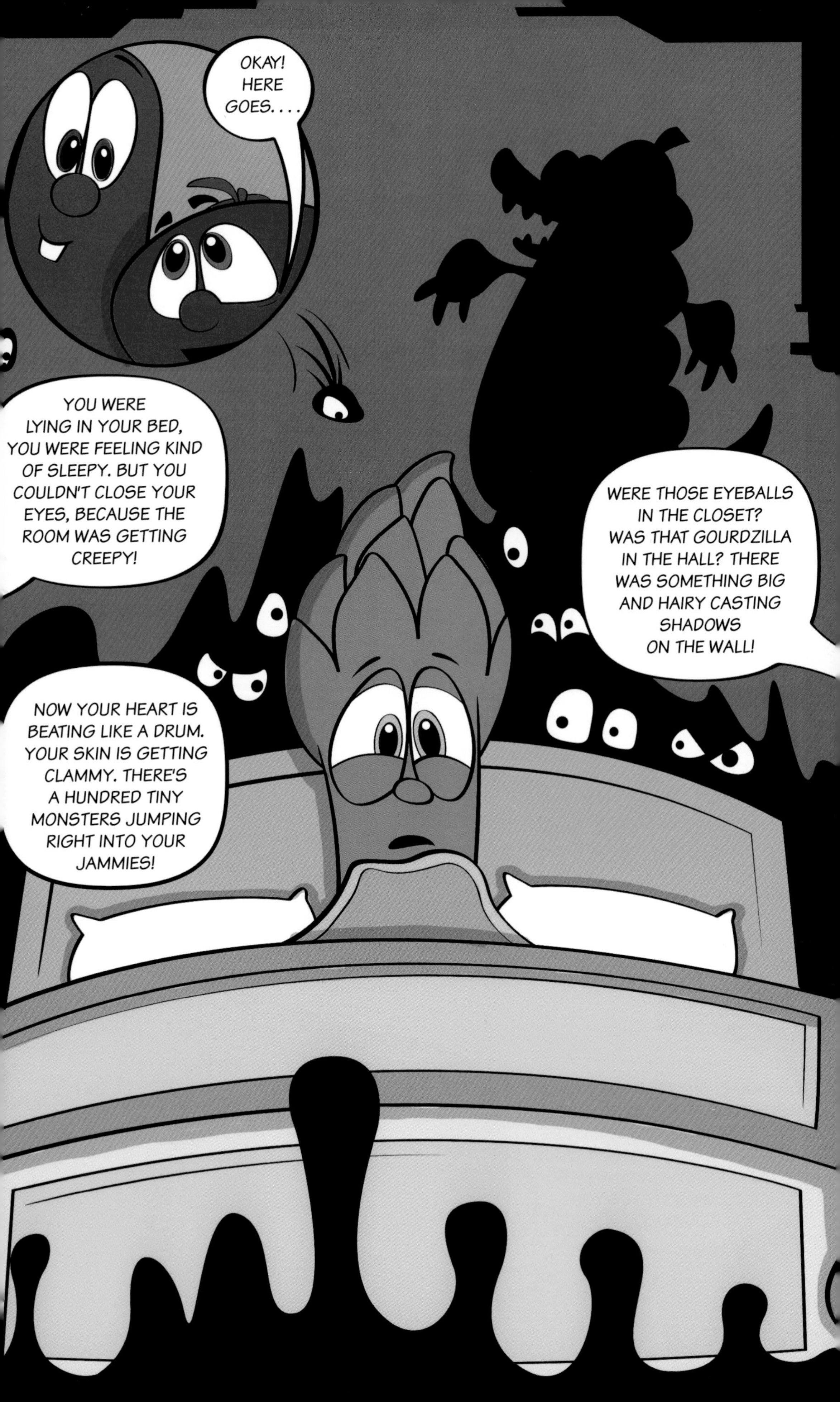
OKAY! HERE GOES. . . .
YOU WERE LYING IN YOUR BED, YOU WERE FEELING KIND OF SLEEPY. BUT YOU COULDN'T CLOSE YOUR EYES, BECAUSE THE ROOM WAS GETTING CREEPY!
WERE THOSE EYEBALLS IN THE CLOSET? WAS THAT GOURDZILLA IN THE HALL? THERE WAS SOMETHING BIG AND HAIRY CASTING SHADOWS ON THE WALL!
NOW YOUR HEART IS BEATING LIKE A DRUM. YOUR SKIN IS GETTING CLAMMY. THERE'S A HUNDRED TINY MONSTERS JUMPING RIGHT INTO YOUR JAMMIES!

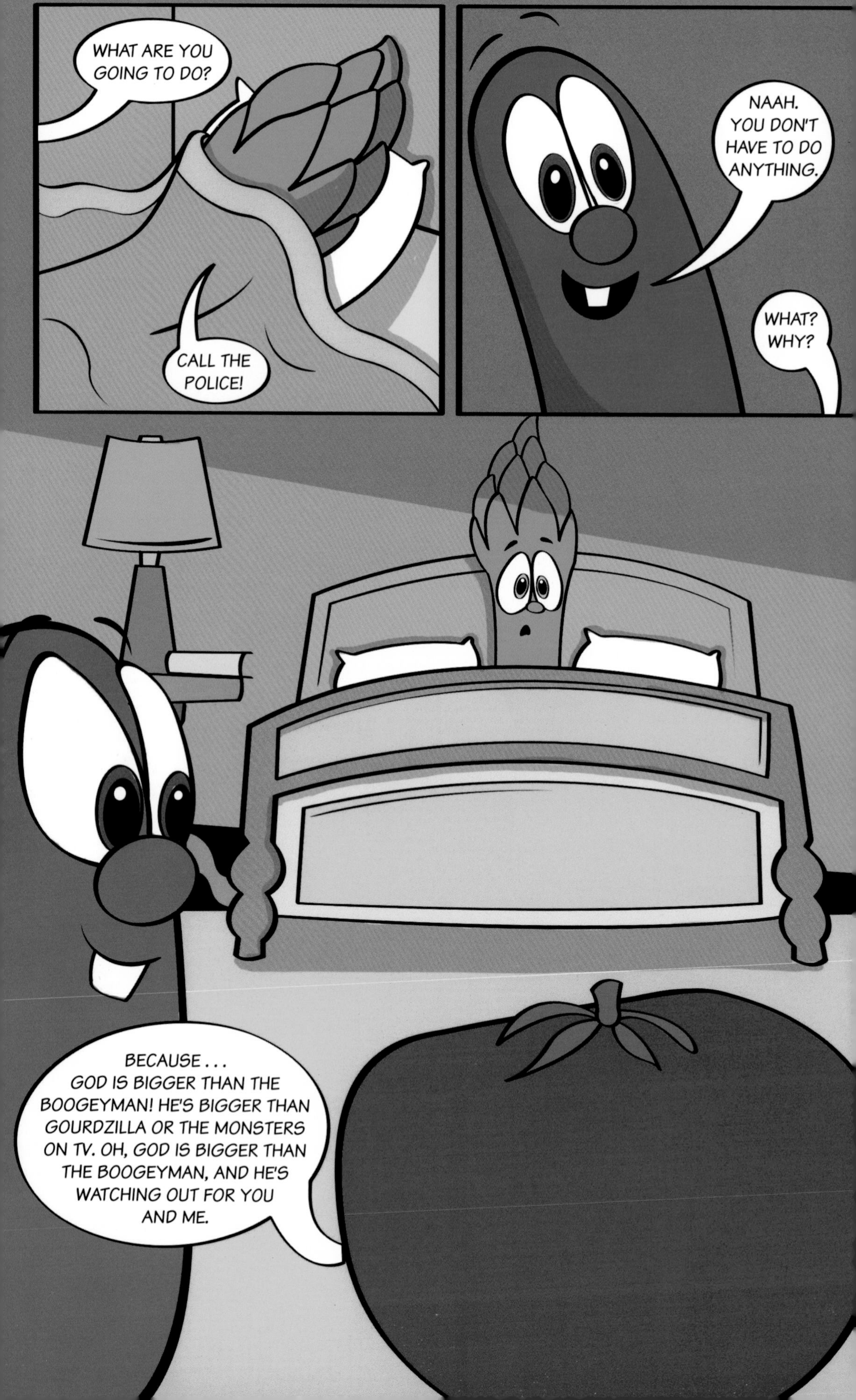
WHAT ARE YOU GOING TO DO?
CALL THE POLICE!
NAAH. YOU DON'T HAVE TO DO ANYTHING.
WHAT? WHY?
BECAUSE . . . GOD IS BIGGER THAN THE BOOGEYMAN! HE'S BIGGER THAN GOURDZILLA OR THE MONSTERS ON TV. OH, GOD IS BIGGER THAN THE BOOGEYMAN, AND HE'S WATCHING OUT FOR YOU AND ME.

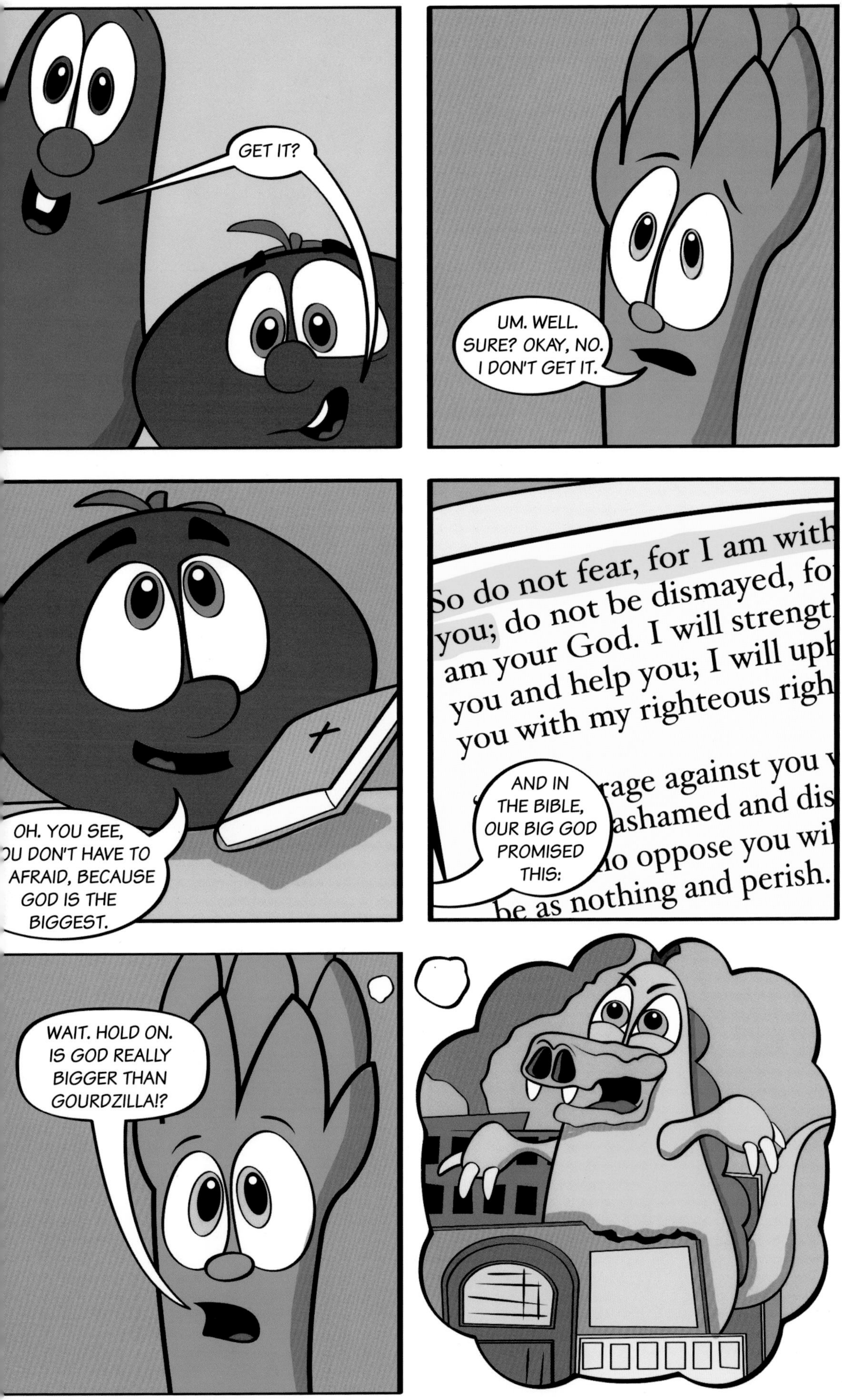
GET IT?
UM. WELL. SURE? OKAY, NO. I DON'T GET IT.
OH. YOU SEE, OU DON'T HAVE TO AFRAID, BECAUSE GOD IS THE BIGGEST.
So do not fear, for I am with
you; do not be dismayed, fo
am your God. I will strengt
you and help you; I will uph
you with my righteous righ
rage against you
ashamed and dis
oppose you wi
as nothing and perish.
AND IN THE BIBLE, OUR BIG GOD PROMISED THIS:
WAIT. HOLD ON. IS GOD REALLY BIGGER THAN GOURDZILLA!?

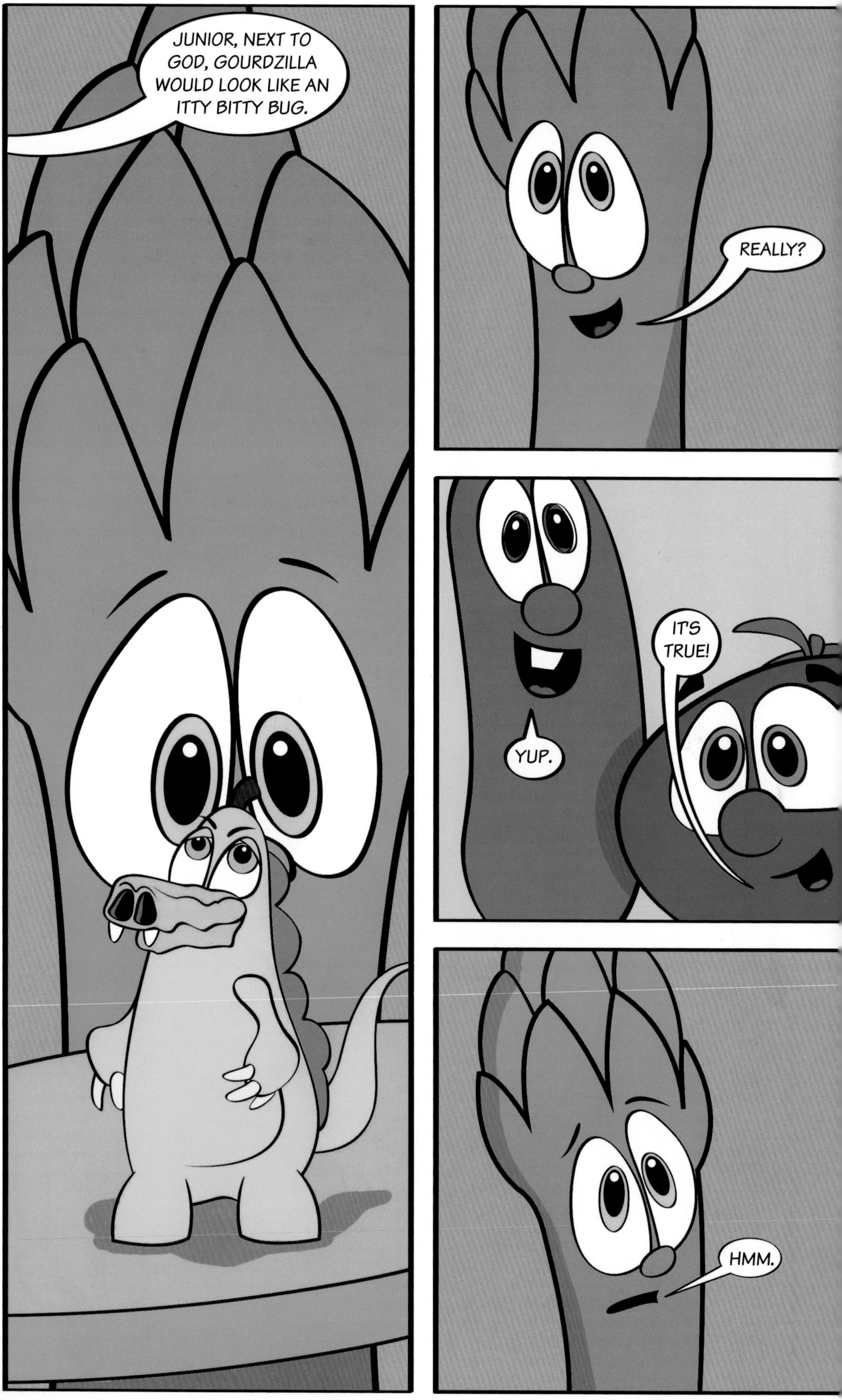
JUNIOR, NEXT TO GOD, GOURDZILLA WOULD LOOK LIKE AN ITTY BITTY BUG.
REALLY?
YUP.
IT'S TRUE!
HMM.

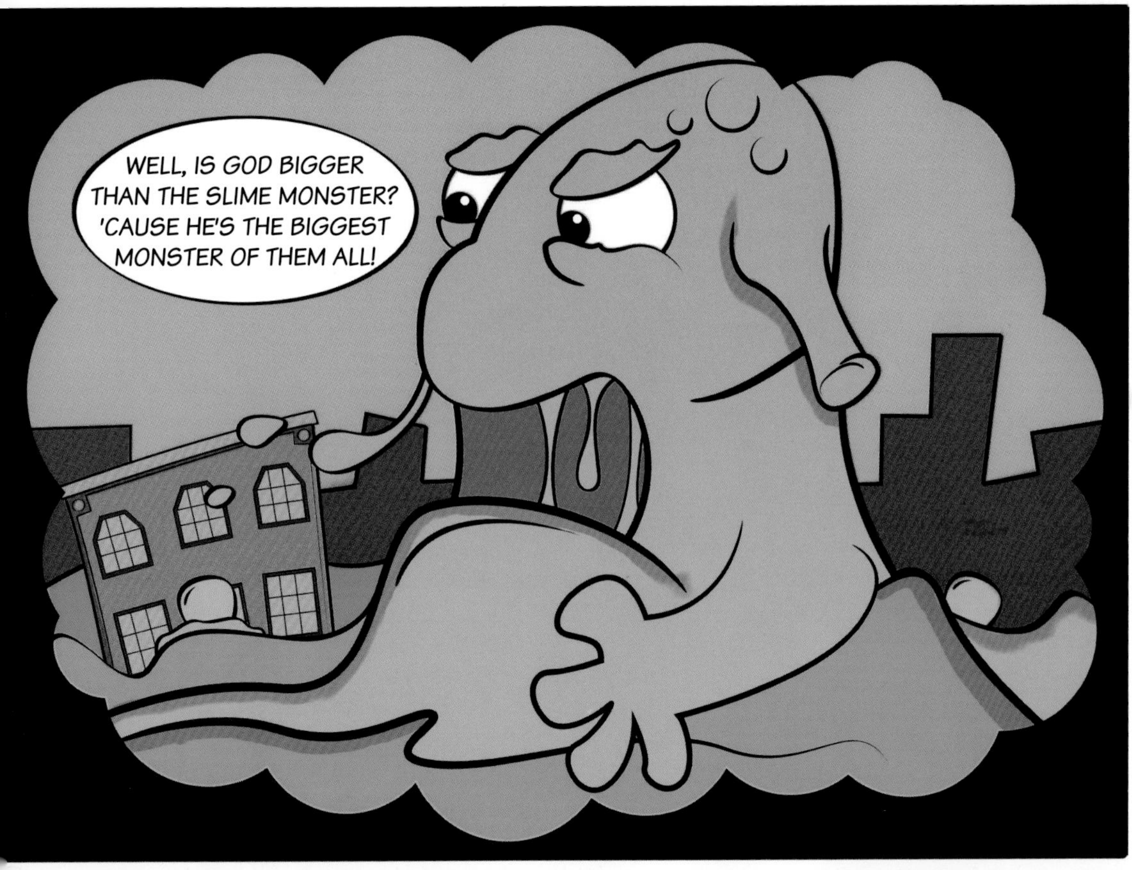
WELL, IS GOD BIGGER THAN THE SLIME MONSTER? 'CAUSE HE'S THE BIGGEST MONSTER OF THEM ALL!

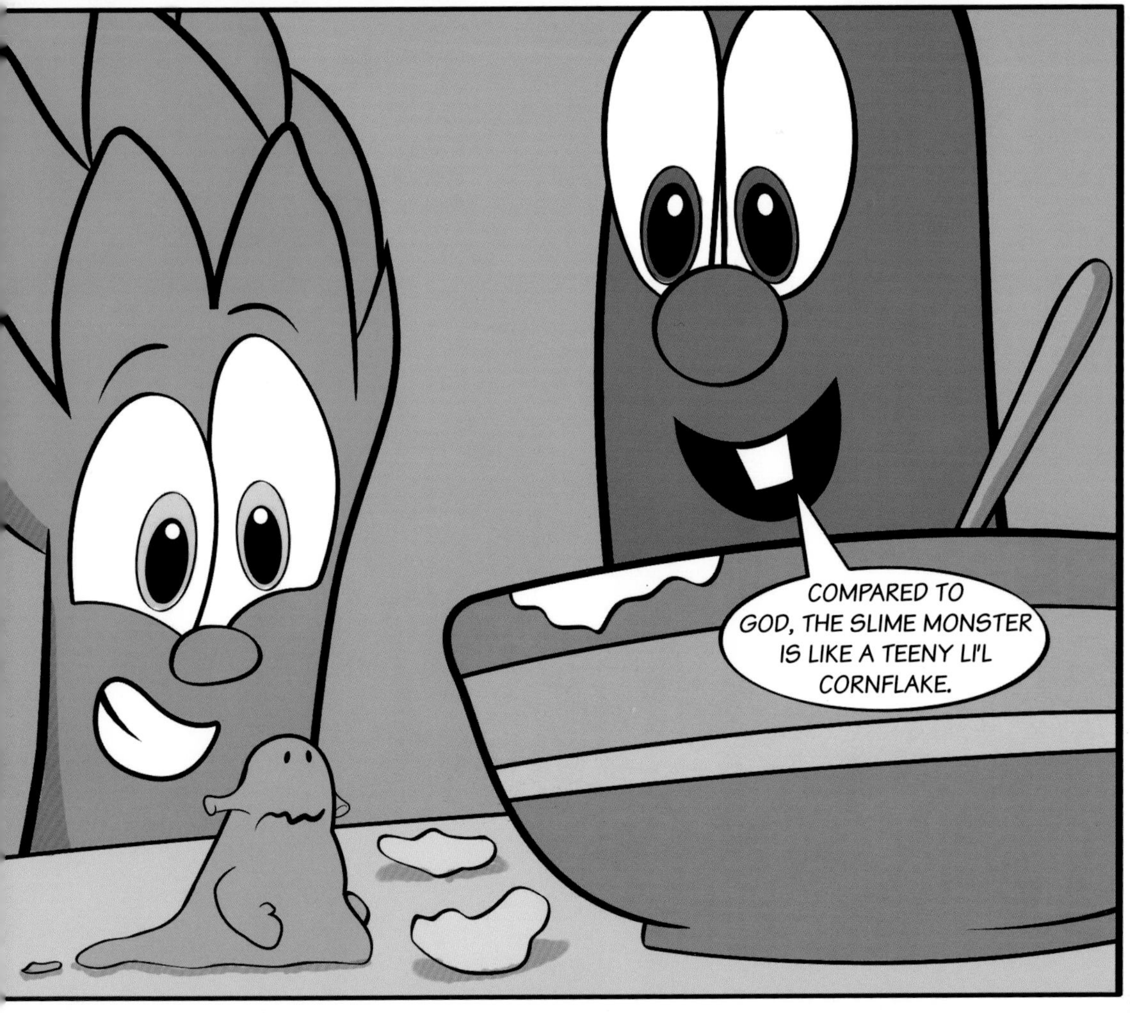
COMPARED TO GOD, THE SLIME MONSTER IS LIKE A TEENY LI'L CORNFLAKE.

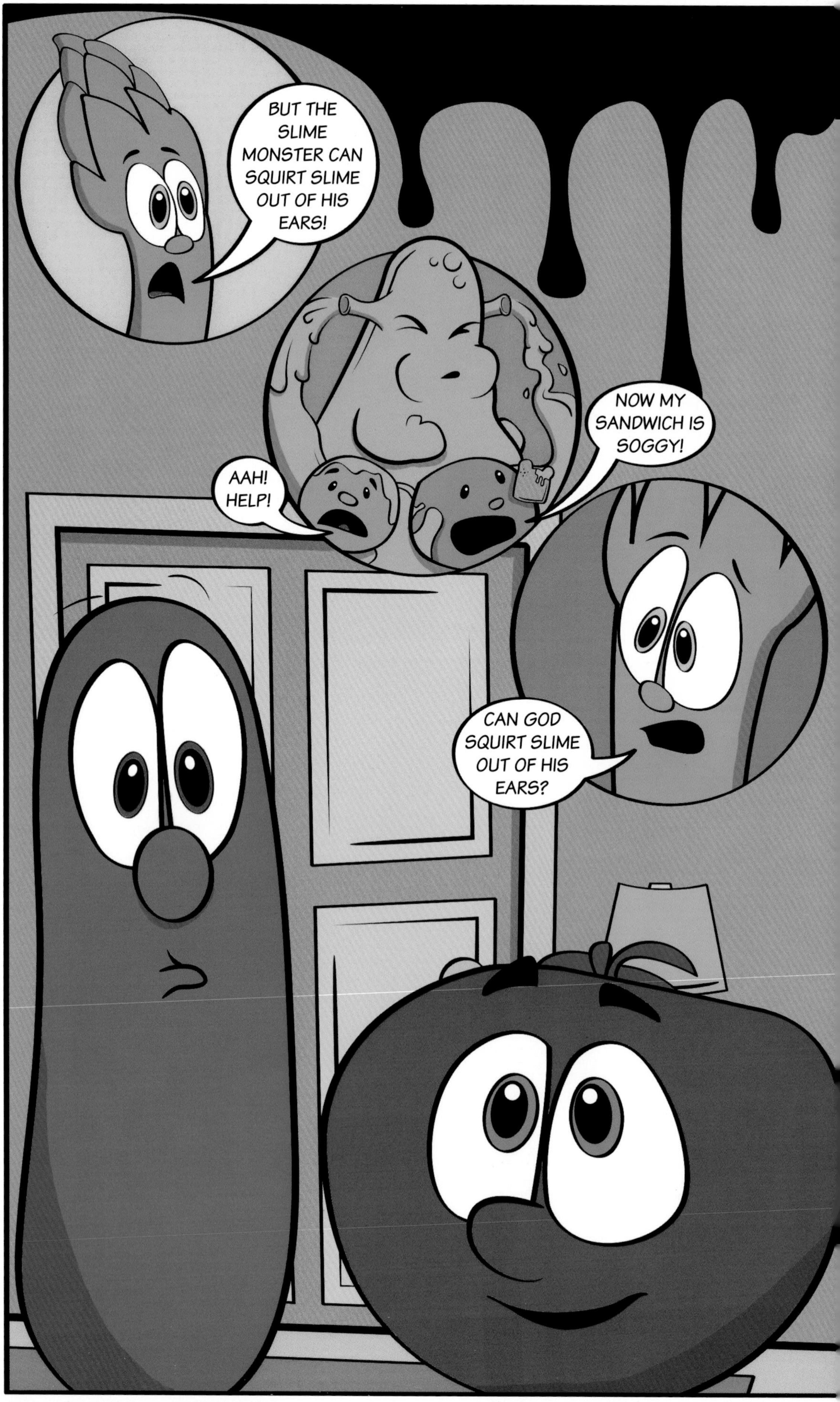
BUT THE SLIME MONSTER CAN SQUIRT SLIME OUT OF HIS EARS!
AAH! HELP!
NOW MY SANDWICH IS SOGGY!
CAN GOD SQUIRT SLIME OUT OF HIS EARS?

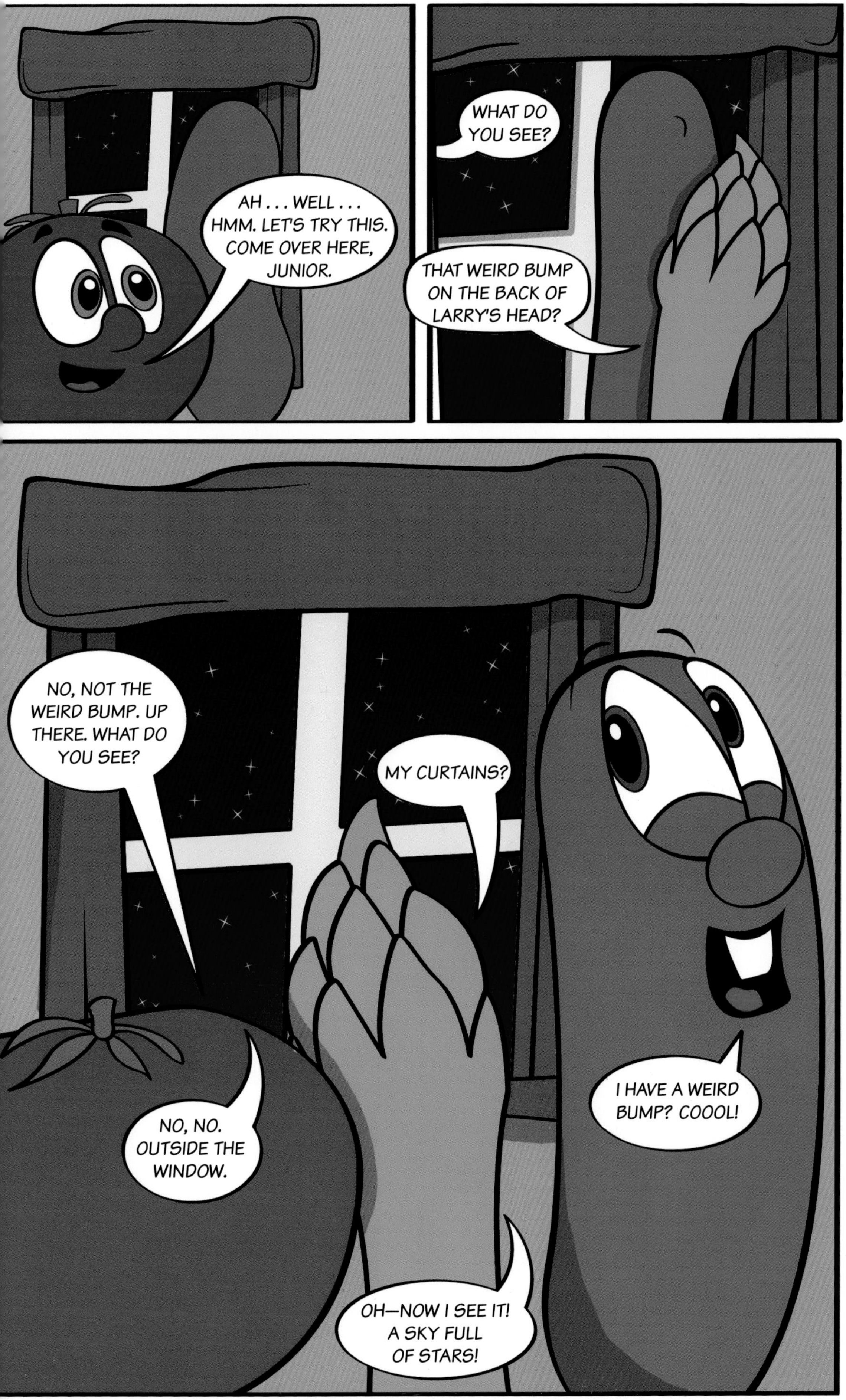
AH . . . WELL . . . HMM. LET'S TRY THIS. COME OVER HERE, JUNIOR.
WHAT DO YOU SEE?
THAT WEIRD BUMP ON THE BACK OF LARRY'S HEAD?
NO, NOT THE WEIRD BUMP. UP THERE. WHAT DO YOU SEE?
MY CURTAINS?
I HAVE A WEIRD BUMP? COOOL!
NO, NO. OUTSIDE THE WINDOW.
OH—NOW I SEE IT! A SKY FULL OF STARS!

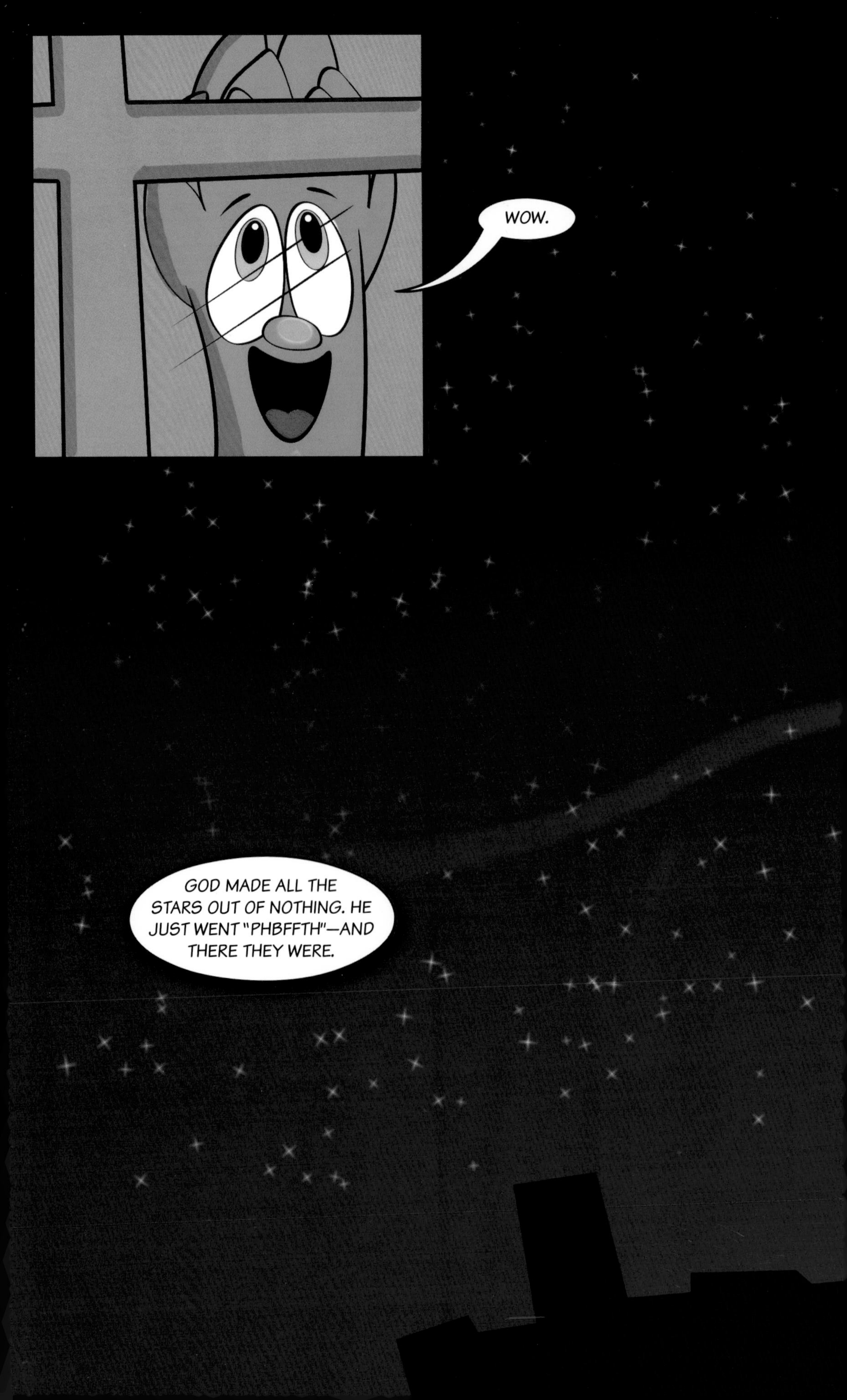
WOW.
GOD MADE ALL THE STARS OUT OF NOTHING. HE JUST WENT "PHBFFTH"—AND THERE THEY WERE.

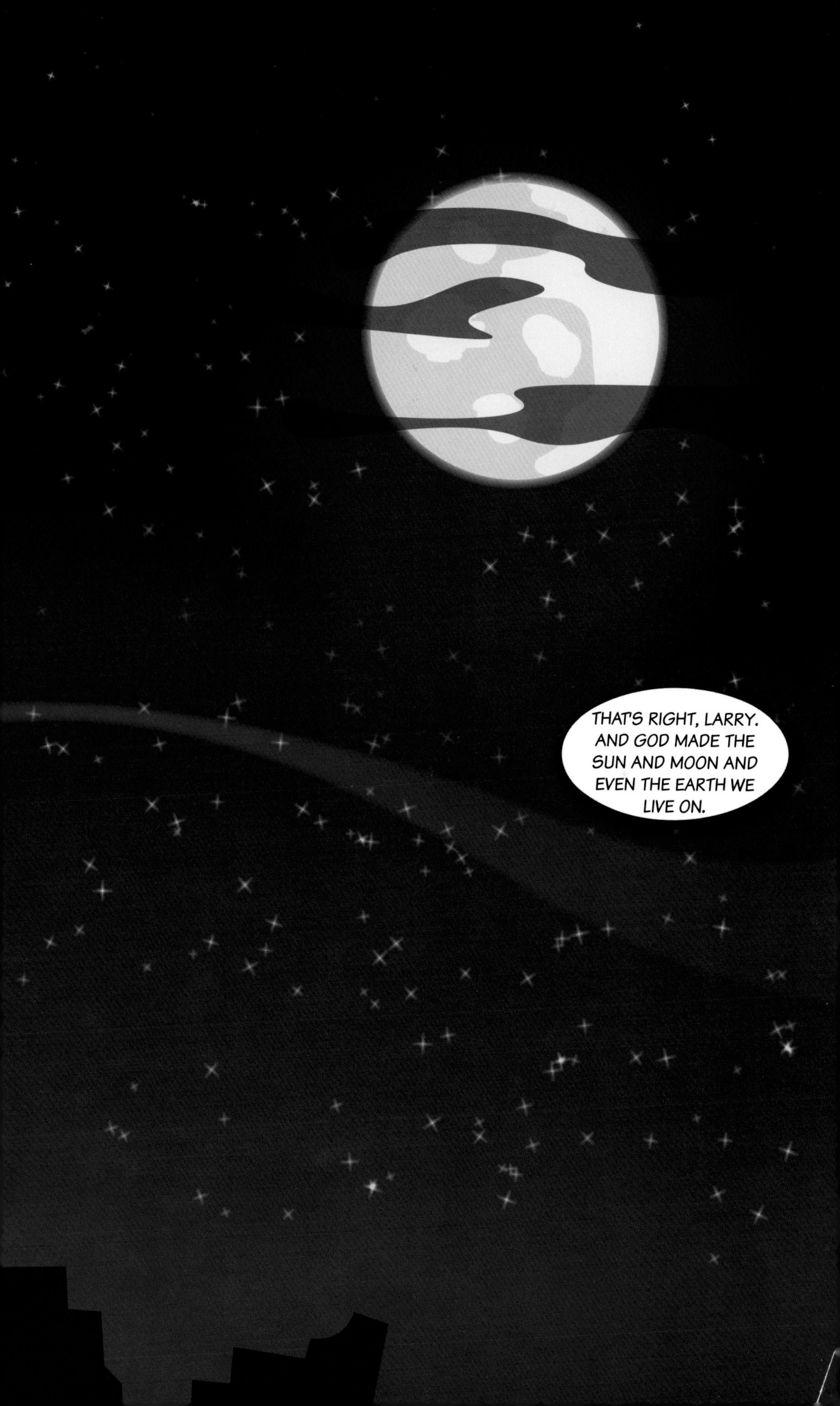
THAT'S RIGHT, LARRY. AND GOD MADE THE SUN AND MOON AND EVEN THE EARTH WE LIVE ON.

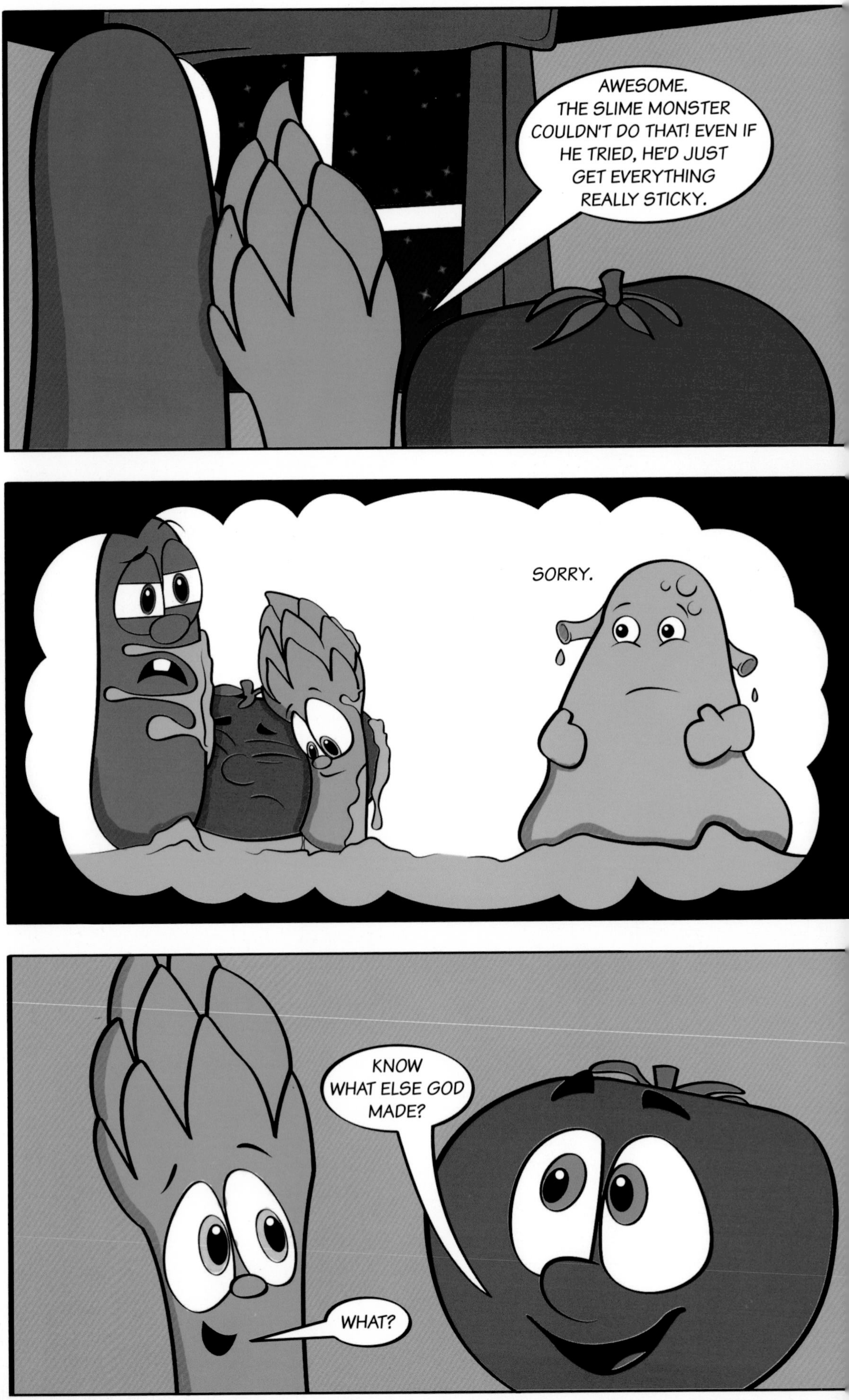
AWESOME. THE SLIME MONSTER COULDN'T DO THAT! EVEN IF HE TRIED, HE'D JUST GET EVERYTHING REALLY STICKY.
SORRY.
KNOW WHAT ELSE GOD MADE?
WHAT?

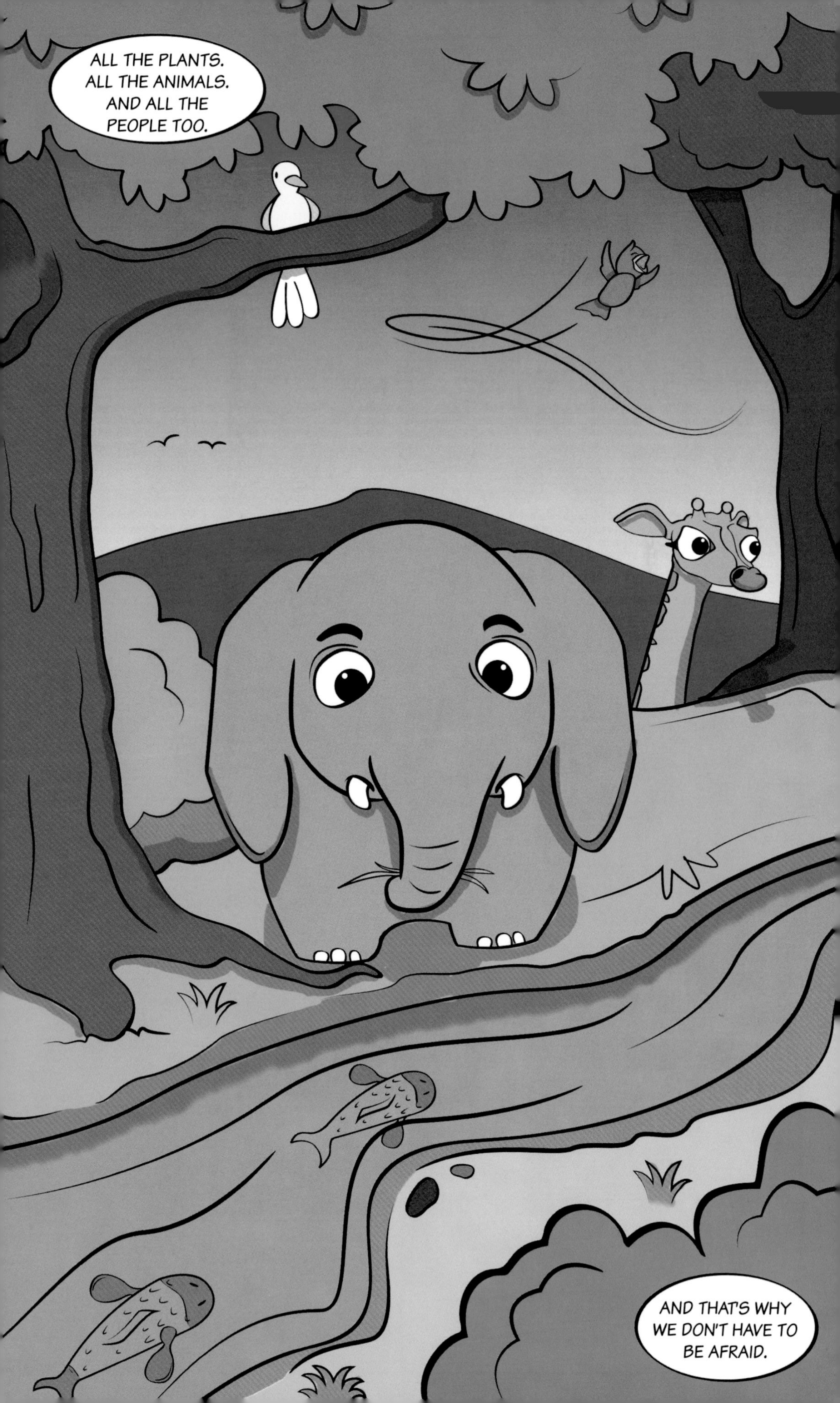
ALL THE PLANTS.
ALL THE ANIMALS.
AND ALL THE
PEOPLE TOO.
AND THAT'S WHY
WE DON'T HAVE TO
BE AFRAID.

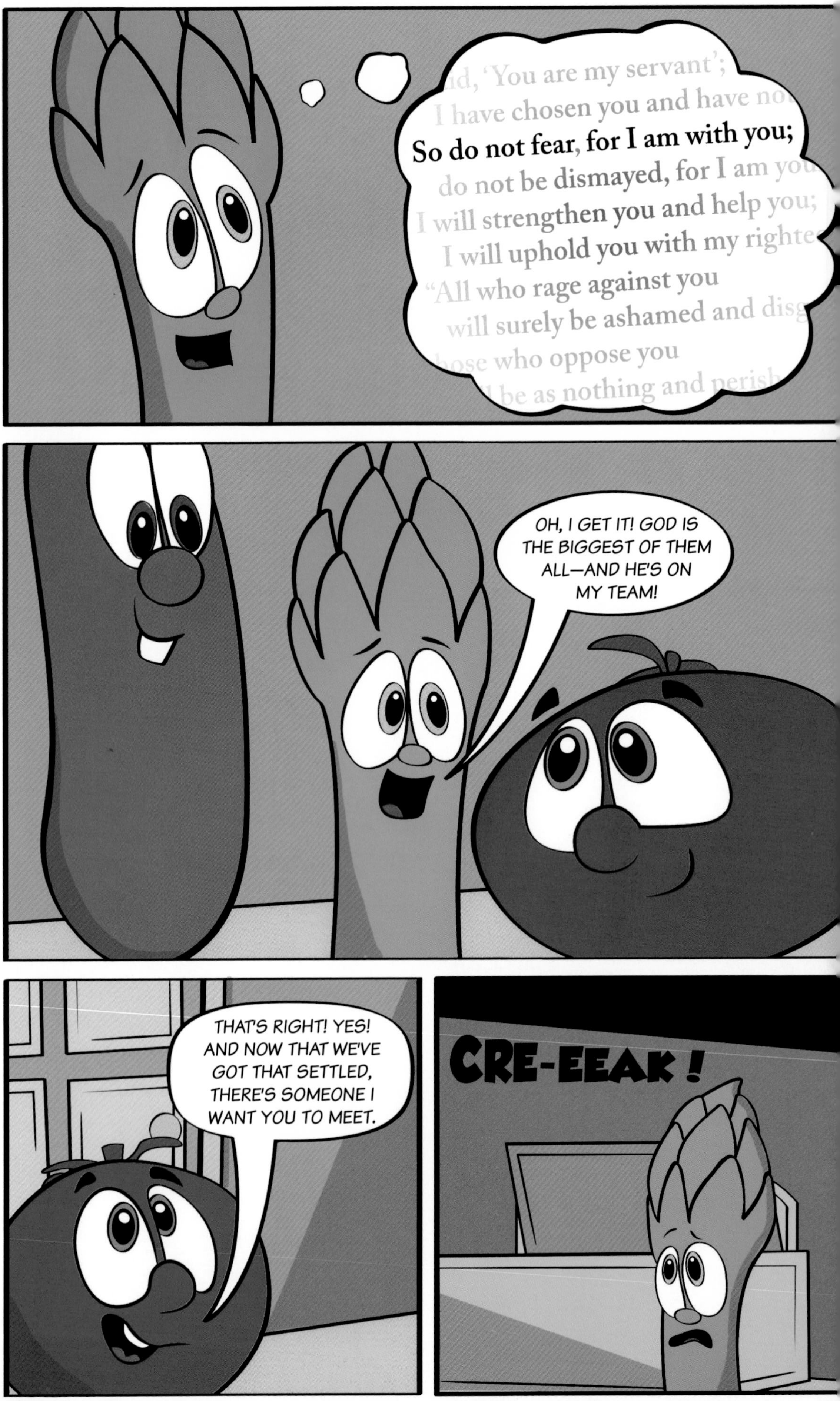

'You are my servant';
I have chosen you and have
So do not fear, for I am with you;
do not be dismayed, for I am
I will strengthen you and help you;
I will uphold you with my
"All who rage against you
will surely be ashamed and
who oppose you
be as nothing and
OH, I GET IT! GOD IS THE BIGGEST OF THEM ALL—AND HE'S ON MY TEAM!
THAT'S RIGHT! YES! AND NOW THAT WE'VE GOT THAT SETTLED, THERE'S SOMEONE I WANT YOU TO MEET.
CRE-EEAK!

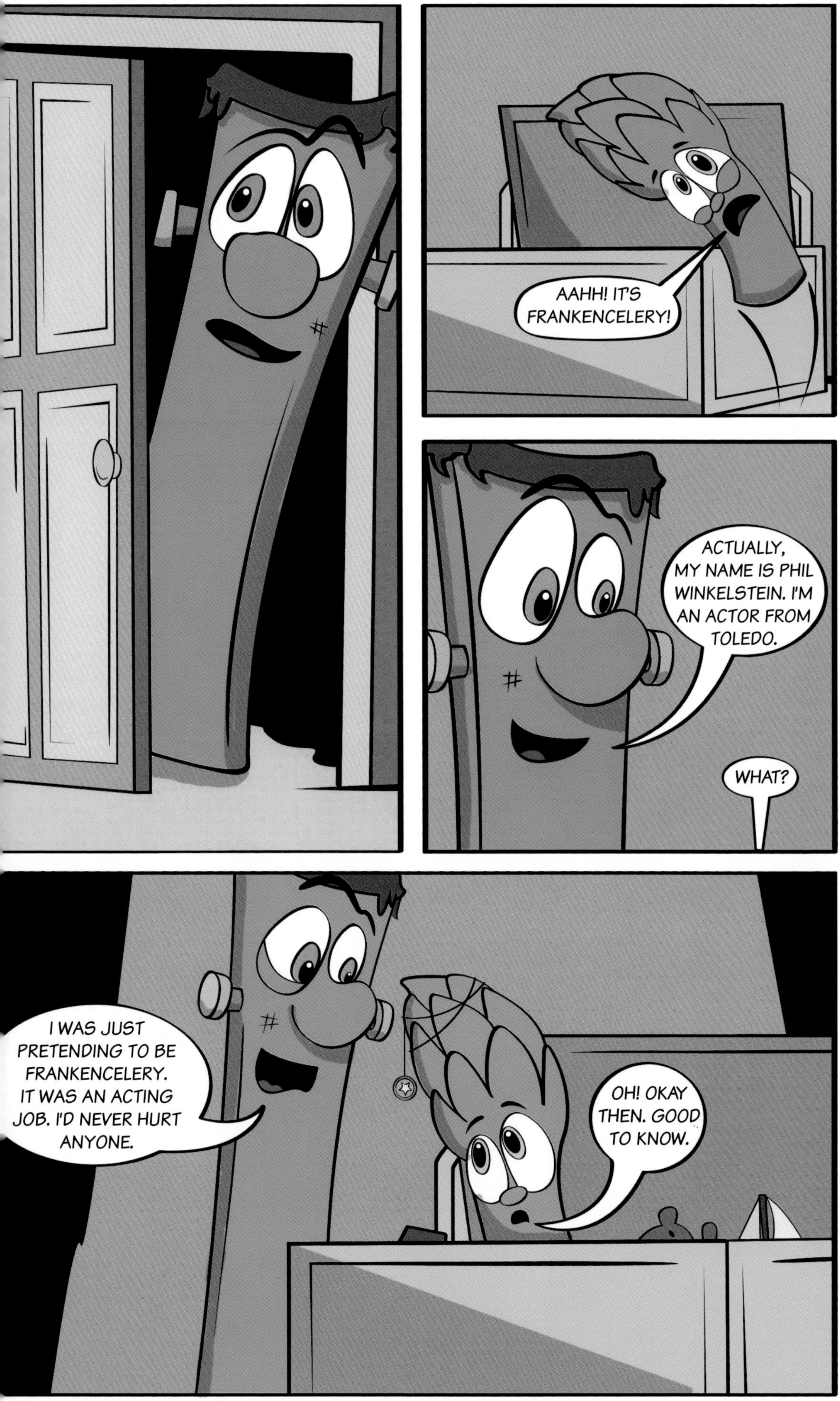
AAHH! IT'S FRANKENCELERY!
ACTUALLY, MY NAME IS PHIL WINKELSTEIN. I'M AN ACTOR FROM TOLEDO.
WHAT?
I WAS JUST PRETENDING TO BE FRANKENCELERY. IT WAS AN ACTING JOB. I'D NEVER HURT ANYONE.
OH! OKAY THEN. GOOD TO KNOW.

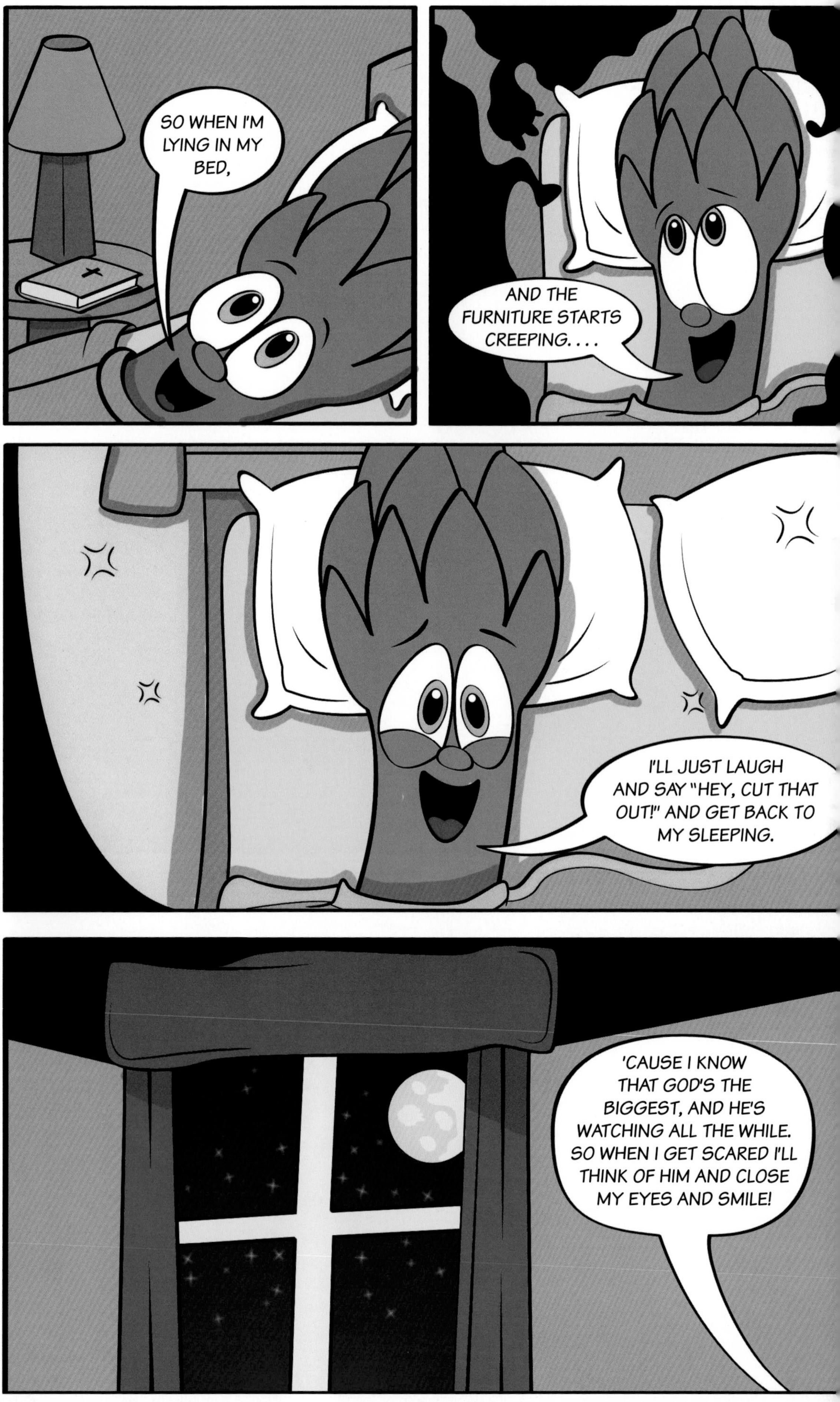
SO WHEN I'M LYING IN MY BED,
AND THE FURNITURE STARTS CREEPING. . . .
I'LL JUST LAUGH AND SAY "HEY, CUT THAT OUT!" AND GET BACK TO MY SLEEPING.
'CAUSE I KNOW THAT GOD'S THE BIGGEST, AND HE'S WATCHING ALL THE WHILE. SO WHEN I GET SCARED I'LL THINK OF HIM AND CLOSE MY EYES AND SMILE!

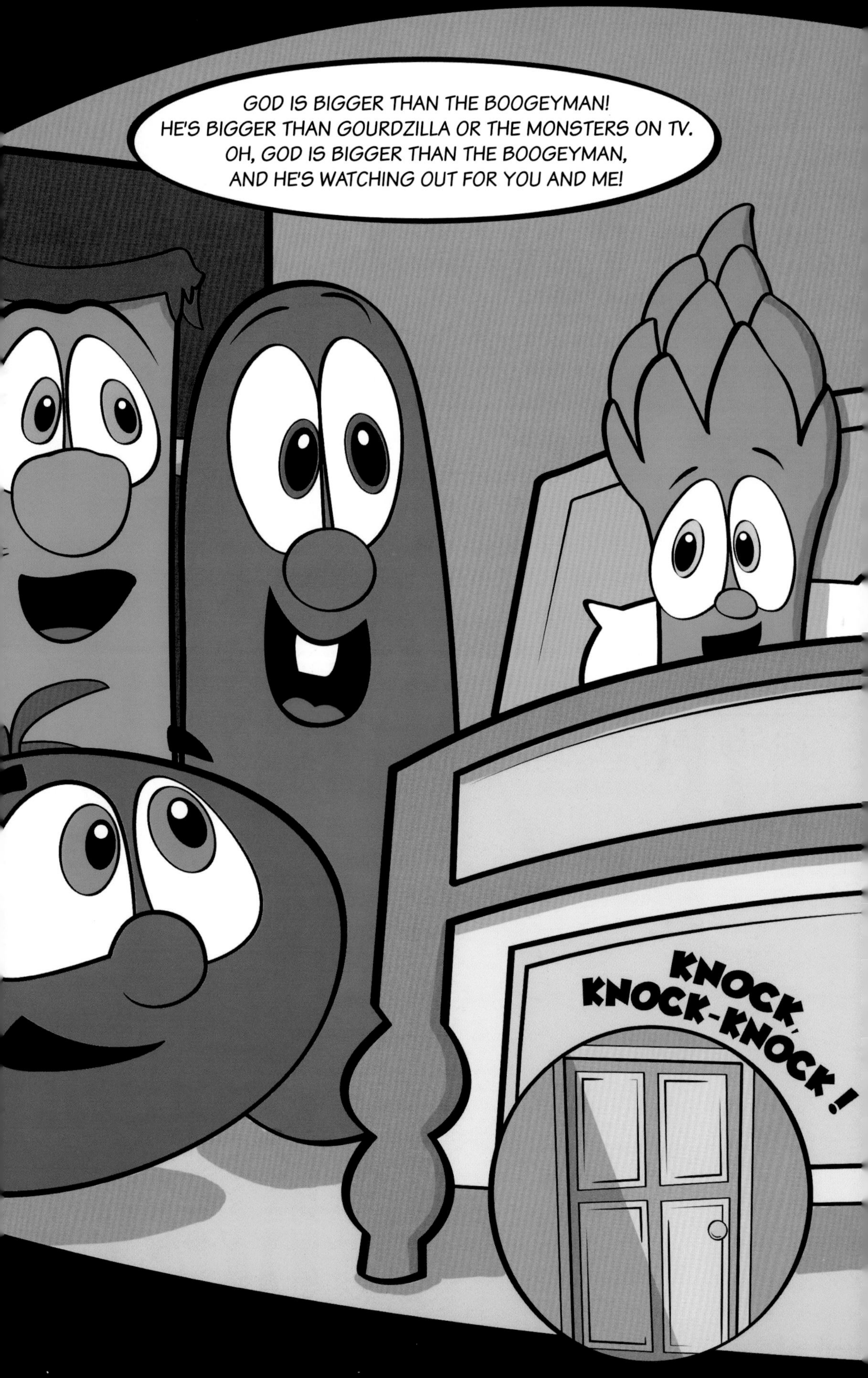
GOD IS BIGGER THAN THE BOOGEYMAN! HE'S BIGGER THAN GOURDZILLA OR THE MONSTERS ON TV. OH, GOD IS BIGGER THAN THE BOOGEYMAN, AND HE'S WATCHING OUT FOR YOU AND ME!
KNOCK, KNOCK-KNOCK!

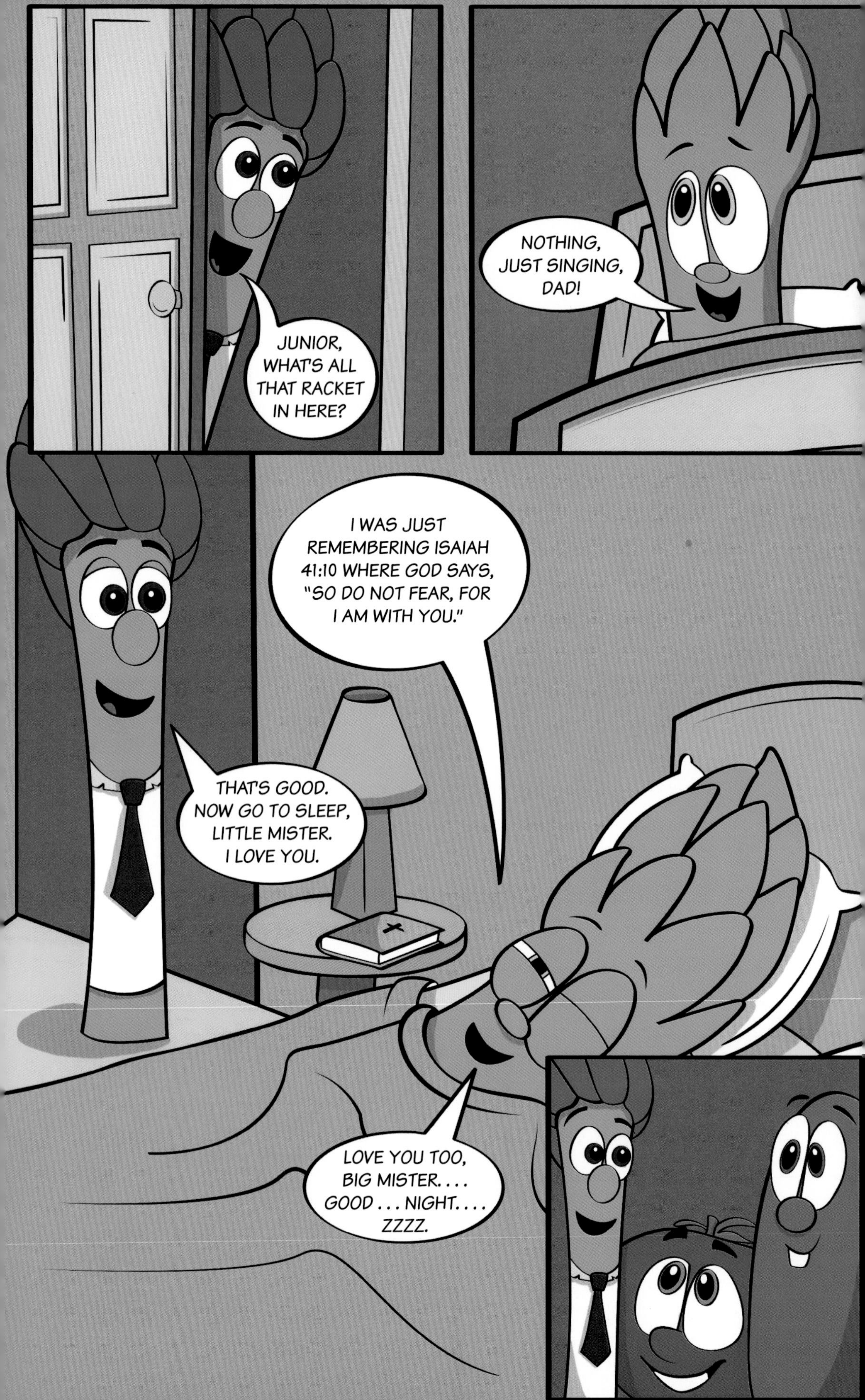
JUNIOR, WHAT'S ALL THAT RACKET IN HERE?
NOTHING, JUST SINGING, DAD!
I WAS JUST REMEMBERING ISAIAH 41:10 WHERE GOD SAYS, "SO DO NOT FEAR, FOR I AM WITH YOU."
THAT'S GOOD. NOW GO TO SLEEP, LITTLE MISTER. I LOVE YOU.
LOVE YOU TOO, BIG MISTER. . . . GOOD . . . NIGHT. . . . ZZZZ.

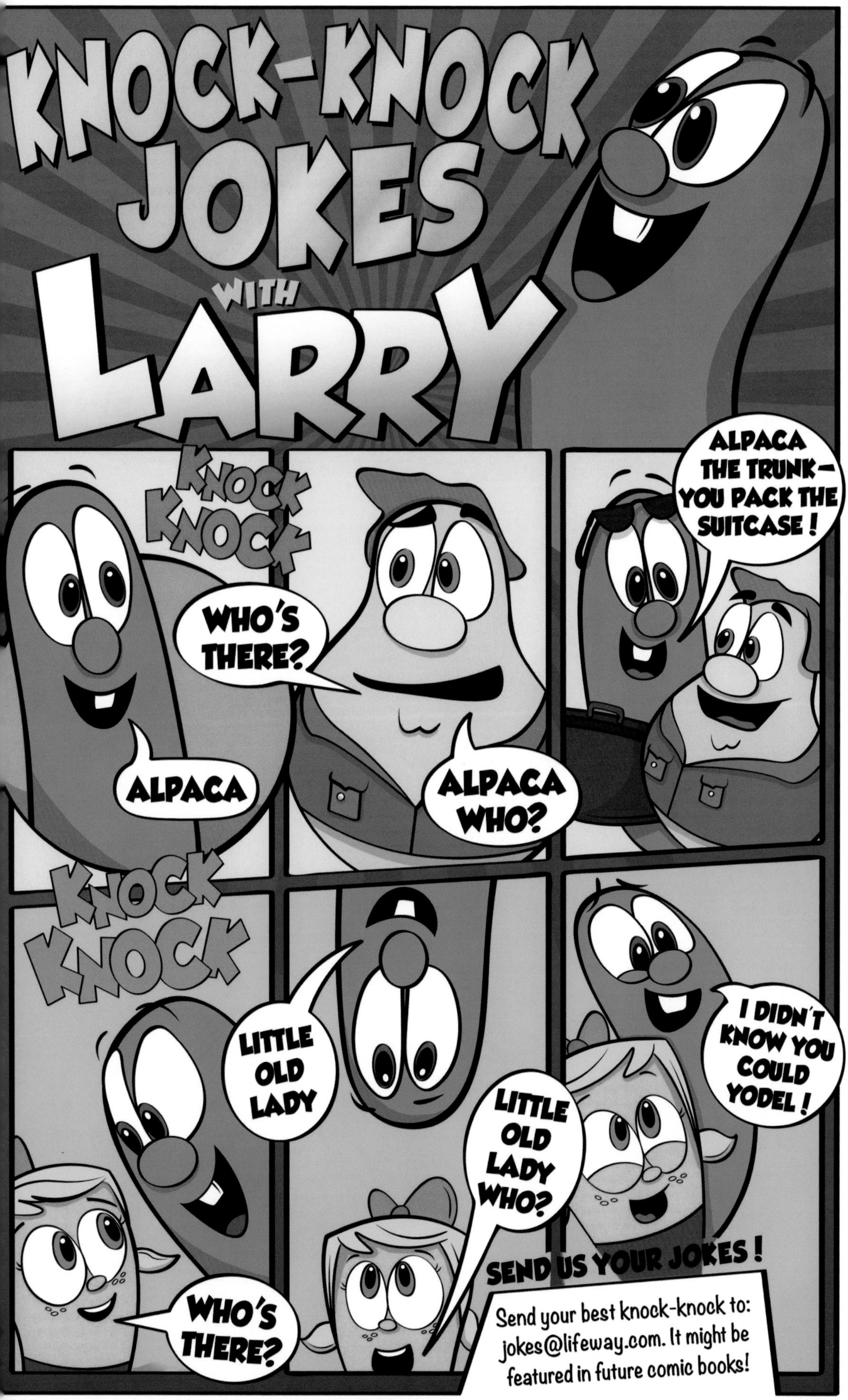
KNOCK-KNOCK JOKES WITH LARRY
KNOCK KNOCK
WHO'S THERE?
ALPACA
ALPACA WHO?
ALPACA THE TRUNK—YOU PACK THE SUITCASE!
KNOCK KNOCK
WHO'S THERE?
LITTLE OLD LADY
LITTLE OLD LADY WHO?
I DIDN'T KNOW YOU COULD YODEL!
SEND US YOUR JOKES!
Send your best knock-knock to: jokes@lifeway.com. It might be featured in future comic books!

NETFLIX

VeggieTales
in the house

A NETFLIX ORIGINAL SERIES

NOW STREAMING!

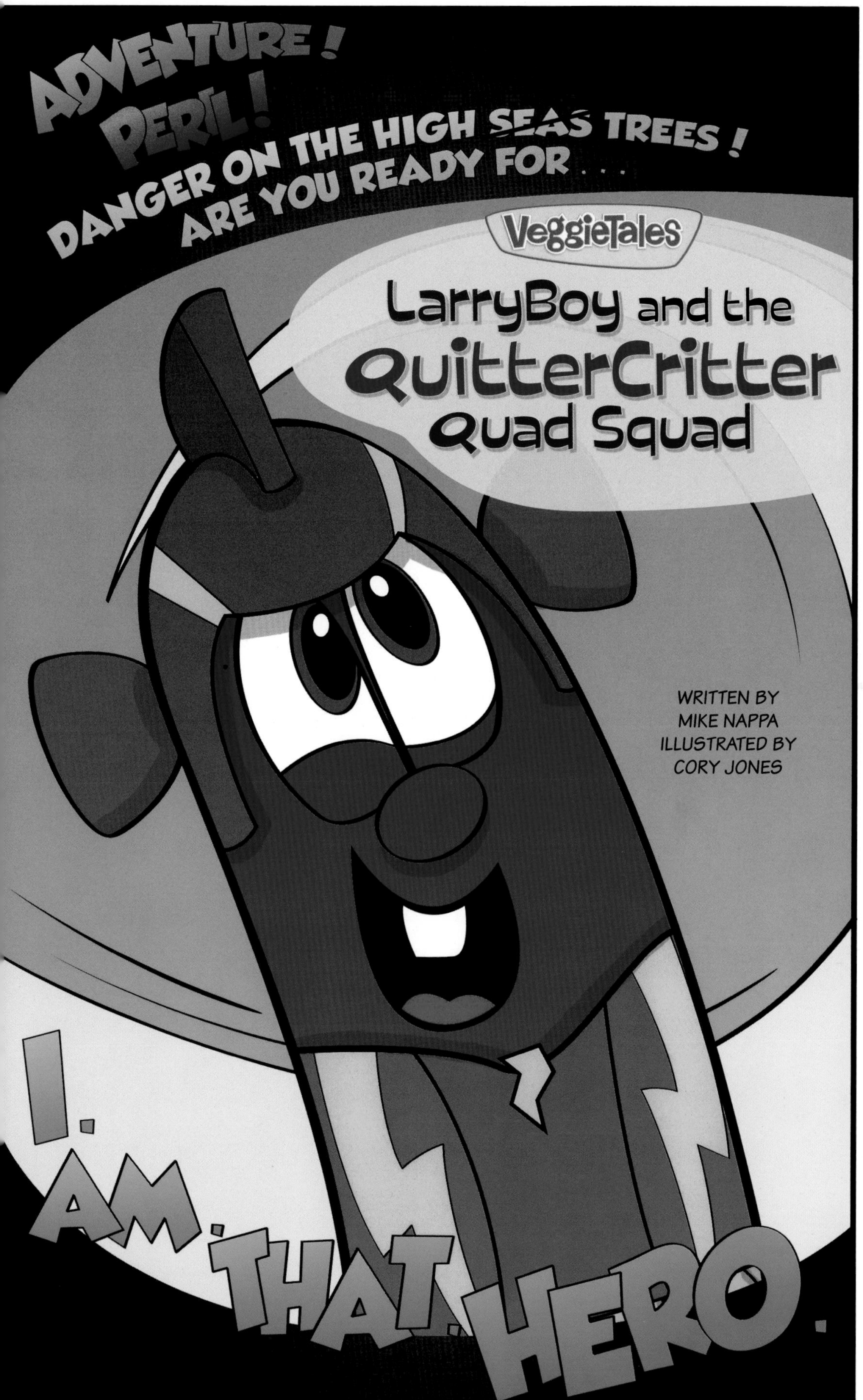
ADVENTURE!
PERIL!
DANGER ON THE HIGH ~~SEAS~~ TREES!
ARE YOU READY FOR . . .
VeggieTales
LarryBoy and the QuitterCritter Quad Squad
WRITTEN BY
MIKE NAPPA
ILLUSTRATED BY
CORY JONES
I. AM. THAT. HERO.

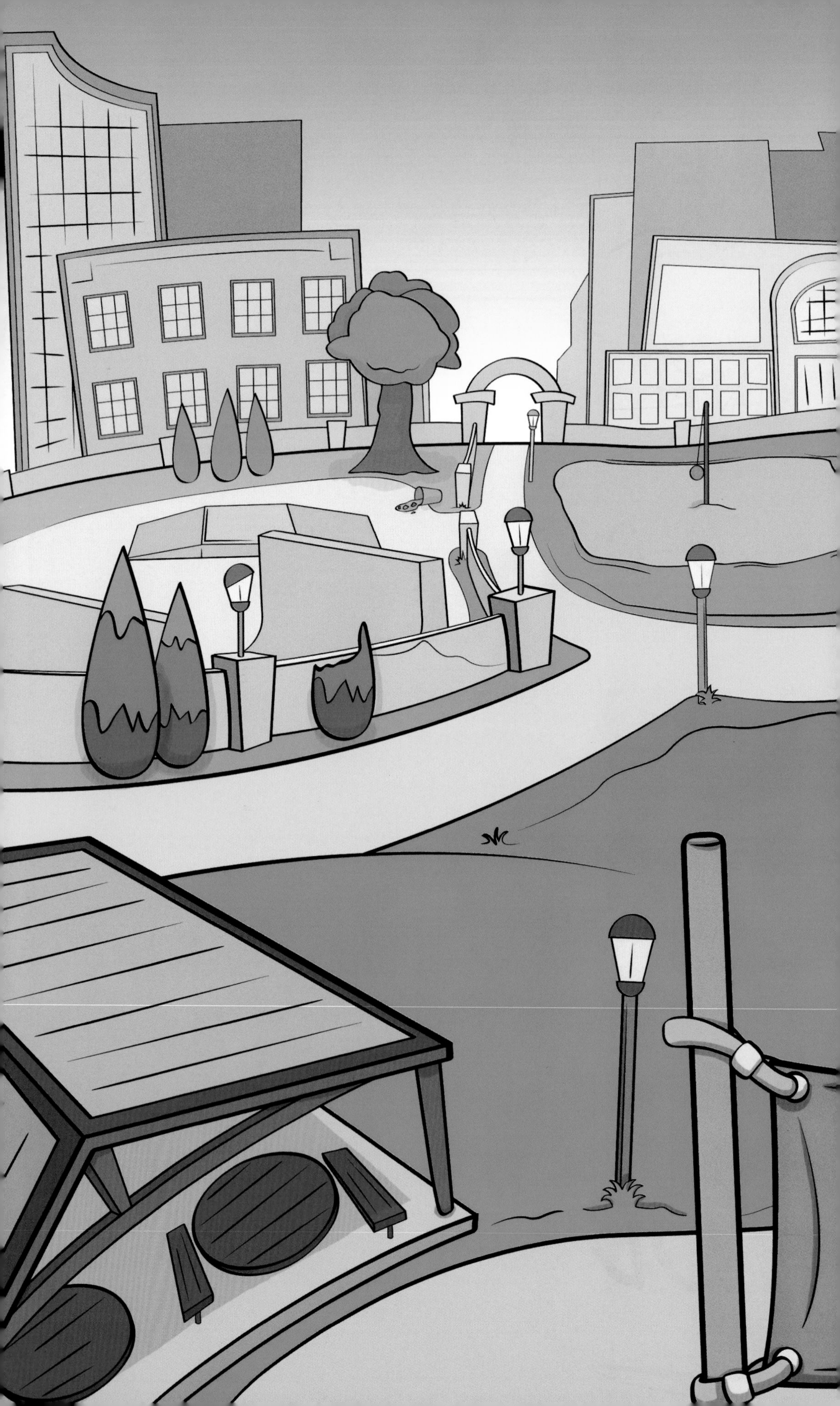

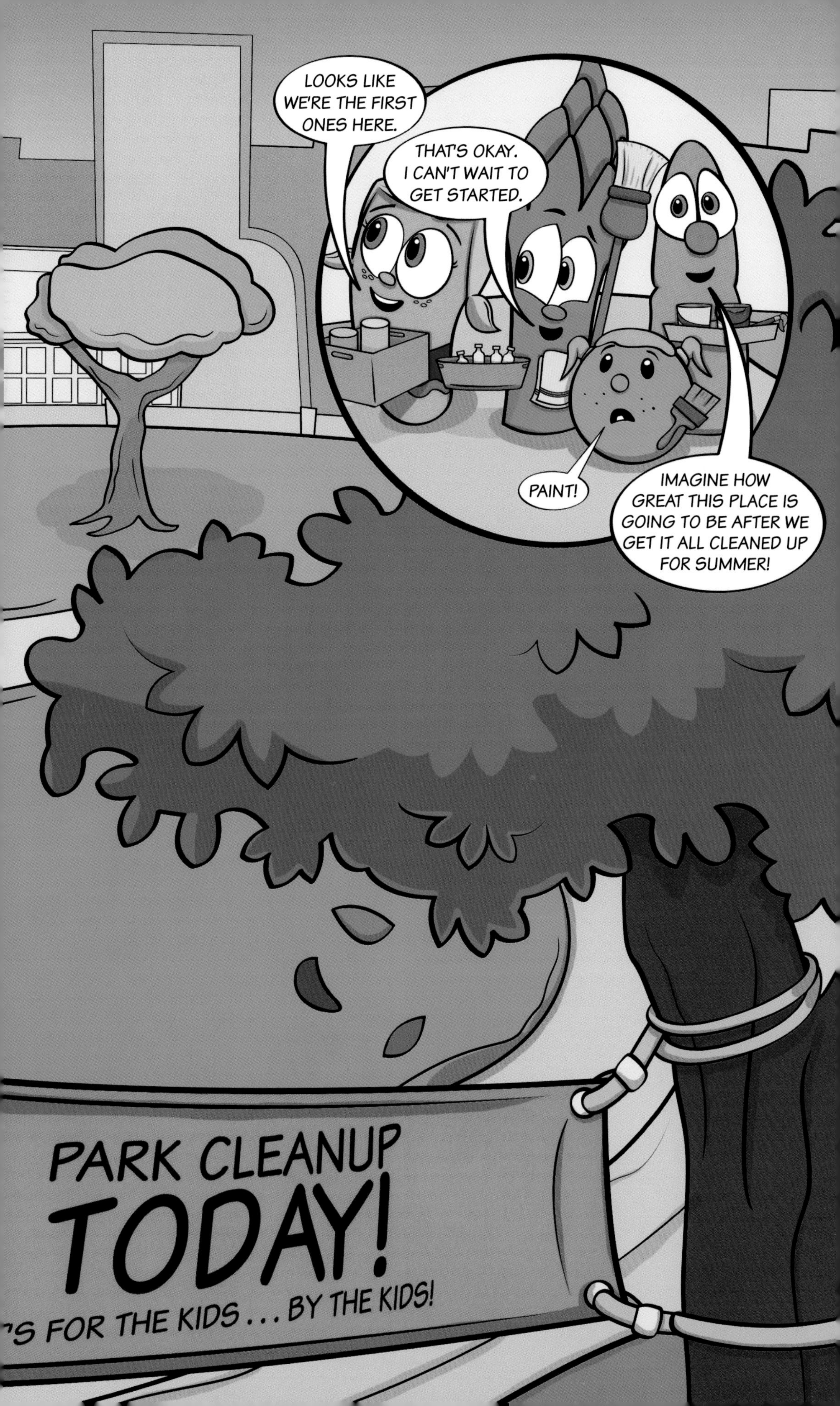
LOOKS LIKE WE'RE THE FIRST ONES HERE.
THAT'S OKAY. I CAN'T WAIT TO GET STARTED.
PAINT!
IMAGINE HOW GREAT THIS PLACE IS GOING TO BE AFTER WE GET IT ALL CLEANED UP FOR SUMMER!
PARK CLEANUP
TODAY!
'S FOR THE KIDS . . . BY THE KIDS!

WE'RE HERE!
YEAH! WHO SAYS KIDS CAN'T DO GREAT THINGS?
LET'S GET THIS PLAYGROUND IN SUMMER-SHAPE!
WE'LL RAKE AND MOW THE LAWNS.
WE'LL CLEAR THE TRASH OFF THE BASKETBALL COURT AND SKATE RAMPS.
WE'LL CLEAN AND WAX THE PLAYGROUND EQUIPMENT.
AND WE'LL PUT A FRESH COAT OF PAINT ON THE PICNIC PAVILION!
PAINT!

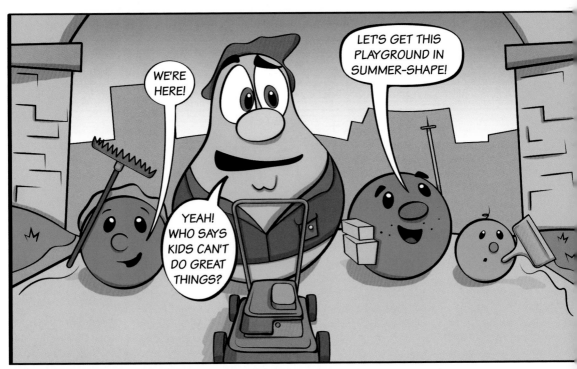

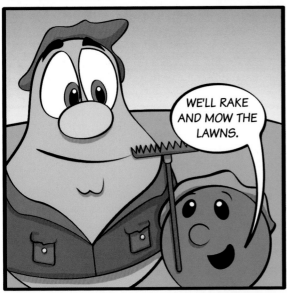

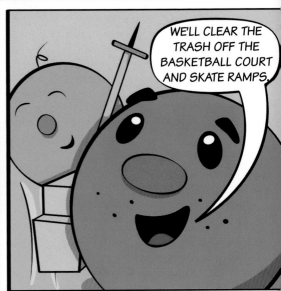

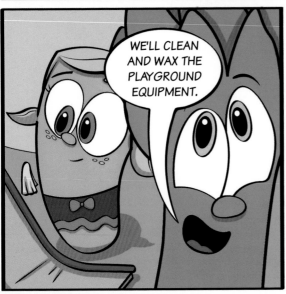

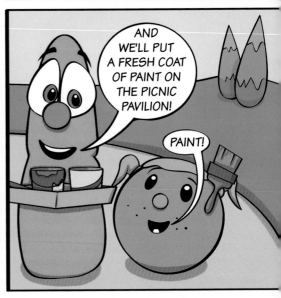

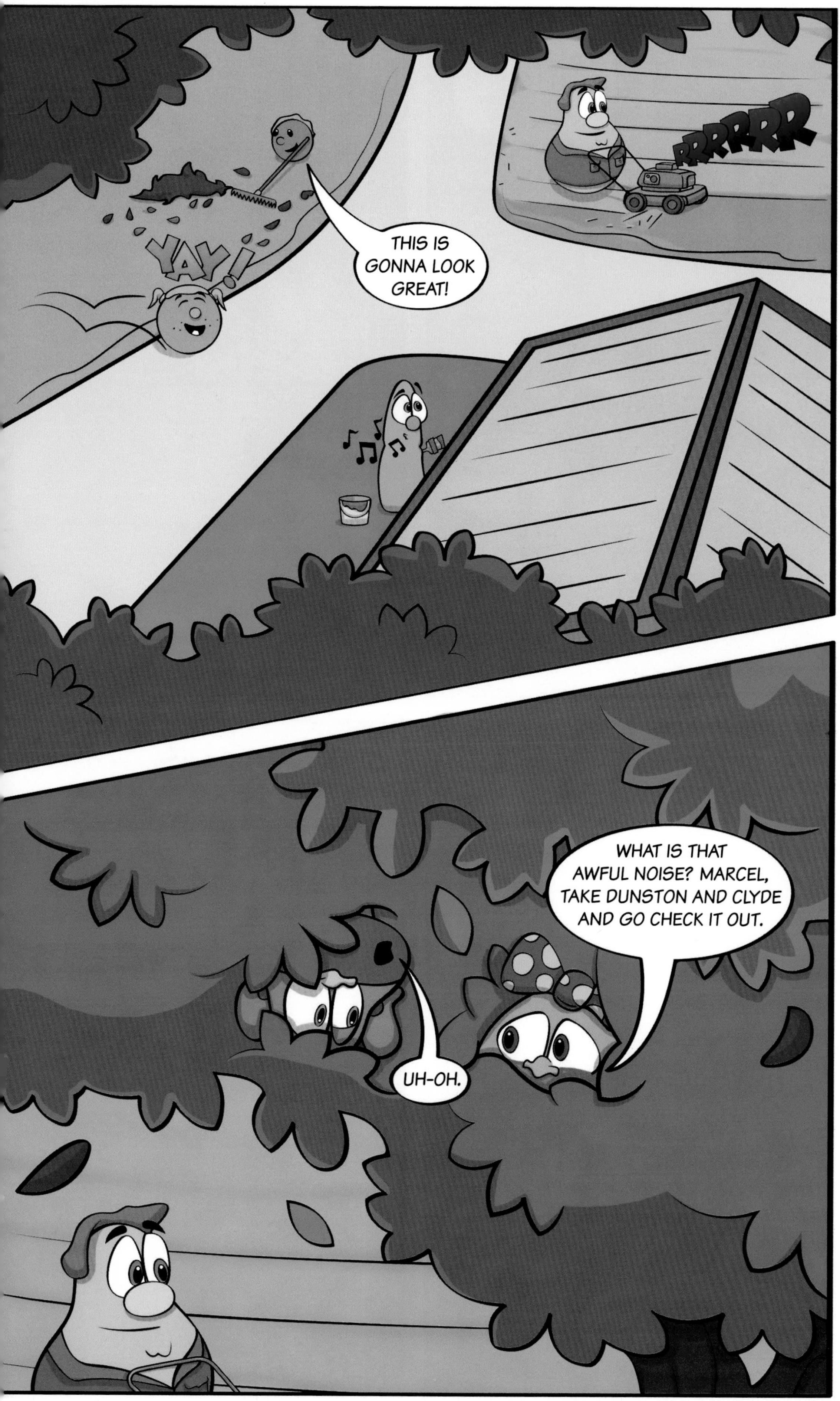
RRRRRR
YAY!
THIS IS GONNA LOOK GREAT!
WHAT IS THAT AWFUL NOISE? MARCEL, TAKE DUNSTON AND CLYDE AND GO CHECK IT OUT.
UH-OH.

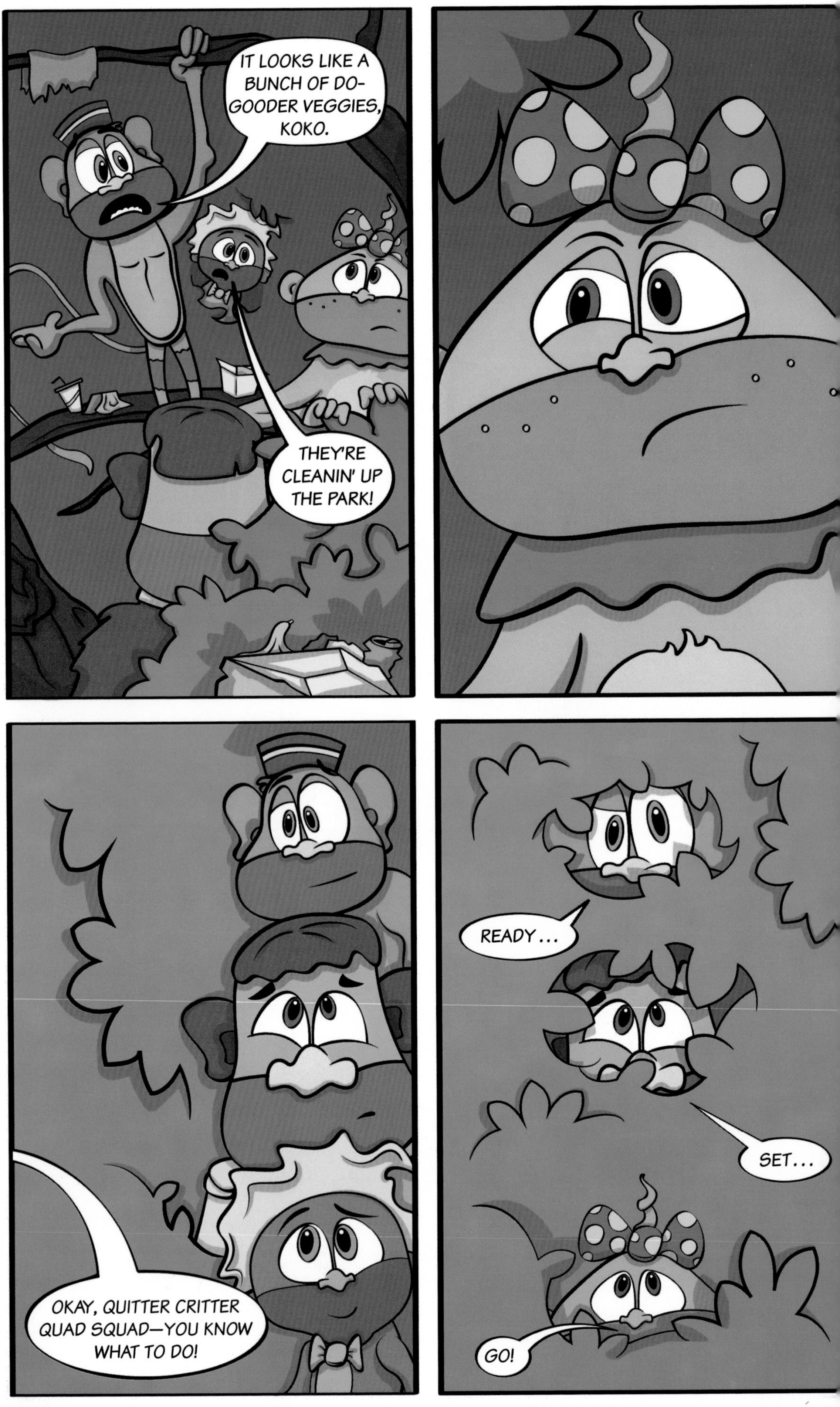
IT LOOKS LIKE A BUNCH OF DO-GOODER VEGGIES, KOKO.
THEY'RE CLEANIN' UP THE PARK!
OKAY, QUITTER CRITTER QUAD SQUAD—YOU KNOW WHAT TO DO!
READY...
SET...
GO!

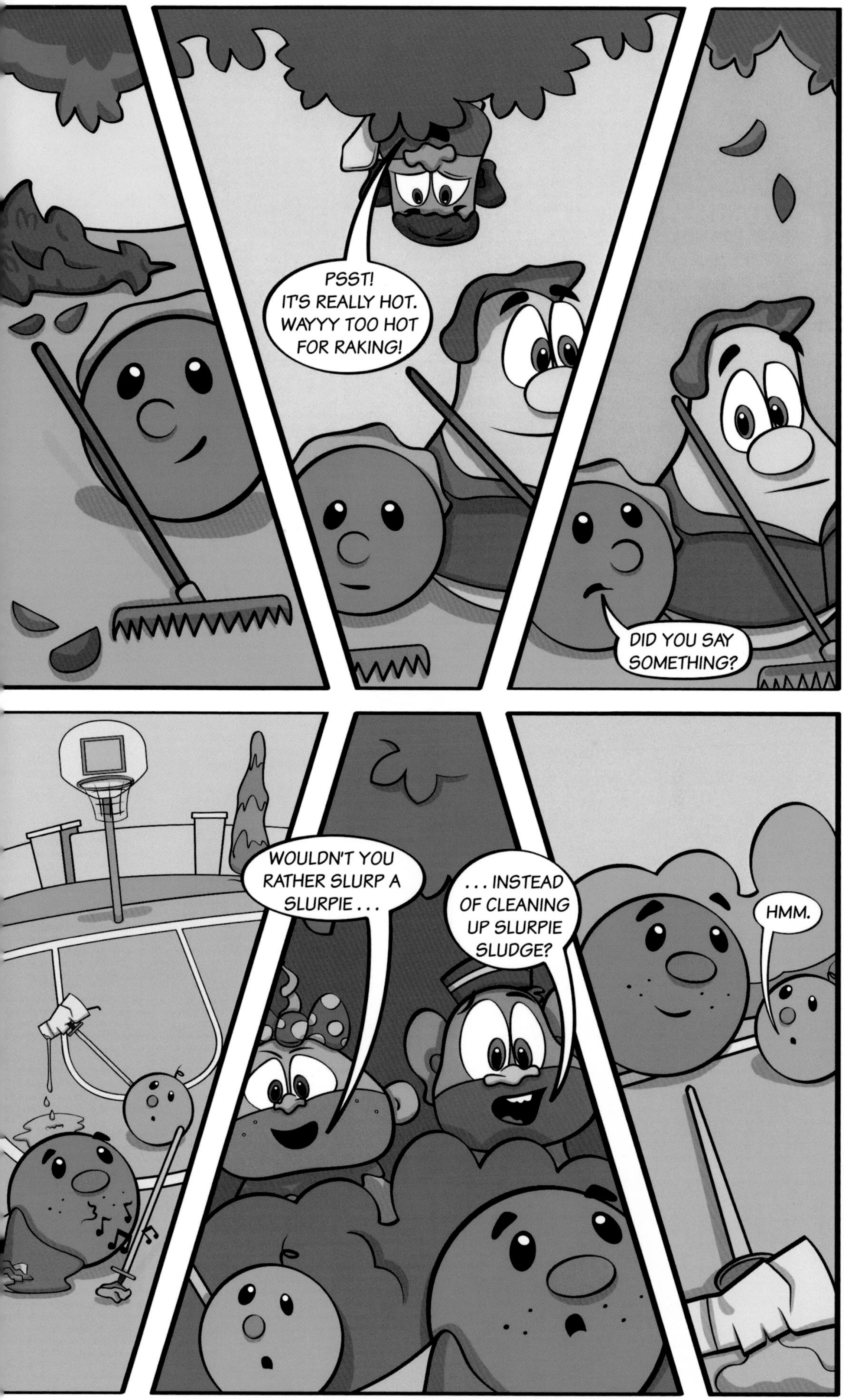
PSST!
IT'S REALLY HOT.
WAYYY TOO HOT
FOR RAKING!
DID YOU SAY
SOMETHING?
WOULDN'T YOU
RATHER SLURP A
SLURPIE . . .
. . . INSTEAD
OF CLEANING
UP SLURPIE
SLUDGE?
HMM.

ISN'T IT TIME FOR A SLURPIE BREAK? I BET THOSE PEAS OVER THERE WOULD JOIN YOU.
I AM GETTING THIRSTY. . . .
NOBODY PLAYS ON SWINGS ANYMORE. WHY NOT MAKE A DAISY CHAIN INSTEAD?
UMM. . . .
YOU'VE DONE ENOUGH ALREADY. DON'T YOU DESERVE A BREAK? A LITTLE NAP WOULDN'T HURT ANYBODY.
PAINT!
YAWN. . . .
NAP! NAP! NAP!
TOO HOT! SO HOT! WAYYY HOT!
SLURPIE! SLURPIE! SLURPIE!
DAISIES! PRETTY, PRETTY DAISIES!

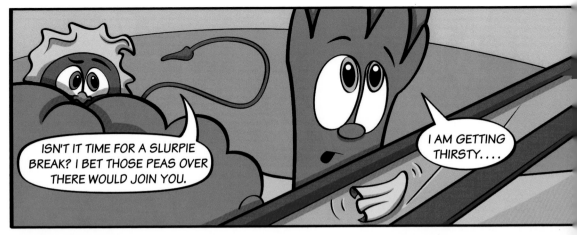

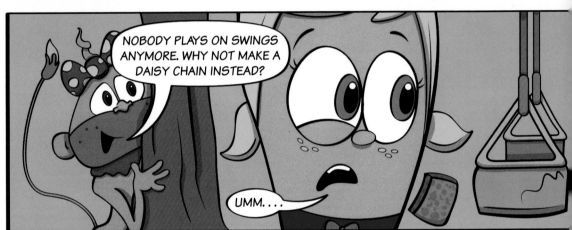

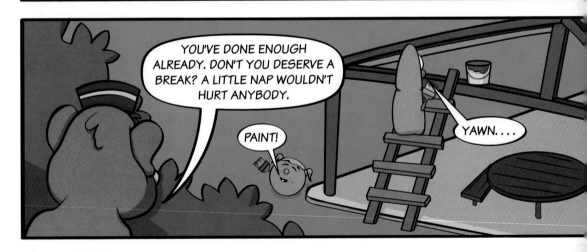

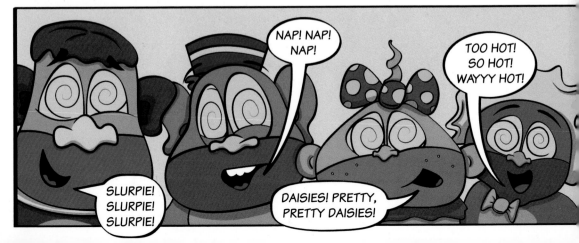

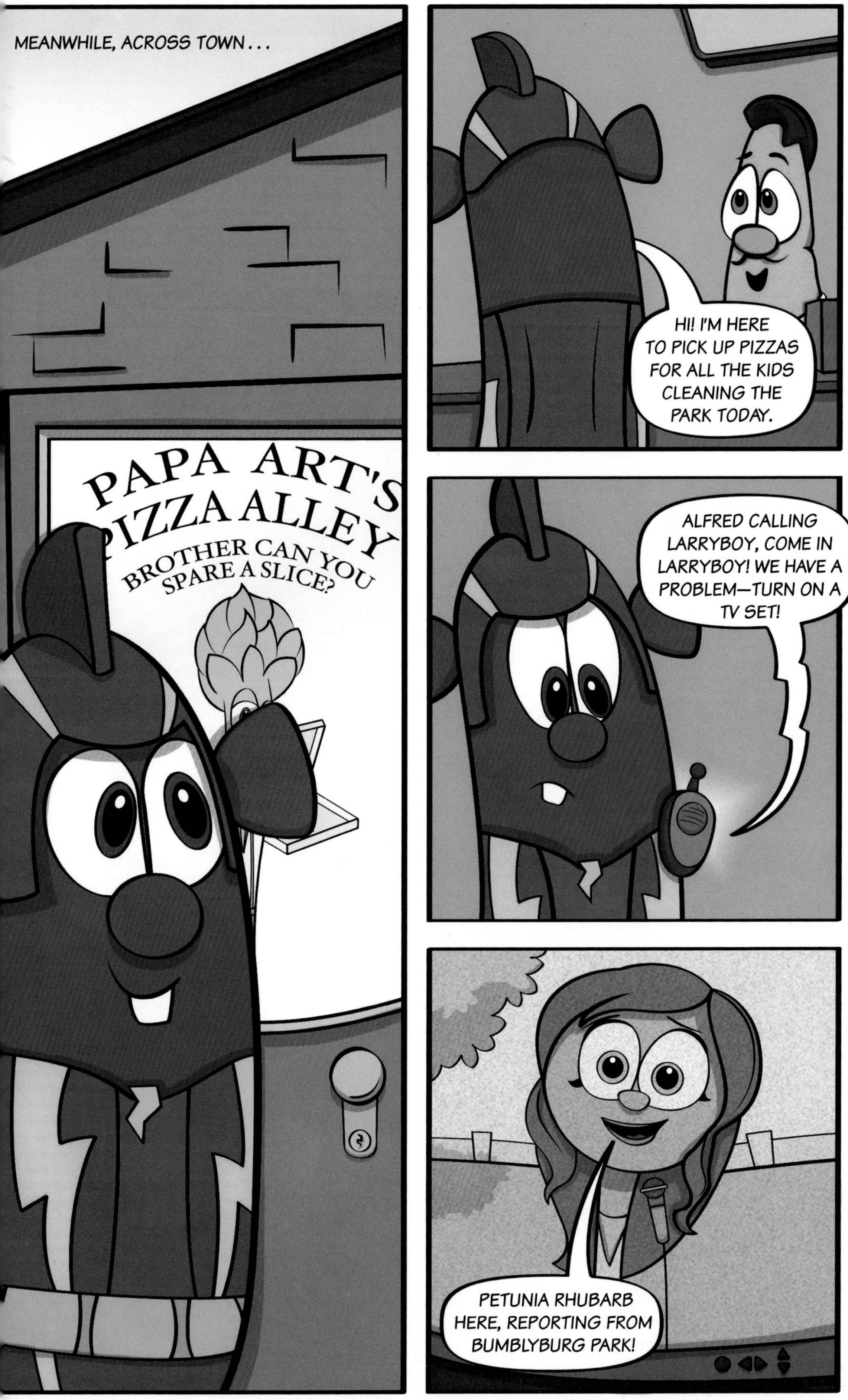
MEANWHILE, ACROSS TOWN...
PAPA ART'S PIZZA ALLEY
BROTHER CAN YOU SPARE A SLICE?
HI! I'M HERE TO PICK UP PIZZAS FOR ALL THE KIDS CLEANING THE PARK TODAY.
ALFRED CALLING LARRYBOY, COME IN LARRYBOY! WE HAVE A PROBLEM—TURN ON A TV SET!
PETUNIA RHUBARB HERE, REPORTING FROM BUMBLYBURG PARK!

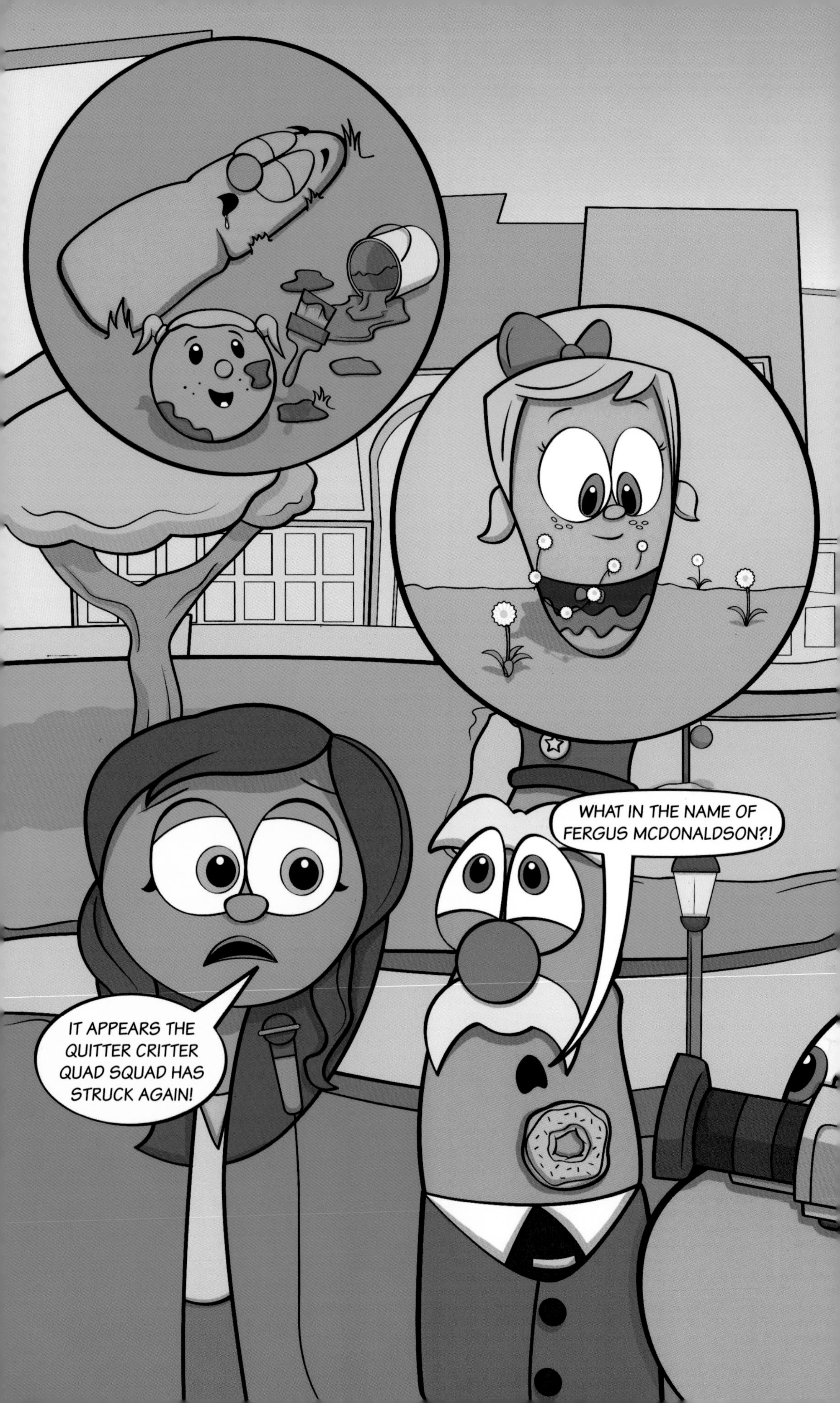
WHAT IN THE NAME OF FERGUS MCDONALDSON?!
IT APPEARS THE QUITTER CRITTER QUAD SQUAD HAS STRUCK AGAIN!

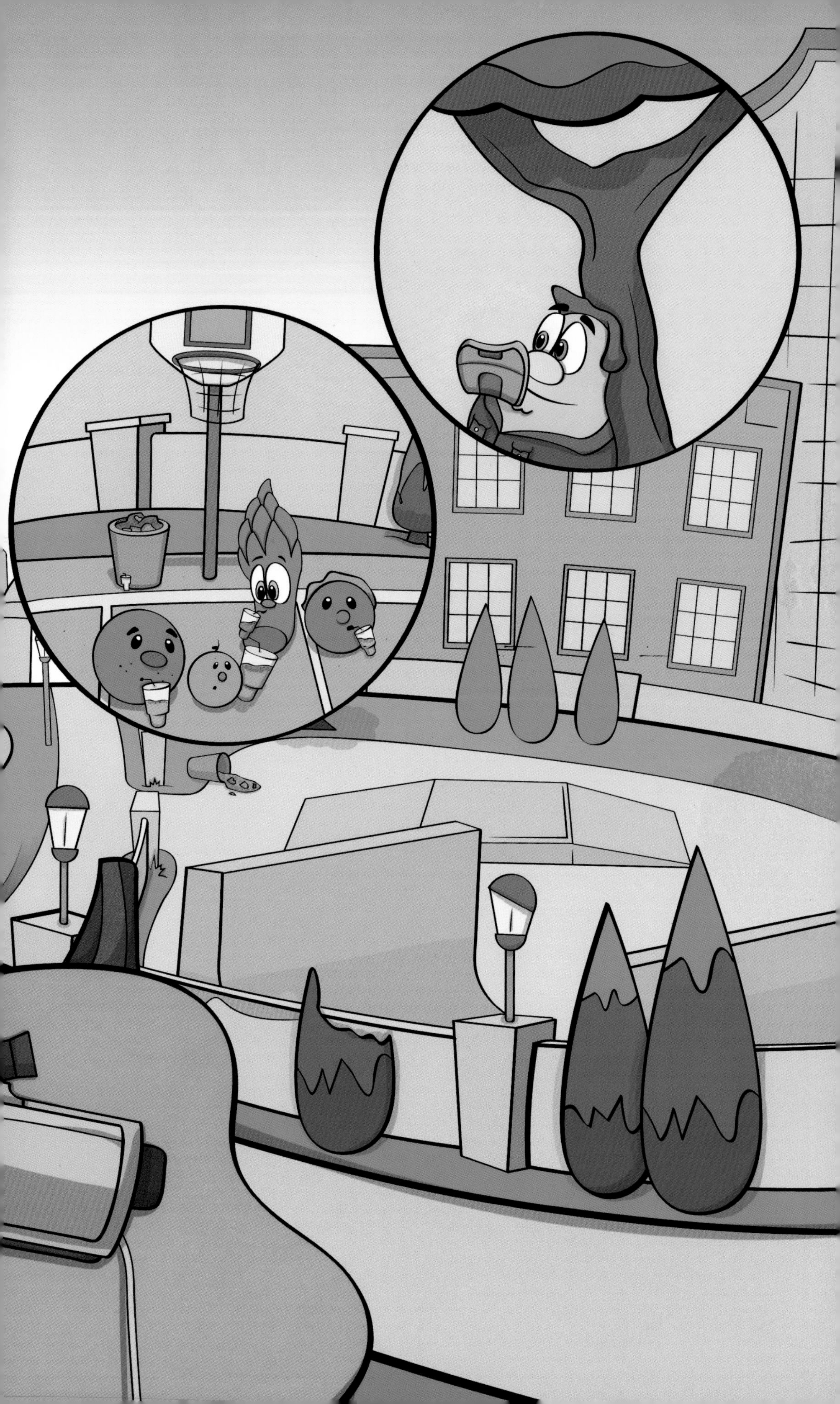

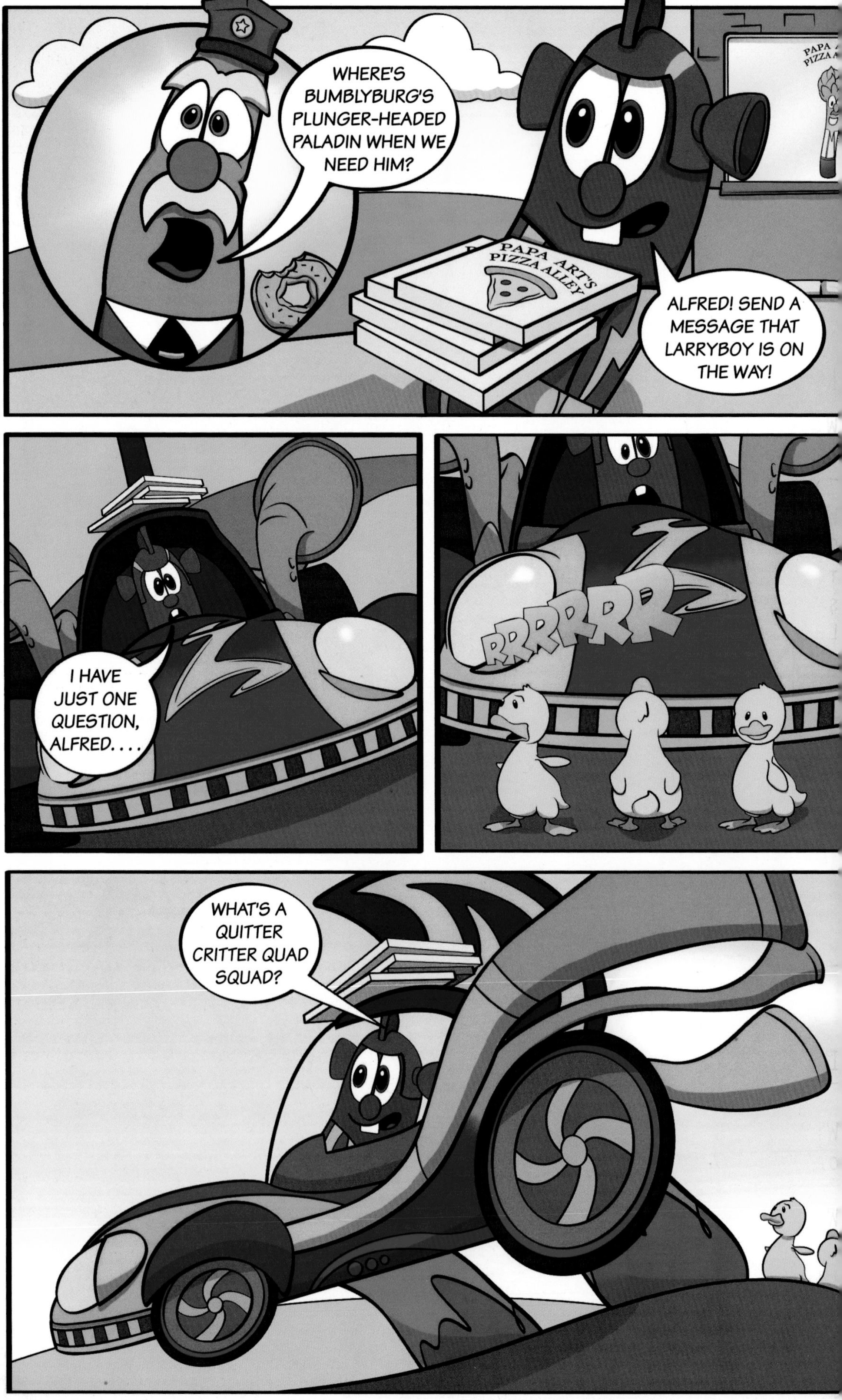

WHERE'S BUMBLYBURG'S PLUNGER-HEADED PALADIN WHEN WE NEED HIM?
PAPA ART'S PIZZA ALLEY
ALFRED! SEND A MESSAGE THAT LARRYBOY IS ON THE WAY!
I HAVE JUST ONE QUESTION, ALFRED. . . .
RRRRRR
WHAT'S A QUITTER CRITTER QUAD SQUAD?

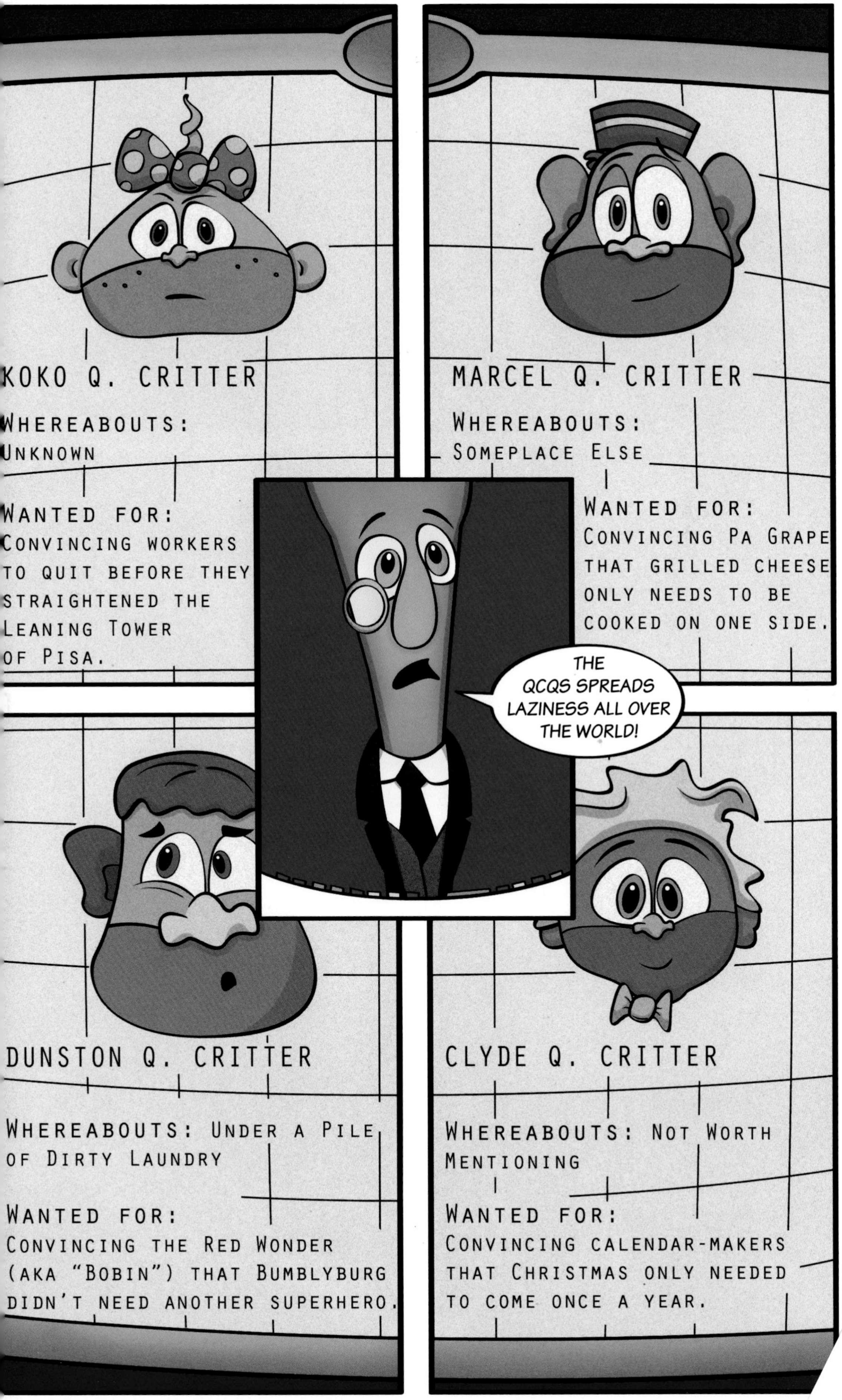
KOKO Q. CRITTER
WHEREABOUTS: UNKNOWN
WANTED FOR: CONVINCING WORKERS TO QUIT BEFORE THEY STRAIGHTENED THE LEANING TOWER OF PISA.
MARCEL Q. CRITTER
WHEREABOUTS: SOMEPLACE ELSE
WANTED FOR: CONVINCING PA GRAPE THAT GRILLED CHEESE ONLY NEEDS TO BE COOKED ON ONE SIDE.
THE QCQS SPREADS LAZINESS ALL OVER THE WORLD!
DUNSTON Q. CRITTER
WHEREABOUTS: UNDER A PILE OF DIRTY LAUNDRY
WANTED FOR: CONVINCING THE RED WONDER (AKA "BOBIN") THAT BUMBLYBURG DIDN'T NEED ANOTHER SUPERHERO.
CLYDE Q. CRITTER
WHEREABOUTS: NOT WORTH MENTIONING
WANTED FOR: CONVINCING CALENDAR-MAKERS THAT CHRISTMAS ONLY NEEDED TO COME ONCE A YEAR.

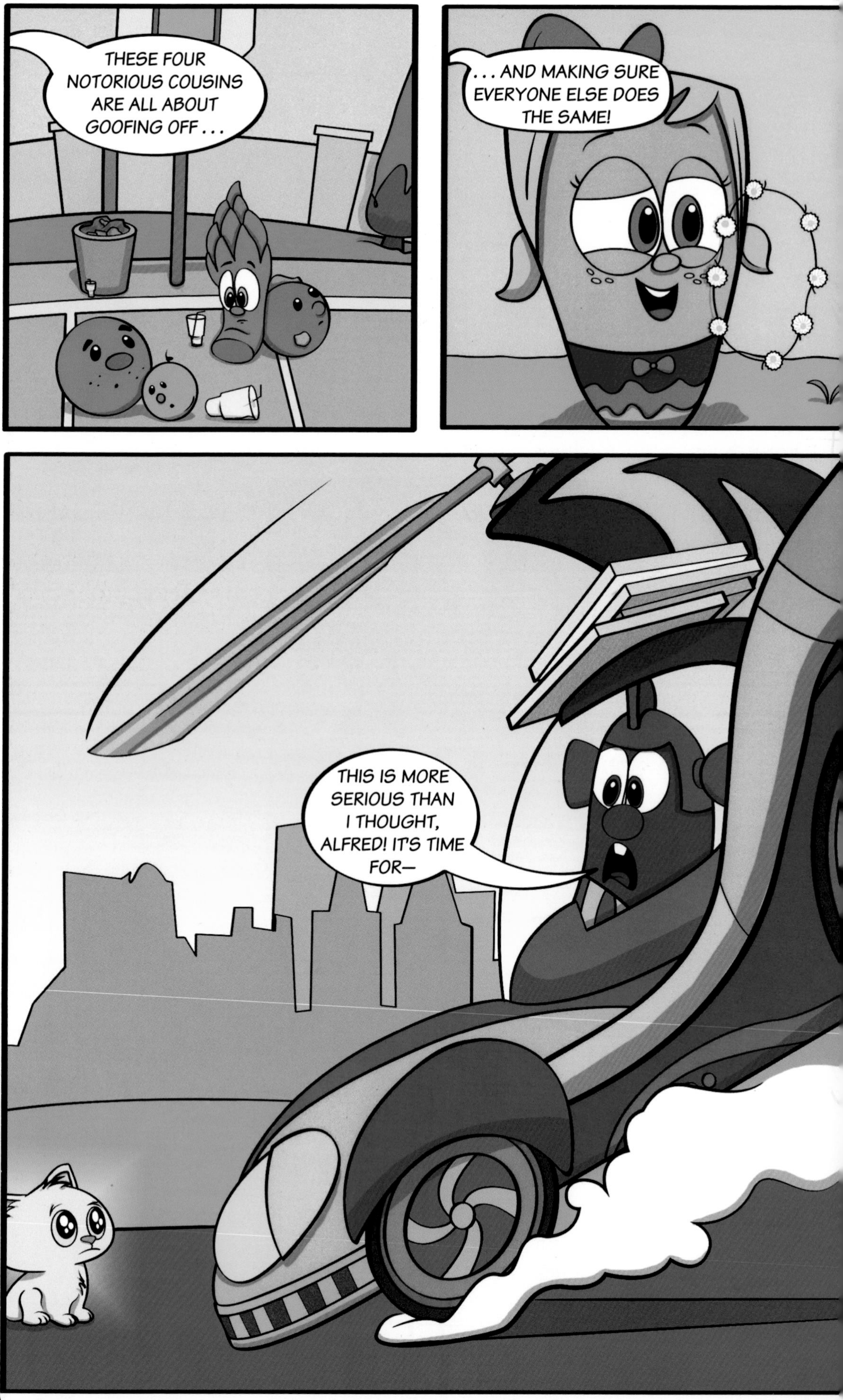
THESE FOUR NOTORIOUS COUSINS ARE ALL ABOUT GOOFING OFF . . .
. . . AND MAKING SURE EVERYONE ELSE DOES THE SAME!
THIS IS MORE SERIOUS THAN I THOUGHT, ALFRED! IT'S TIME FOR—

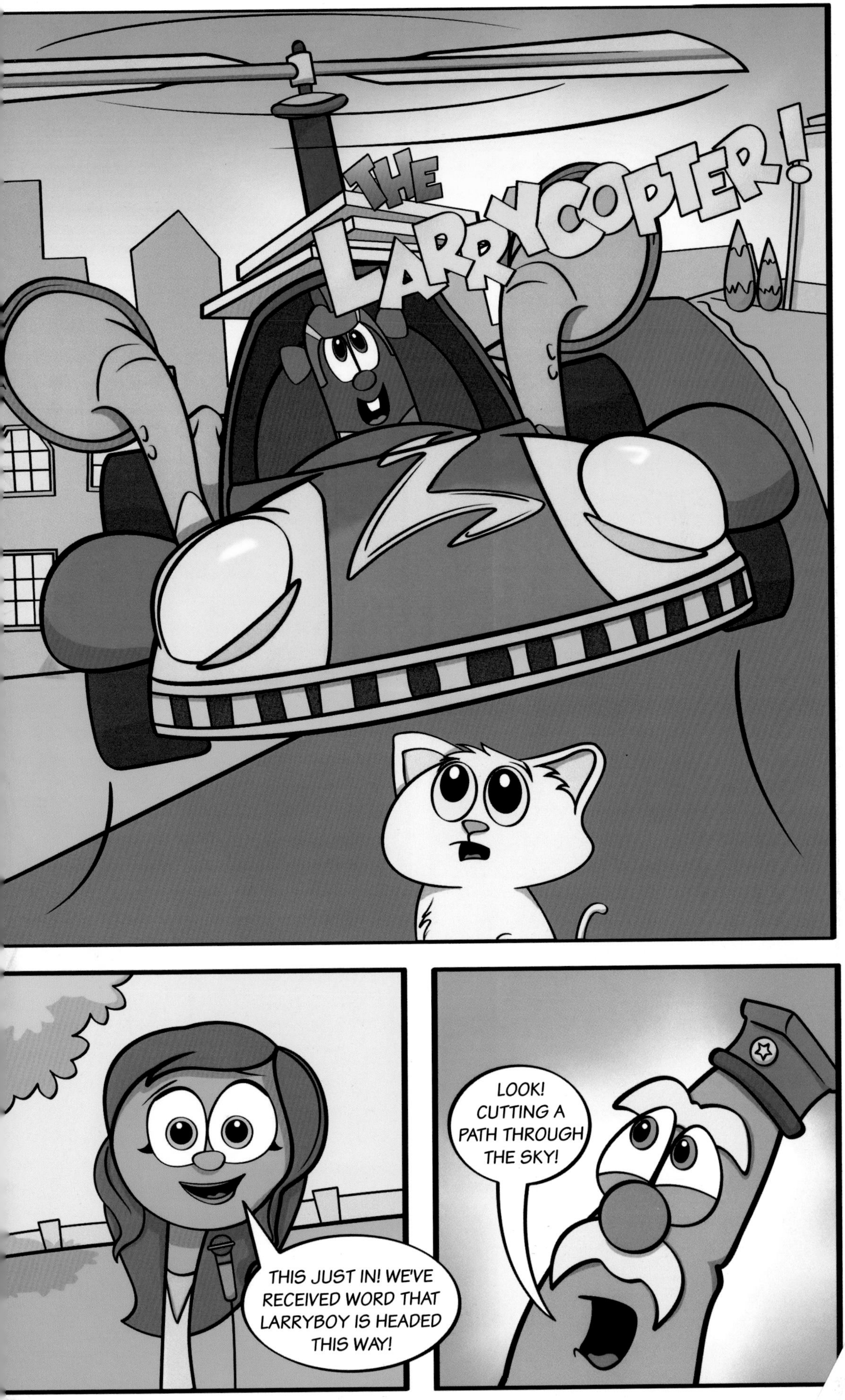
THE LARRYCOPTER!
THIS JUST IN! WE'VE RECEIVED WORD THAT LARRYBOY IS HEADED THIS WAY!
LOOK! CUTTING A PATH THROUGH THE SKY!

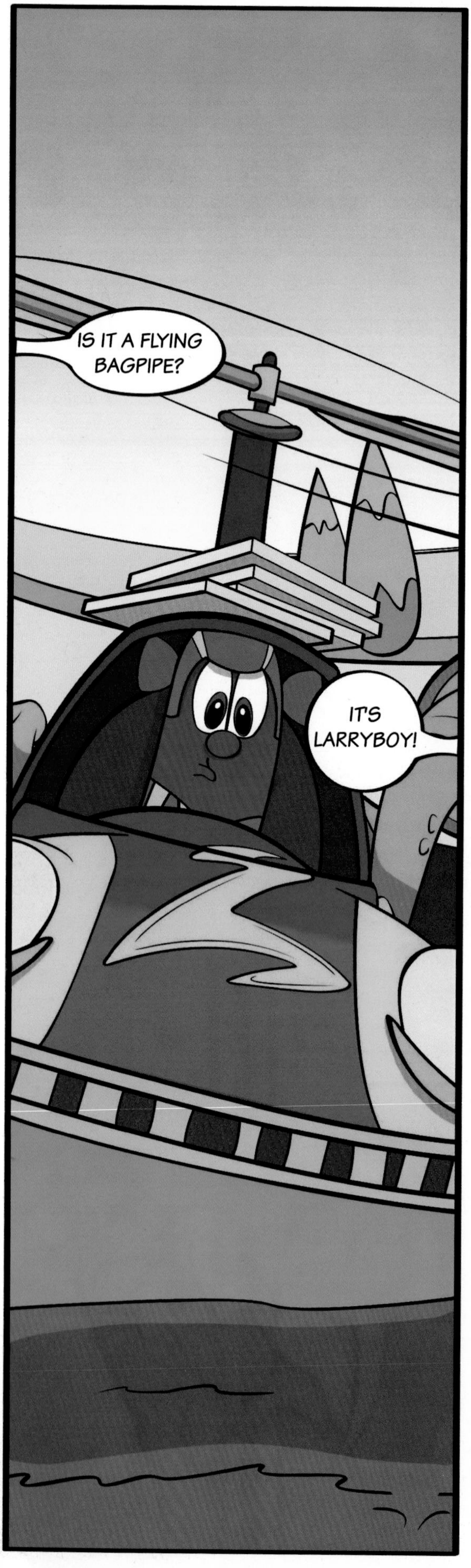
IS IT A FLYING BAGPIPE?
IT'S LARRYBOY!

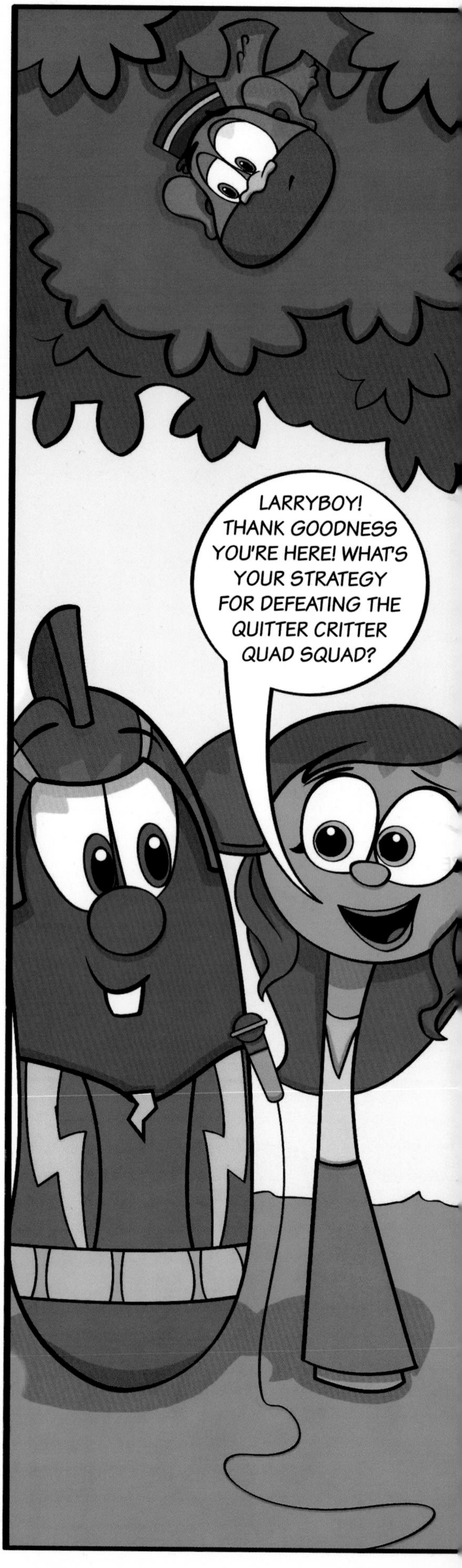
LARRYBOY! THANK GOODNESS YOU'RE HERE! WHAT'S YOUR STRATEGY FOR DEFEATING THE QUITTER CRITTER QUAD SQUAD?

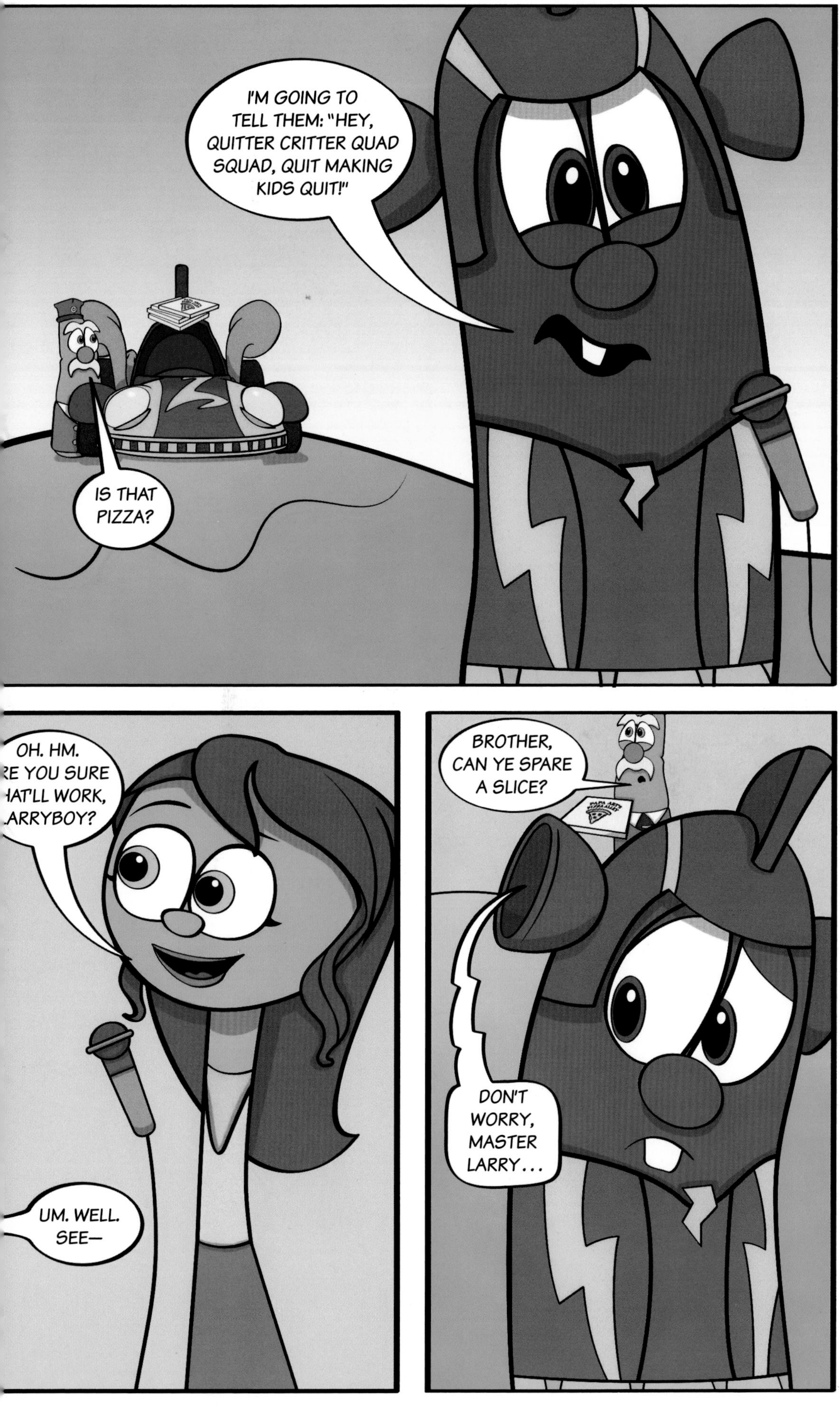

I'M GOING TO TELL THEM: "HEY, QUITTER CRITTER QUAD SQUAD, QUIT MAKING KIDS QUIT!"
IS THAT PIZZA?
OH. HM. RE YOU SURE HAT'LL WORK, ARRYBOY?
UM. WELL. SEE—
BROTHER, CAN YE SPARE A SLICE?
DON'T WORRY, MASTER LARRY...

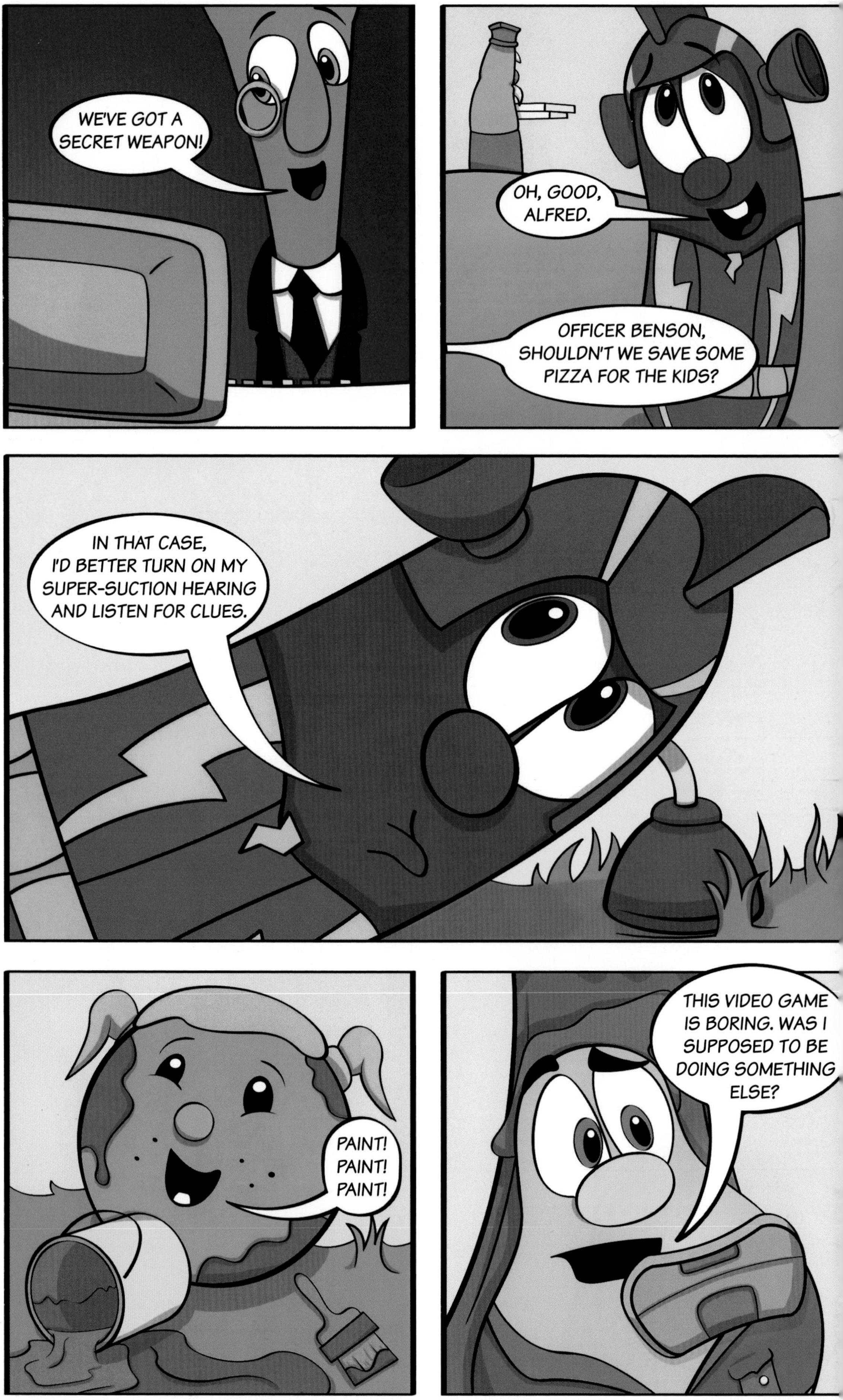

WE'VE GOT A SECRET WEAPON!
OH, GOOD, ALFRED.
OFFICER BENSON, SHOULDN'T WE SAVE SOME PIZZA FOR THE KIDS?
IN THAT CASE, I'D BETTER TURN ON MY SUPER-SUCTION HEARING AND LISTEN FOR CLUES.
PAINT! PAINT! PAINT!
THIS VIDEO GAME IS BORING. WAS I SUPPOSED TO BE DOING SOMETHING ELSE?

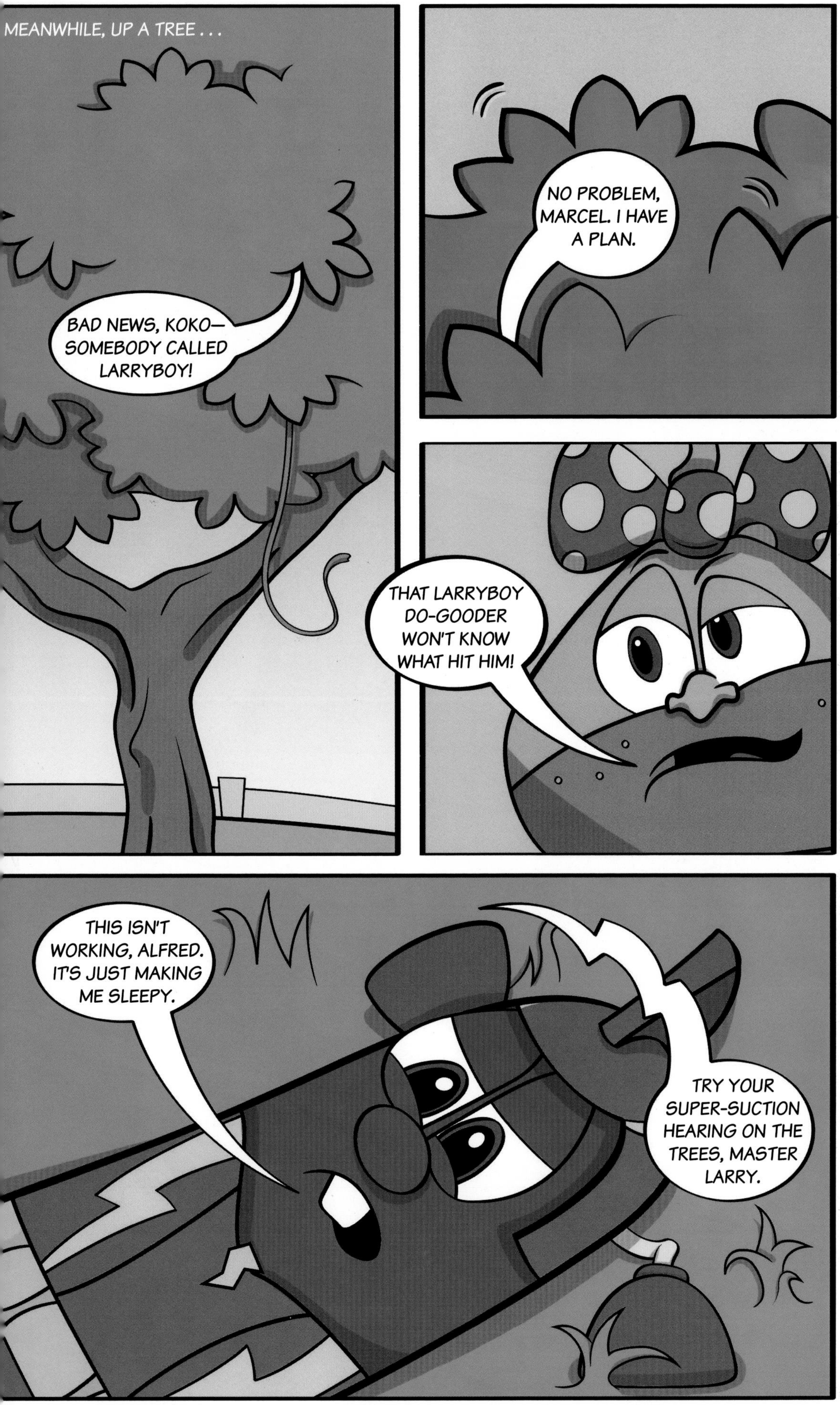
MEANWHILE, UP A TREE . . .
BAD NEWS, KOKO—SOMEBODY CALLED LARRYBOY!
NO PROBLEM, MARCEL. I HAVE A PLAN.
THAT LARRYBOY DO-GOODER WON'T KNOW WHAT HIT HIM!
THIS ISN'T WORKING, ALFRED. IT'S JUST MAKING ME SLEEPY.
TRY YOUR SUPER-SUCTION HEARING ON THE TREES, MASTER LARRY.

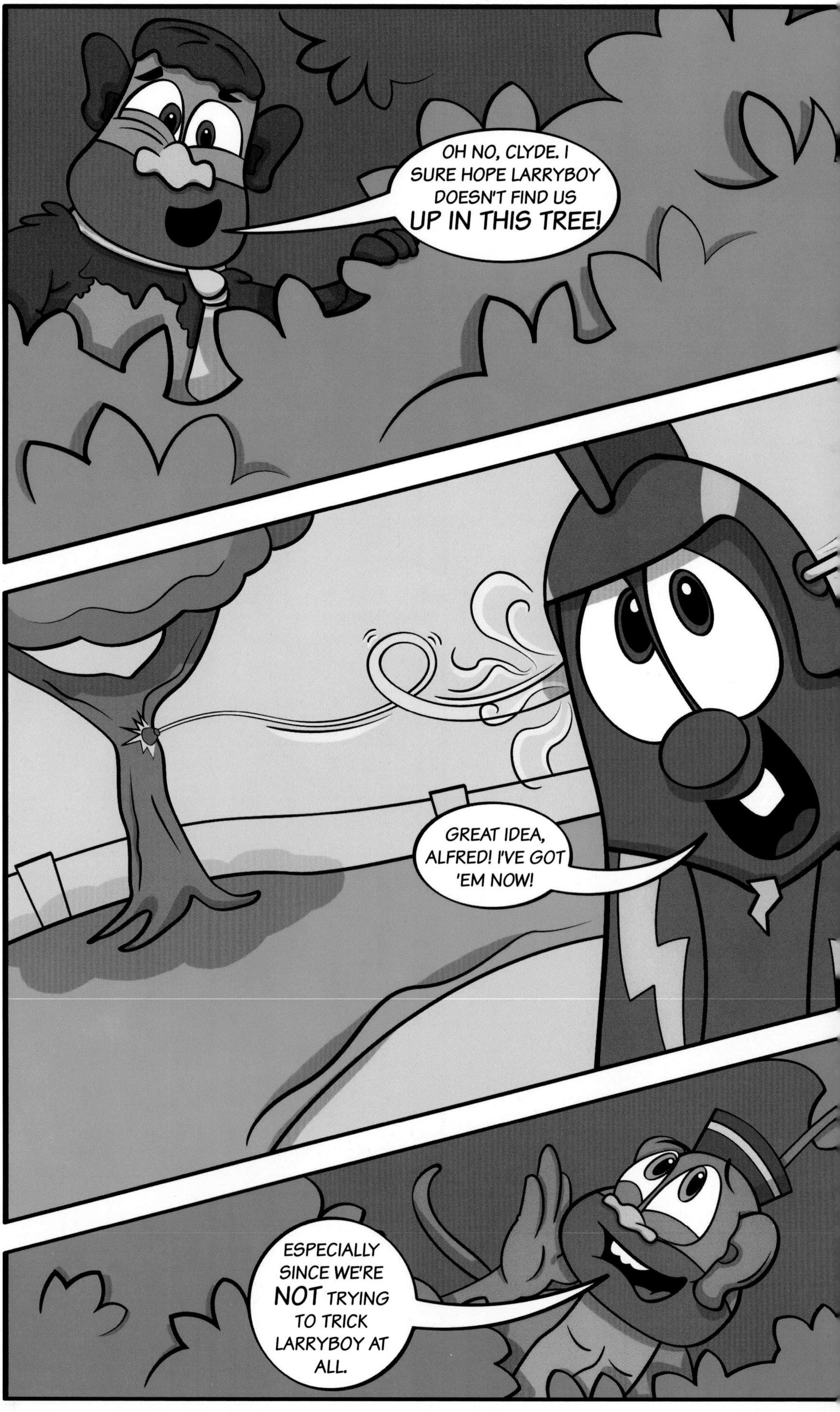
OH NO, CLYDE. I SURE HOPE LARRYBOY DOESN'T FIND US UP IN THIS TREE!
GREAT IDEA, ALFRED! I'VE GOT 'EM NOW!
ESPECIALLY SINCE WE'RE NOT TRYING TO TRICK LARRYBOY AT ALL.

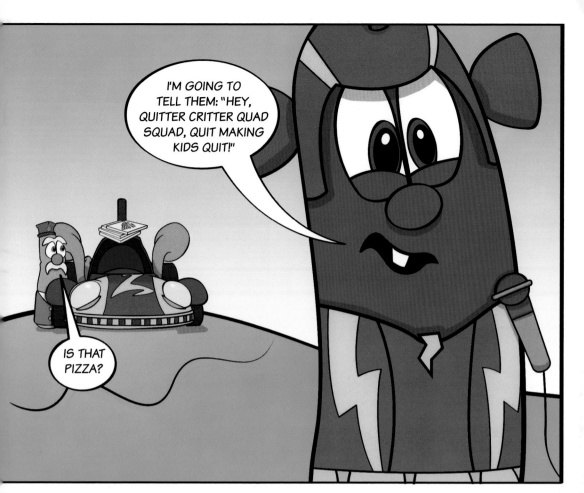

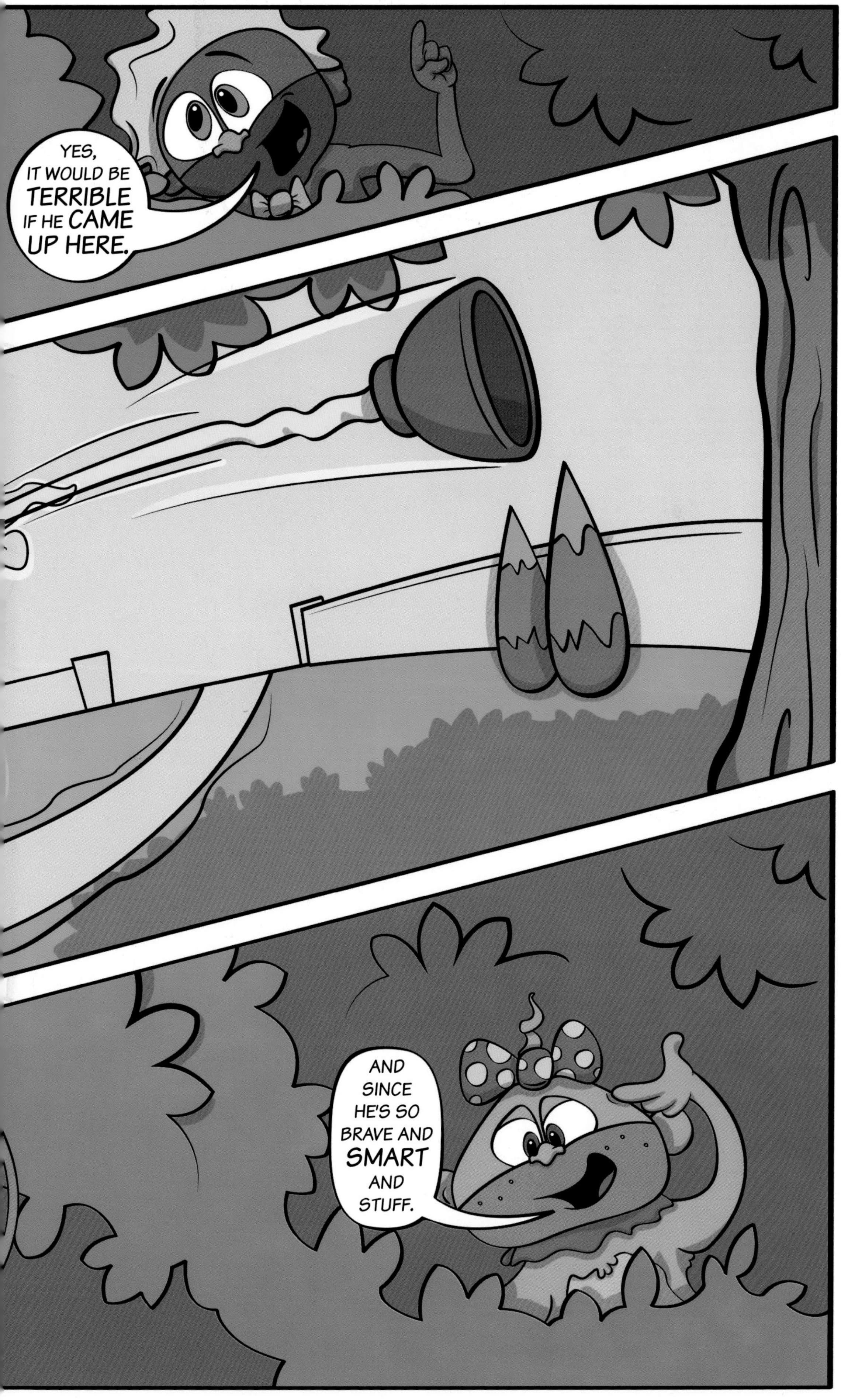
YES, IT WOULD BE TERRIBLE IF HE CAME UP HERE.
AND SINCE HE'S SO BRAVE AND SMART AND STUFF.

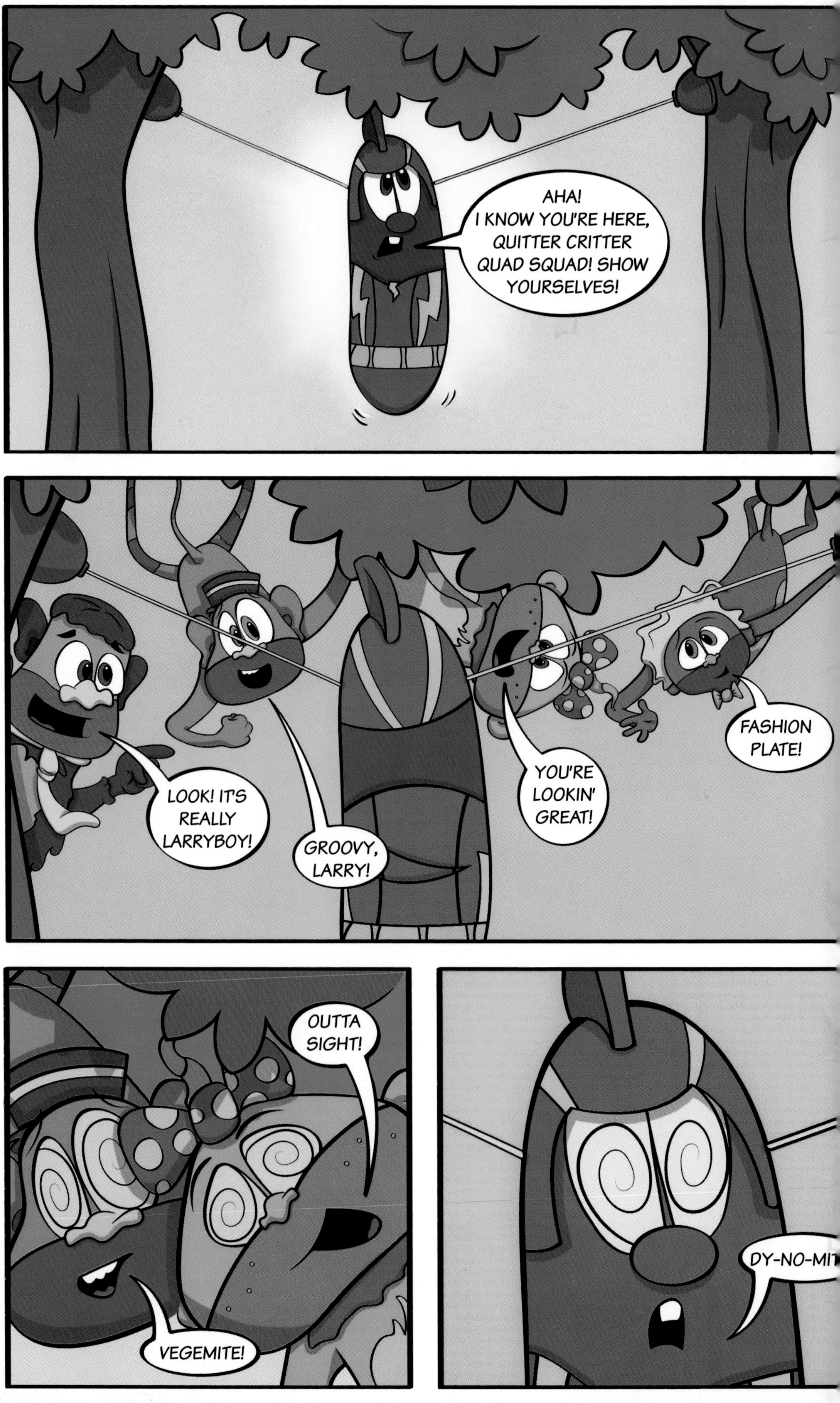
AHA!
I KNOW YOU'RE HERE, QUITTER CRITTER QUAD SQUAD! SHOW YOURSELVES!
LOOK! IT'S REALLY LARRYBOY!
GROOVY, LARRY!
YOU'RE LOOKIN' GREAT!
FASHION PLATE!
OUTTA SIGHT!
VEGEMITE!
DY-NO-MI

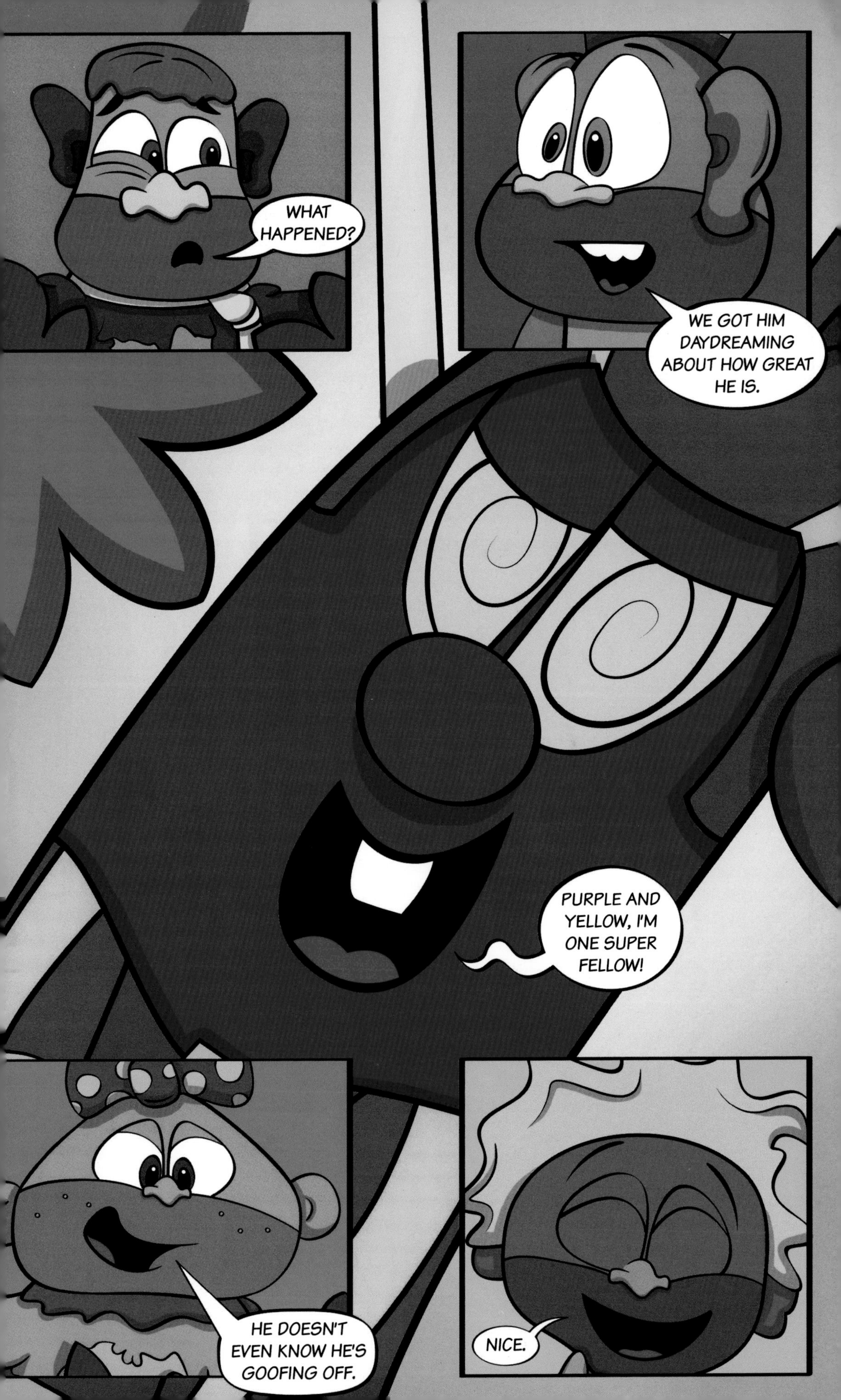
WHAT HAPPENED?
WE GOT HIM DAYDREAMING ABOUT HOW GREAT HE IS.
PURPLE AND YELLOW, I'M ONE SUPER FELLOW!
HE DOESN'T EVEN KNOW HE'S GOOFING OFF.
NICE.

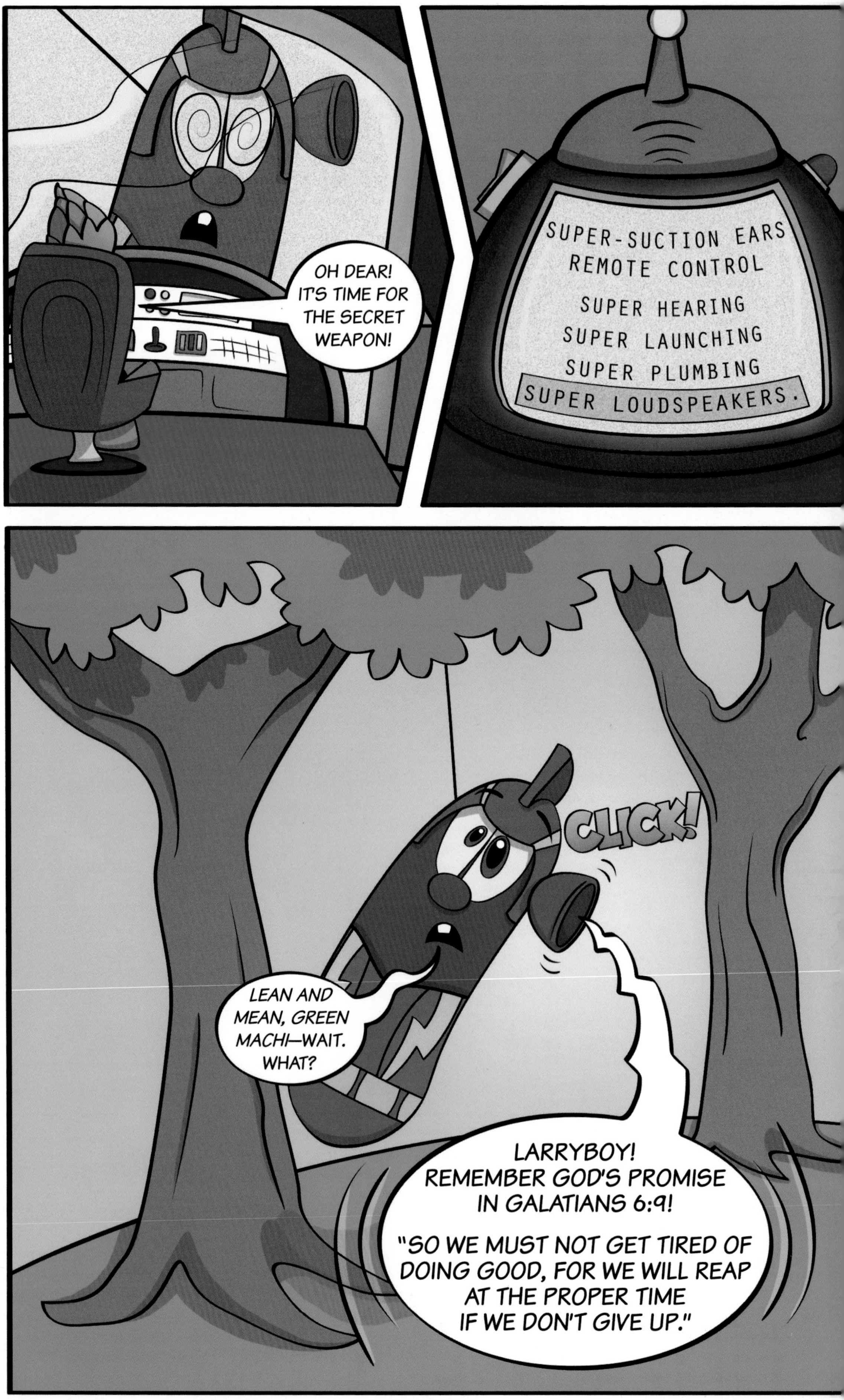
OH DEAR! IT'S TIME FOR THE SECRET WEAPON!
SUPER-SUCTION EARS
REMOTE CONTROL
SUPER HEARING
SUPER LAUNCHING
SUPER PLUMBING
SUPER LOUDSPEAKERS.
CLICK!
LEAN AND MEAN, GREEN MACHI—WAIT. WHAT?
LARRYBOY! REMEMBER GOD'S PROMISE IN GALATIANS 6:9!
"SO WE MUST NOT GET TIRED OF DOING GOOD, FOR WE WILL REAP AT THE PROPER TIME IF WE DON'T GIVE UP."

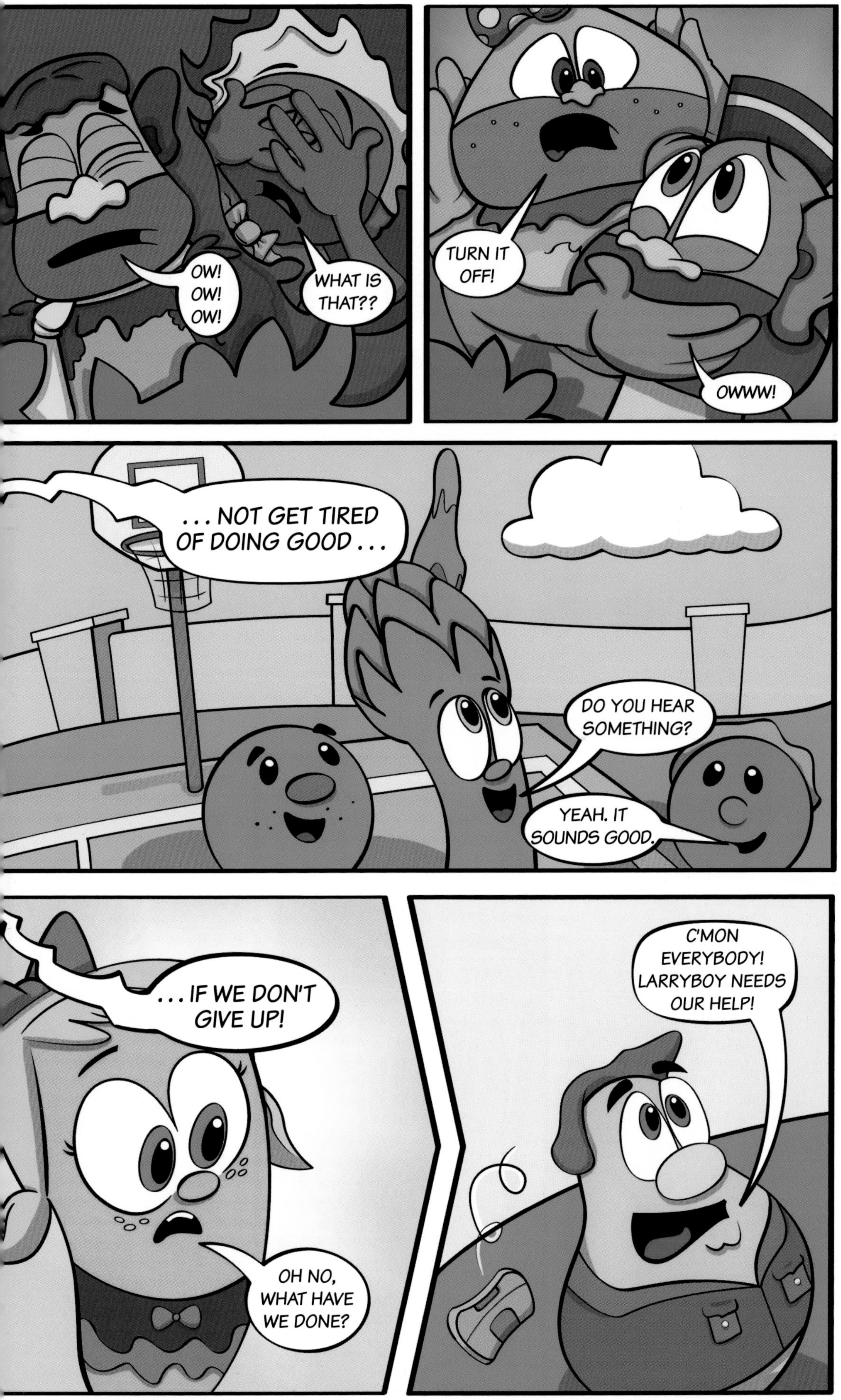
OW! OW! OW!
WHAT IS THAT??
TURN IT OFF!
OWWW!
. . . NOT GET TIRED OF DOING GOOD . . .
DO YOU HEAR SOMETHING?
YEAH. IT SOUNDS GOOD.
. . . IF WE DON'T GIVE UP!
OH NO, WHAT HAVE WE DONE?
C'MON EVERYBODY! LARRYBOY NEEDS OUR HELP!

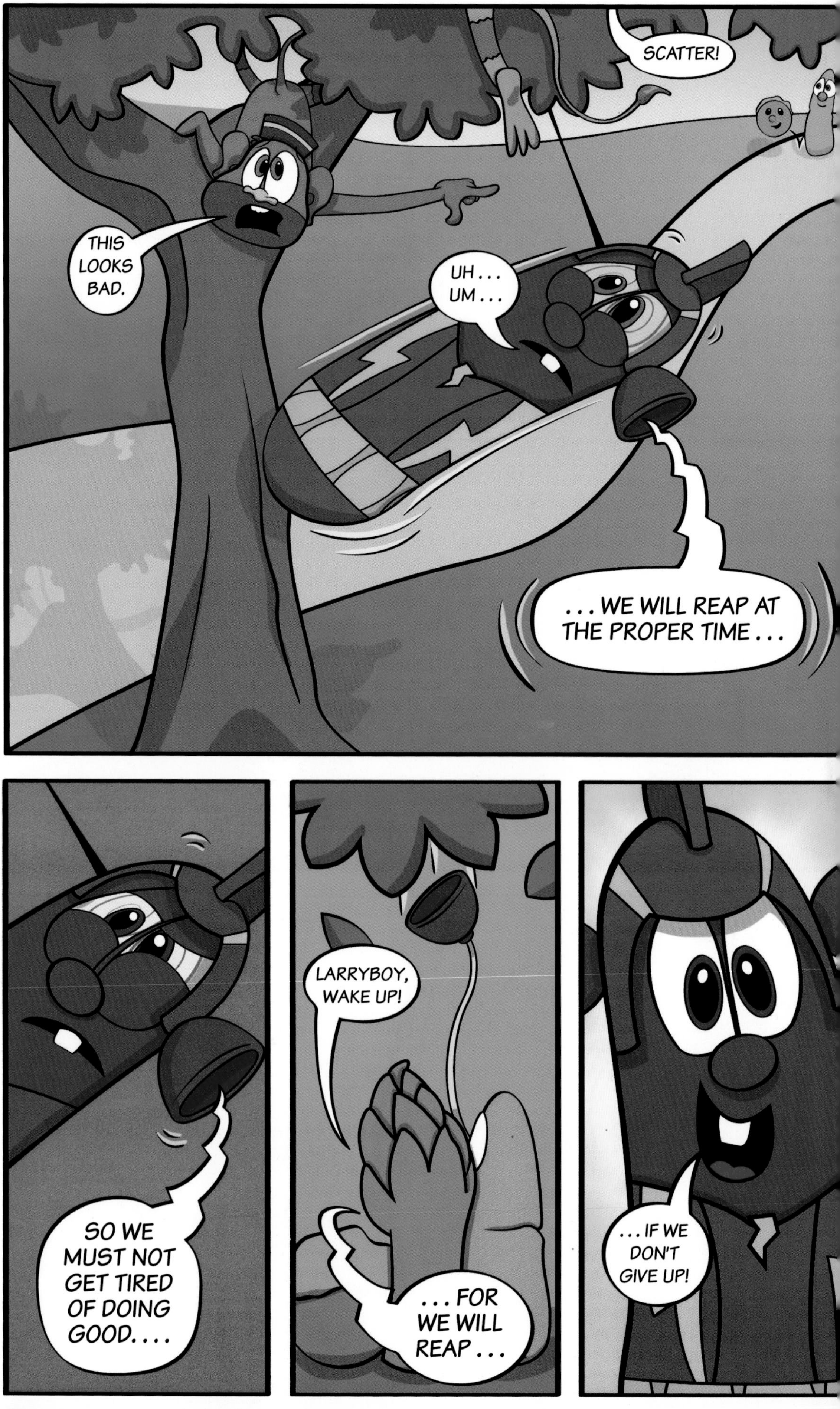
SCATTER!
THIS LOOKS BAD.
UH . . . UM . . .
. . . WE WILL REAP AT THE PROPER TIME . . .
SO WE MUST NOT GET TIRED OF DOING GOOD. . . .
LARRYBOY, WAKE UP!
. . . FOR WE WILL REAP . . .
. . . IF WE DON'T GIVE UP!

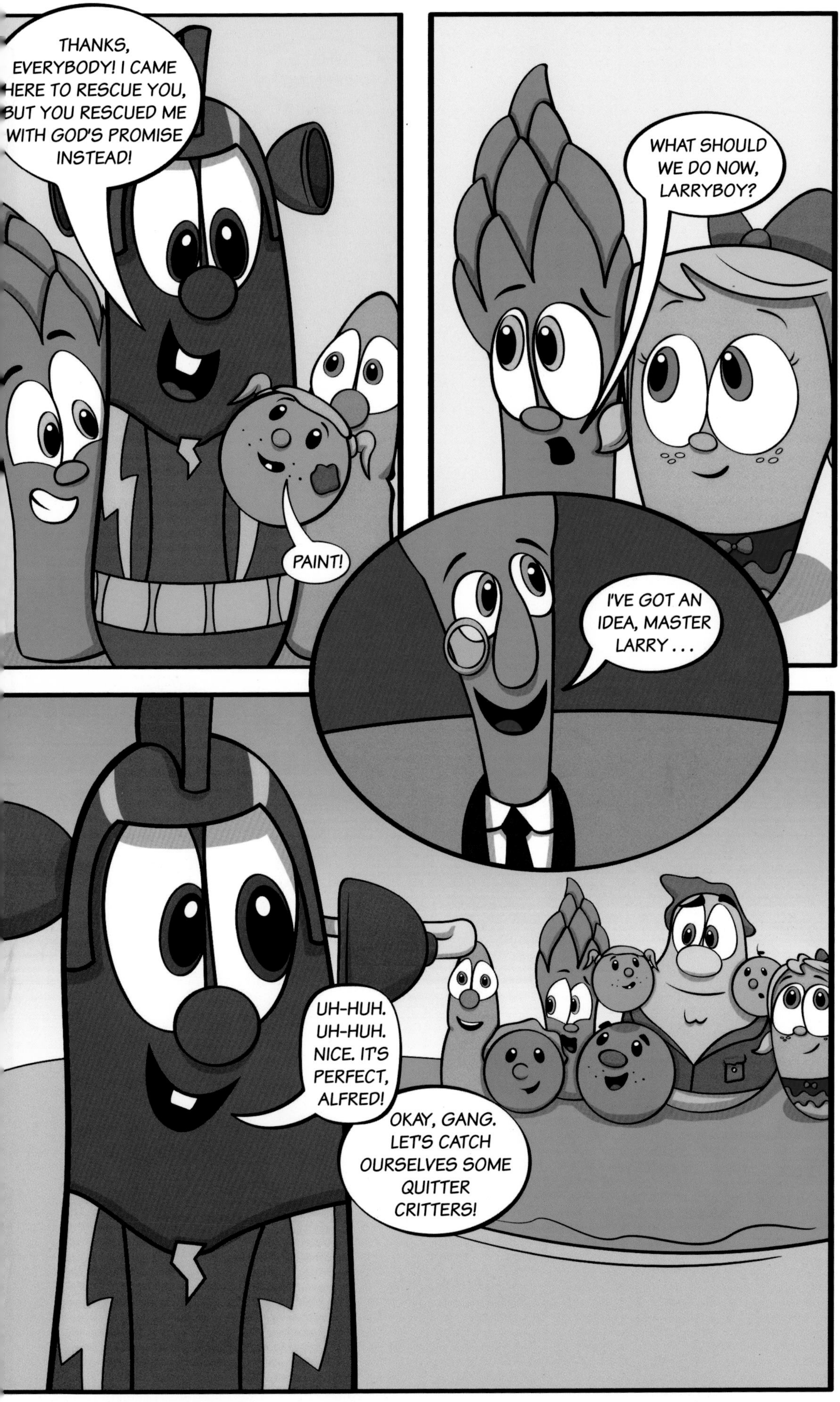
THANKS, EVERYBODY! I CAME HERE TO RESCUE YOU, BUT YOU RESCUED ME WITH GOD'S PROMISE INSTEAD!
PAINT!
WHAT SHOULD WE DO NOW, LARRYBOY?
I'VE GOT AN IDEA, MASTER LARRY . . .
UH-HUH. UH-HUH. NICE. IT'S PERFECT, ALFRED!
OKAY, GANG. LET'S CATCH OURSELVES SOME QUITTER CRITTERS!

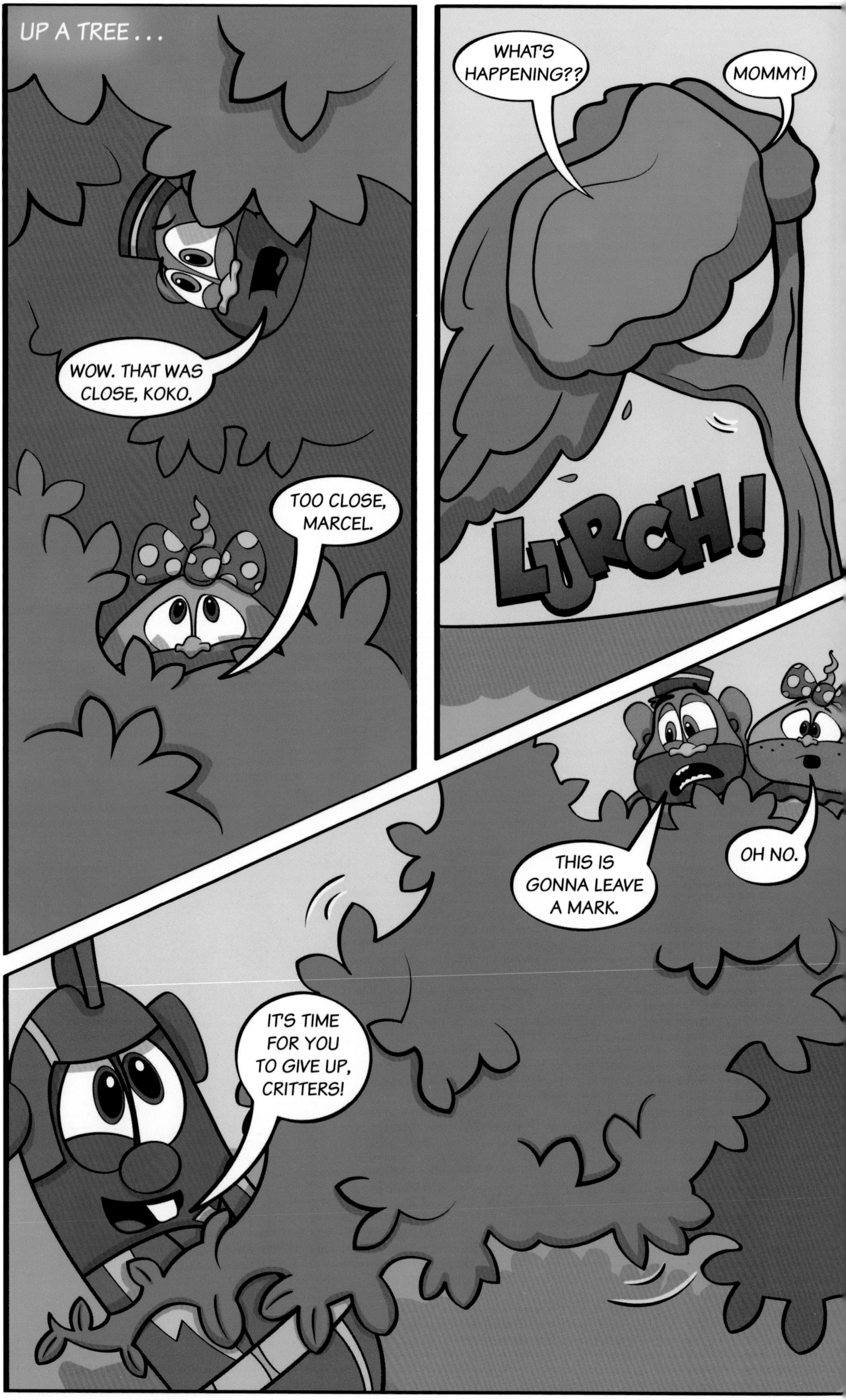
UP A TREE . . .
WOW. THAT WAS CLOSE, KOKO.
TOO CLOSE, MARCEL.
WHAT'S HAPPENING??
MOMMY!
LURCH!
THIS IS GONNA LEAVE A MARK.
OH NO.
IT'S TIME FOR YOU TO GIVE UP, CRITTERS!

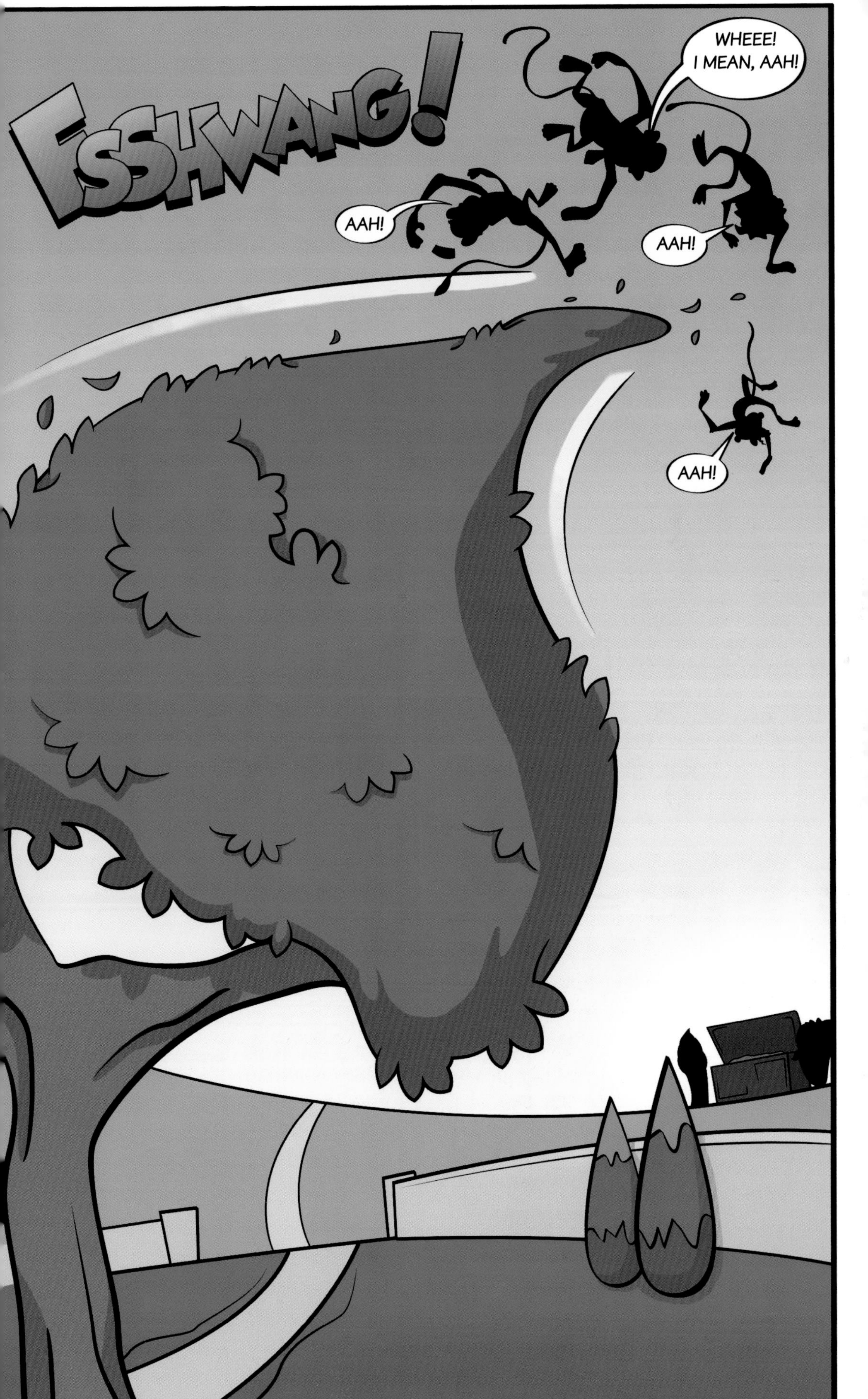
ESSHWANG!
WHEEE!
I MEAN, AAH!
AAH!
AAH!
AAH!

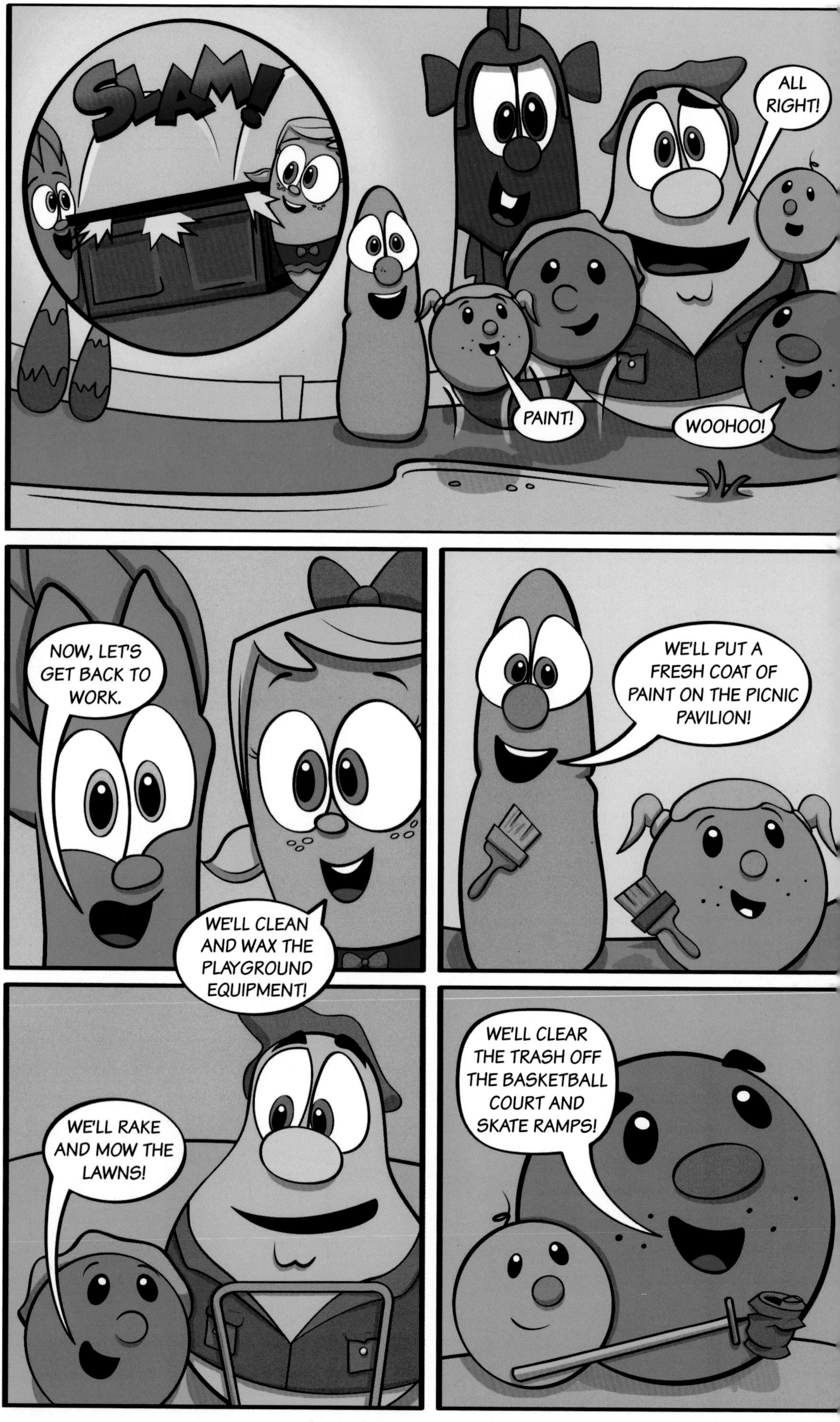
SLAM!
ALL RIGHT!
PAINT!
WOOHOO!
NOW, LET'S GET BACK TO WORK.
WE'LL CLEAN AND WAX THE PLAYGROUND EQUIPMENT!
WE'LL PUT A FRESH COAT OF PAINT ON THE PICNIC PAVILION!
WE'LL RAKE AND MOW THE LAWNS!
WE'LL CLEAR THE TRASH OFF THE BASKETBALL COURT AND SKATE RAMPS!

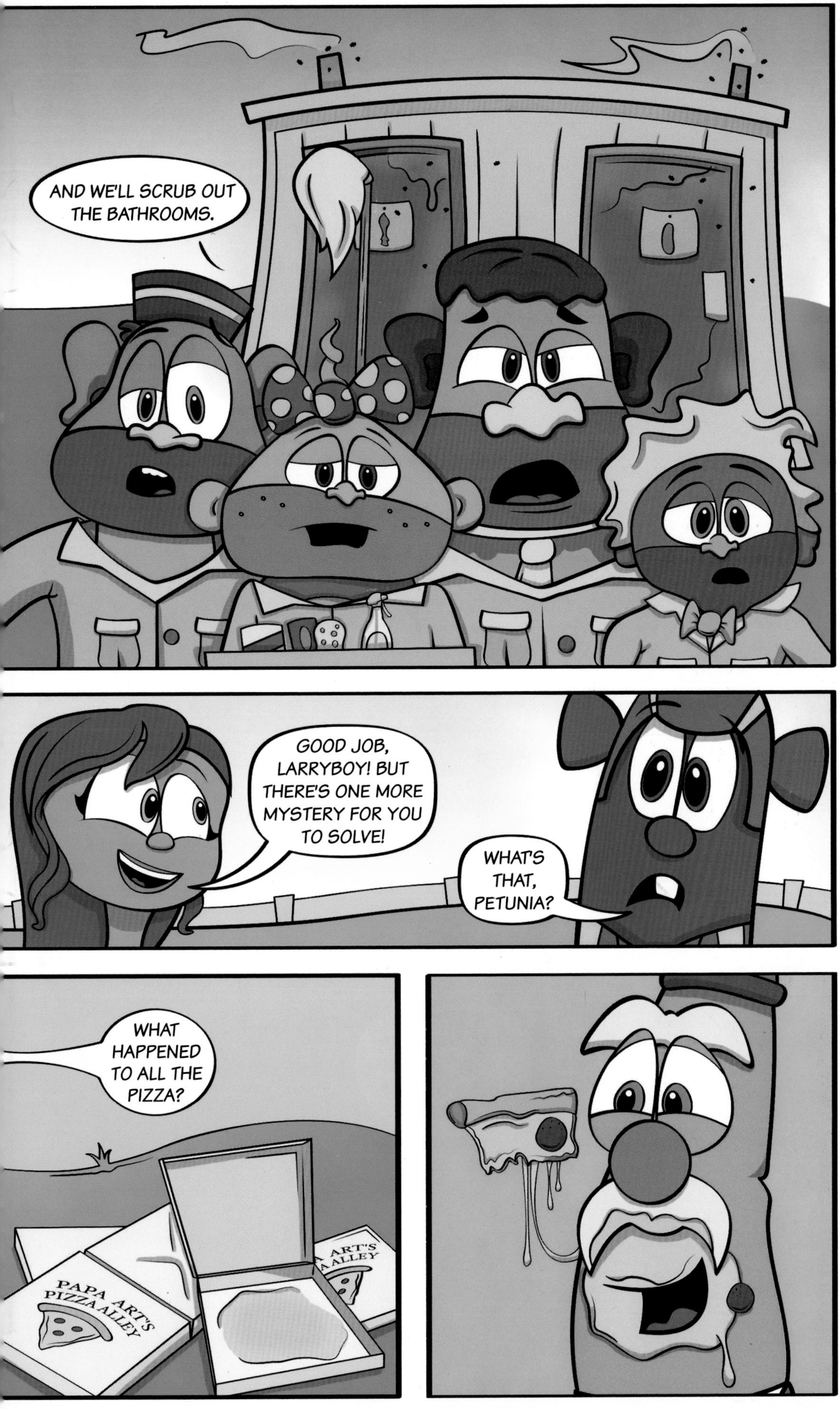
AND WE'LL SCRUB OUT THE BATHROOMS.
GOOD JOB, LARRYBOY! BUT THERE'S ONE MORE MYSTERY FOR YOU TO SOLVE!
WHAT'S THAT, PETUNIA?
WHAT HAPPENED TO ALL THE PIZZA?
PAPA ART'S PIZZA ALLEY

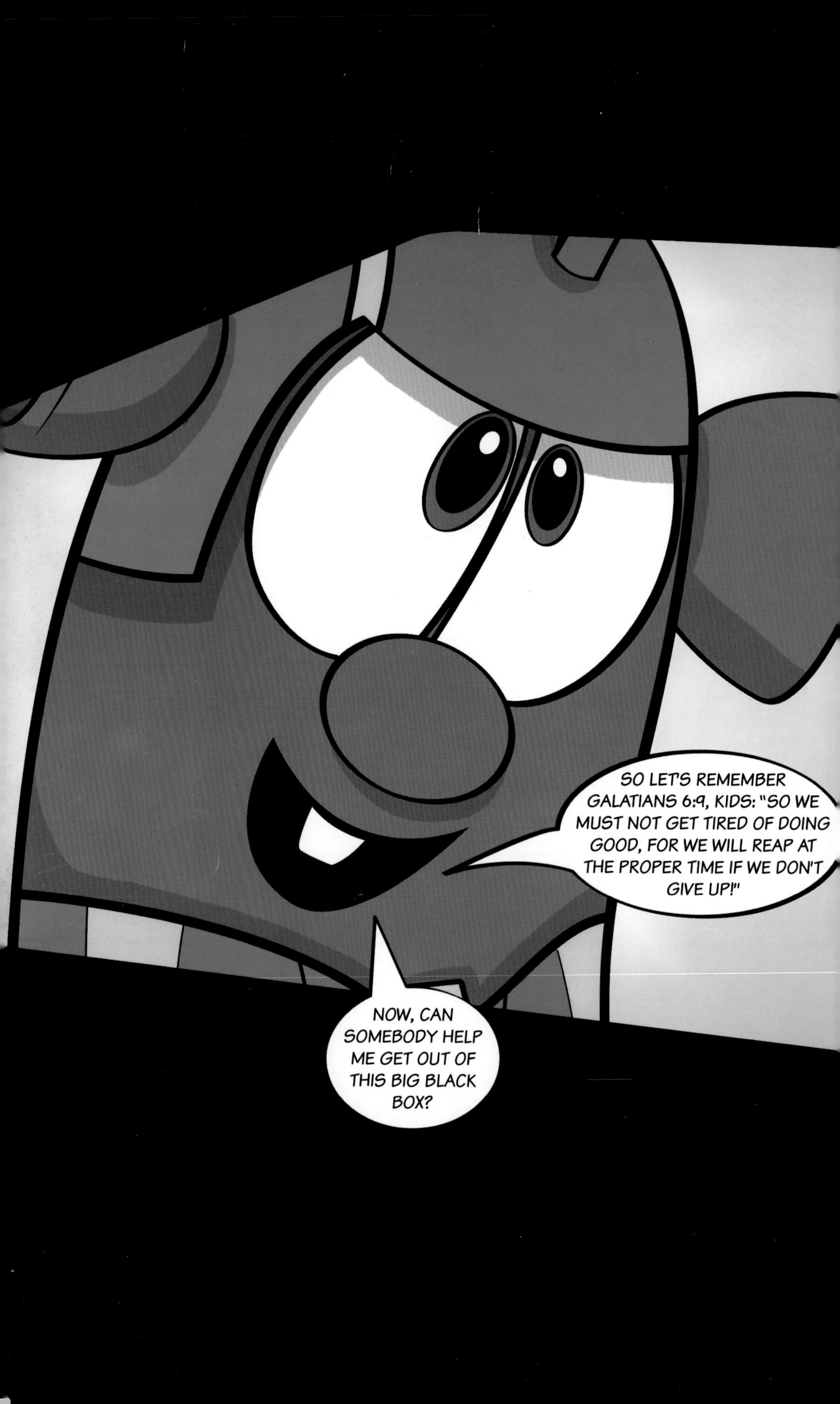
SO LET'S REMEMBER GALATIANS 6:9, KIDS: "SO WE MUST NOT GET TIRED OF DOING GOOD, FOR WE WILL REAP AT THE PROPER TIME IF WE DON'T GIVE UP!"
NOW, CAN SOMEBODY HELP ME GET OUT OF THIS BIG BLACK BOX?